"Edge of your seat and nail-bitingly thrilling."
— Readers' Favorite

"A brilliant read."
— NaturalBri Reviews

"What an amazing book! Can't wait to read the next book in the series."
— Pepper S via NetGalley

"This is one wild ride. A very good psychological thriller that will keep you up until the wee hours of the morning."
— The Cubicle Escapee

"Loved, loved, loved, this book."
— Kate H via NetGalley

"A thrilling, suspenseful novel that had me hooked from the first page to the last."
— Mary T, Amazon Reviewer

"A sassy, edgy page-turner."
— Wall to Wall Books

"I absolutely loved this book! It was my first read from this author and I instantly became a fan."
— Sarah R, Goodreads Reviewer

"An intensively satisfying read! Looking forward to exploring more writing from this talented author in the future!"
— Krystal K via NetGalley

ALSO BY GLEDE BROWNE KABONGO

Mark of Deceit (a short story)
Swan Deception
Conspiracy of Silence

GAME OF FEAR

A FEARLESS NOVEL

GLEDÉ BROWNE KABONGO

GAME OF FEAR
Copyright © 2016 Gledé Browne Kabongo

To learn more about Gledé and her work,
visit www.gledekabongo.com

Cover Design by Najla Qamber Designs

ISBN: 978-069-2539-729

For Donat, Amini and Max

PROLOGUE

I'LL NEVER TELL

Two years earlier

THEY WERE GOING to kick me out. That's what the meeting was about. The last piece of my lousy existence was about to crumple like a paper doll. Two weeks ago, Dad called a family meeting and announced that he would resign as chief financial officer of Orphion—a multi-billion dollar global technology company. He would have been CEO in a year. This crisis was a greedy little monster that couldn't be satisfied. The sensational and relentless media coverage, the sly, not-so-kind comments from classmates, and the possibility that Mom was facing life in prison were enough to make me want to crawl into a rabbit hole and never come out.

I pulled my shoulders back, stuck my chin out, and put on my game face. The door opened on the first knock. When I entered the office, my guidance counselor, Ms. Morris, and the school psychologist, Dr. Burns, were already seated. Our Headmaster, Dr. Stephen Kellogg, gestured for me to take the empty chair. He sat behind his desk, cleared his throat, and adjusted his glasses. A bunch of documents was spread out before him.

"None of us wants to see you in here," he began. "You've been an exemplary student in every way, and we're all proud of your accomplishments."

I waited for the proverbial shoe to drop. Their solemn faces made my stomach heave.

"Dr. Kellogg is right," my guidance counselor said. "We understand you're facing difficult circumstances. It's our job to help you stay on track. This meeting is about your support system here at school."

"I appreciate the support, Ms. Morris, but I've already met with everyone in this room and the school chaplain."

Dr. Kellogg cleared his throat again and picked up one of the papers in front of him. "We're concerned about your academic performance as of late," he said, scanning the paper. "You're well aware of our high standards here. Our reputation is built on it. You're part of it. We think it's best to take action now before it's too late."

I blinked a couple of times. "You mean before you have to expel me."

Dr. Burns stared straight ahead, and Ms. Morris opened her mouth to speak. Nothing came out. She just looked like a fish on dry land gasping for air.

"Goodness, no." Dr. Kellogg gave off a forced laugh

and adjusted his tie. "We want to formulate a plan to get you through these tough times."

Dr. Burns spoke for the first time, "Processing your emotions and having the proper tools in place is critical. A parent incarcerated, awaiting trial, and an uncertain future ahead is a lot for a young person to handle. We're here to help you cope successfully within the walls of Saint Matthews and beyond."

I sat ramrod straight in my chair. My anger bubbled over. "My mother didn't kill that man. She was set up and doesn't deserve to be in jail. We'll prove it. When we do, she'll come home where she belongs."

I saw the doubt in their eyes, the challenge to my statement. I could practically read their thoughts. *Poor, delusional kid.*

"Your teachers say you've been unfocused and withdrawn," Ms. Morris continued. "They tell me you've given up. It's our responsibility to make certain you don't fall any further behind. You're one of the best students we have. We don't want to see you lose your edge. I'm sure your parents would agree."

I smoothed out my skirt as I struggled to hold back the tears. They were right. I couldn't allow school to fall apart too, along with the rest of my life. If I didn't get myself together, Mom would be heart-broken. Dr. Kellogg handed me a box of tissue from his desk. I placed it on my lap without using a single sheet.

"We can talk right now if you need to," Dr. Burns offered.

Dr. Kellogg and Ms. Morris took the hint and left the room.

I turned to Dr. Burns. "May I have a few minutes alone, please? We'll chat. I promise."

When he left, I took deep breaths to wash away the humiliation threatening to strangle me. I couldn't make excuses anymore. The time had come to take drastic measures. I searched my bag for the piece of paper I'd carried around for weeks—the phone number of a classmate with an easy-going disposition, and a reputation as the guy who could make your troubles go away. I fished out my phone and dialed the number. He answered on the first ring.

"Need your help," I said.

"I am surprised to hear from you. But I understand why you called."

"Good. I don't want to go to The Pit. Someone might see me."

"You won't have to. I can hook you up. How much?"

"As much as you can get."

"Whoa. Are you sure about that?"

"Yes. I lost a lot of ground. It's time to make up for it."

"I can get you a discount, but it's still going to cost."

"Just do it."

"At your service, Mademoiselle."

"And one more thing."

"Yes?"

"This stays between us. Forever."

"I'll never tell."

PART ONE

THE GOOD GIRL

CHAPTER 1

I ATTRACT TROUBLE like a magnet, despite my best intentions. Perhaps it's because I attend Saint Matthews Academy, where the pressure is overwhelming, the secrets are dirty, and the games are wicked. But I don't let it get to me. My path to becoming one of the world's top neurosurgeons is already mapped out: Princeton for college, then off to Harvard or Stanford for medical school. I'll complete my internship and residency at the Mayo Clinic and Massachusetts General Hospital. My life is orderly, focused, and predictable, the way I like it. But some people have other ideas.

"What's up, Abbie?" he asks, making sexually suggestive motions with the lollipop in his mouth. I'm talking about Christian Wheeler, the resident bad boy.

For the past few weeks, since school started in September, he's been appearing at my locker every morning, asking me out like it's his new religion. I roll my eyes at him and then turn my attention to swapping the books I need for my first-period class. A couple of sophomore girls pass by and giggle as their friend tries to flirt with him. The lollipop comes out of his mouth, and he pushes a blond lock of hair away from his eyes—a luminous shade of Spanish blue that's so hypnotic I've heard girls faint when they look at him too long. Whatever.

"You're so gross," I say, hostility rolling off me in waves. "Isn't there some poor girl on this campus waiting to get dumped by you? Oh, wait, I don't think there's anyone left. You've been with every girl at Saint Matthews. Man-whore." I glare at him.

"Since we never hooked up, does that mean you're not a girl?"

I flip him the bird, but it doesn't faze him. He makes obnoxious kissing noises with his lips.

"That ice princess thing you do is all an act, isn't it? I know you want me."

"No, thanks. I have standards, and an aversion to STDs."

"Ouch. Watch where you point that thing you call a tongue. Somebody could get hurt."

I snort in disgust and stuff a couple of books in my backpack. "Why are you all over me, Christian? I'm not interested in joining your fan club. Get lost."

"I'm an enlightened man."

Christian turned eighteen over the summer and thinks that makes him a man.

"You're still a boy. Let's not get it twisted."

"I should get points for bravery. Every guy at this school is afraid to ask you out."

10

"I'm fresh out of brownie points. Besides, you don't want to date me."

"Why not? If you stopped hiding your, um, considerable assets," he says, ogling me, "you'd be a total babe."

"I find that statement deeply offensive."

The corners of his mouth turn up into a smile, revealing perfectly even white teeth. I can't help it, so I grin too. I zip up my backpack and sling it over my shoulders. I'm about to close my locker, but my hand stops in mid-air. I see Sidney Bailey Shepard sauntering toward us, elbowing people out of her way. Her eyes laser in on Christian like a lioness about to pounce on its prey. Sidney is a fellow senior, but that's where our similarities end. She plants herself in front of Christian and tosses her hair back, the long auburn locks coming to rest in a perfect cascade past her shoulders. I've seen her do this a million times, her come-hither ritual.

She hands him a brown paper bag. "You forgot this. I know it's your favorite belt."

Christian's eyes bug out of his head. He doesn't take the bag, so Sidney shoves it into his hands.

"Oh, my bad. I didn't know we were keeping it a secret, us getting back together. You won't tell anyone, will you Abbie?" She gives me what's meant to be a conspiring wink, but it comes off as fake as her surgically enhanced nose.

I give them both a dirty stare. I'm sure they can see the daggers aimed at them. Then Sidney melts into the crowd of kids on their way to first period, as if she wasn't just standing here, staking claim to her territory. I'm steaming mad.

"Sidney's lying," he begins. "It—"

"I don't care." I want to get away from him as fast as possible. I'm about to close my locker when something catches my attention—my psychology textbook at the far right corner of the top shelf, with a glossy, ivory-colored paper sticking out of it. I remove the paper from the book haphazardly, place it in the side pocket of my bag, and shut the locker.

I join the hallway crowd, bobbing and weaving my way to a meeting with my STEM (Science, Technology, Engineering, Math) Advisor. I want to distract myself from my anger at Christian. How dare he think he can play me? Not that I would have accepted a date with him, but it's the principle of the thing. Asking me out when he's still hooking up with Sidney. Eew!

Someone crashes into me and makes a quick apology. My backpack almost slips from my shoulders, but I grab it in time. That's my cue to retrieve the paper before it falls out of the side pocket. Christian catches up to me.

"You don't have to keep showing up at my locker, pretending to be interested," I tell him. "I don't even care what your motive is. Just stop it."

"I swear Sidney's lying. I would never do anything that shady to you."

I shake my head, peeved by his lame attempt at honesty. I open the paper, a standard 8.5x11. What I see written on it stops me cold.

CHAPTER 2

I KNOW WHAT you did. Hypocrite!
Justice will be served.

The Avenger

Someone has a sick sense of humor. Is it that witch, Sidney, stirring up trouble? But how did she get into my locker? How did she figure out the combination? My hands are shaky when I unzip my bag and drop the note inside.

Christian taps me on the shoulder; his face is bursting with worry. "What is it, Abbie? What's wrong?"

"Nothing," I mumble. "I don't want to be late for my meeting with Ms. Lyons."

I increase my pace in a frantic effort to escape his prying eyes and questions. He won't be deterred. He keeps up with me.

"Ms. Lyons can wait. Who sent you that paper? What does it say?"

"It's not a big deal."

"It is a big deal. You froze in your tracks when you read it."

"Stop making a thing out of it," I say, irritated.

"Ookay. Why are you flipping out, then?"

"Can you please drop this?" I ask, scowling at him. "Don't say anything to anyone."

"So, now you want me to do you favors?" he asks, stroking his chin like some evil cartoon villain. "Fine. I won't tell if you go out on a date with me. A real date."

I stare at him, slack-jawed. Why the urgency for a date? What is he up to?

"I'm not desperate enough to go out with you." I make sure my tone is dripping with contempt, sharp enough to cause bodily harm. "It's been amusing for the past few weeks, stalking me daily. Now, the fun is over. Move on to someone else."

He remains stubborn. "If you want me to keep quiet about what you found in your locker, go out with me. Those are my terms. Otherwise, I'll start spreading vicious rumors about what's in the note."

"You're a total scum bag, and I hate you."

He taps the face of his watch. "Need an answer by 3:00 p.m." Then he disappears into the crowd of kids, leaving me to untangle a giant ball of confusion.

I MAKE IT through my morning classes, distracted the whole time. I keep thinking about the message, looking for clues in the tone, the word choices, something that would point to the kind of person who would do this (obviously a psycho). The text is typewritten. There's nothing special about the font. The note could have been printed from any computer. I push the thoughts aside. There's a simple explanation: wrong locker. I feel terrible for the intended victim.

My stomach growls as I enter the dining hall, already buzzing with gossip, socializing, and students making their way through the lunch lines. Hardwood floors, wooden tables and chairs enhance the dining ambiance. Portraits of famous alumni and hunting trophies are mounted on the walls—testaments to the rich and illustrious history of Saint Matthews.

One of my best friends is waving to me. Our group, nicknamed the Rainbow Posse because of our diverse ethnic backgrounds is one member short this year. Anastasia Cruz, our sidekick from Columbia, returned home after her parents were kidnapped and brutally murdered, a crime rumored to be politically motivated. She made the move to Madrid and now lives with her soccer superstar brother and his wife.

Now, our trio is made up of Callie Furi, a free-spirited California girl my mom says reminds her of a young Elizabeth Taylor, and Frances Lin, a tell-it-like-it-is Jersey girl and future Pulitzer Prize winner.

I drop my bag on the floor next to the seat saved for me and sit. My friends started lunch without me.

"Nice earrings. Are they new?" I ask Frances.

She fiddles with the gorgeous, diamond-accented rosebud earrings on her left earlobe and gushes, "Trevor spoils me. He bought them for our six-month anniversary."

"Is it love?" I ask.

"Maybe."

"You're not sure?"

She scoffs. "We don't need to put labels on our relationship, Abbie. We're so past that."

Trevor Forrester is a fellow senior from Philadelphia. His dad founded Forrester International, one of the largest advertising firms in the country. His mother, Grace, is a well-connected socialite. In spite of his pedigree, Trevor is not a snob like most of the kids at our school. He's an all-around good guy whom everyone likes.

I head to the lunch line to grab some food. When I return to our table, the interrogation begins.

"What's up with you and Christian Wheeler?" Frances asks.

My brain seizes for a moment. I wasn't expecting that question since I've told the girls about Christian's habit of asking me out every single day of the school week. It's a running gag, but right now, I have no idea what she's talking about.

"The usual."

"I don't think so."

Callie starts fanning herself with a napkin. "I would pay to see him naked."

"I'm sure he'll show you for free," I say, giggling.

Callie glows like the matter's been settled, then digs into her soup.

Frances isn't about to let the issue drop. "He's staring at you. I see drool coming out the side of his mouth."

"How am I supposed to know what's going on with him? It's not like we're BFFs."

I don't want to look in Christian's direction, but some invisible force compels me to. Major mistake. He points to his watch then smacks his lips. My cheeks burn with embarrassment. When I turn my attention back to our table, inquisitive eyes gaze at me.

"Breaking news," Frances announces, using her fork as a microphone. "Hell has just frozen over. Abbie Cooper has the hots for Christian Wheeler."

"I do not." My denial is quick. The last thing I need is for Frances to make a big deal out of nothing.

"You can be honest with us," Callie says, trying to coax the so-called truth out of me.

"Will you two stop it? Christian is being Christian. He likes playing games, and I let him because I find his antics amusing. Get a grip, people." I roll my eyes for dramatic effect.

The girls aren't convinced.

"He's still looking over here," Frances says, waving to Christian, who has the nerve to wave back. "What happened this morning?"

I weigh the pros and cons of telling my girls about the incident with Sidney and the note. I don't want to worry them, especially since the likelihood that I received it in error is high. We've been a tight-knit group since we met as wide-eyed fourteen-year-olds our freshman year and have seen each other through some tough times. It's Callie's turn. Her parents' pending divorce has been tabloid fodder for the past few months. Our friendship has been her refuge.

I fill them in on my run-in with Sidney and the reason Christian keeps staring at me from his lunch table. I'm not even sure this is his usual lunch period. He probably showed up just to bait me.

"Whoa," Callie says. "Do you still have the note?"

I reach for my bag, and then pull out the note. I flatten it on the table. Frances and Callie lean in to read it. They have identical frowns on their faces. Callie picks it up and reads it again, then hands it back to me.

"I think someone stuck it in the wrong locker," I explain. "I don't know how they got past the combination. They couldn't have pushed it through the vents because I found the note sticking out of my psych textbook."

"You should file a complaint," Frances says. "Someone violated your privacy by opening your locker. That's huge."

"I don't have any proof. Unless there's a witness willing to come forward, we have nothing."

"You're right," Frances says. "I forgot about the no ratting policy. You could get the death penalty for violating that code. We can still ask around, discreetly."

"You're the reporter," Callie says. "Find out if anyone has been lurking around Abbie's locker."

"We might already know who left the note," I point out.

"You just said it was the wrong locker," Callie reminds me.

"Sidney. You know she hates me. Throw in the Christian factor and that's her way of telling me to back off. Is she crazy enough to write a note like that? She isn't, right?"

Callie shrugs and stuffs a piece of fruit in her mouth. Frances isn't so nonchalant. She rakes her fingers through her hair and won't look at me.

"You know something," I say.

She gestures for us to lean in closer as if she's about to reveal state secrets.

"This is off the record. I promised my source I wouldn't say a word to anyone, but since you received this anonymous message, I should tell you." Frances ramps up her dramatic tone as she launches into the story. "Remember that accident last winter, the one that put Willa Schofield in a wheelchair?"

"Someone ran a stop sign and plowed into her. It was horrible," I say, shivering at the memory. Willa and I had creative writing together, and I tutored her in pre-calculus.

"My source says Sidney caused that accident. She was totally wasted, missed the sign, and almost killed Willa."

"Shut up," Callie says. "No way."

The revelation stuns me.

Frances carries on. "Her parents paid a lot of money to the Schofields to keep it quiet. A lot. When your daddy is a former White House Chief of Staff, you can get away with anything. My source also said it's not the first time her parents bailed her out of serious trouble."

"That girl is a walking disaster," I say. "She shouldn't be left alone with sharp objects or cars, apparently."

Frances takes a sip of her drink and then places the glass on the table. "She's capable of sending you that note. Probably got one of her minions to do it. She's jealous that Christian keeps asking you out. The entire school knows her only goal in life is to become Mrs. Christian Wheeler. I mean, where are her self-esteem and ambition?"

"You should go for it with Christian," Callie says, her eyes full of mischief. "Because he's into you, it would piss Sidney off, and because you need to do something crazy before we graduate."

Frances agrees. "Yeah, Abbie. Live a little."

"Says the girl whose idea of acting crazy was burning her sister's fan letter from Tom Cruise."

Frances's older sister, Penny, is a world-renowned concert pianist, and they're involved in a serious case of sibling rivalry.

"Penny had it coming. She's still mad months later, so I got her beat on that round."

I shake my head. "I can't date Christian."

Callie folds her arms and leans back in her chair. "Why not?"

I tick off a list of Christian's transgressions, counting them on my fingers. "There's too much drama with the whole Sidney thing, he has a horrible reputation when it comes to girls, and he was kicked out of two other boarding schools for bad behavior. You know, the stuff that makes Christian, who he is."

"Sounds to me like you're chicken," Callie says.

Frances sighs dramatically. "I know what this is about. It's time to let go, Abbie."

"What do you mean?"

"Ty. He's in college now, and you're in the friend zone."

"This has nothing to do with Ty. I don't want to be one of 'Christian's girls.'"

Callie starts clucking like a chicken and flapping her arms.

"I'm not afraid. I like things a certain way. Christian is a hot mess."

"I have an idea," Frances says. "Come to the party. If he's still chasing you, then you have to go out with him. At least once."

I glance at her, puzzled. "What party?"

"Evan Mueller's senior year kickoff bash at his parents' house in Wellesley," Callie answers. "You have to come."

"I don't know," I say, eyeing the lunch I haven't touched since I sat down. The fries are soggy, and the meat in my burger looks like something that died on the side of the road. I stick a fork in my garden salad and start eating. "I'll have to think about it. Plus, I wasn't invited."

Frances pulls her phone from her purse and presses a few buttons. "Check your email."

I reach for my phone in my bag. I open the email from her and see the evite. "Evan won't mind?"

"He asked me to invite you. He knows we're friends," Frances says.

CHAPTER 3

I EXIT THE main building. An unseasonably warm breeze greets me when I arrive outdoors. Indian summer. I trudge toward the parking lot reserved for non-boarders. Saint Matthews Academy is tucked away from the main road that runs in the direction of downtown. The school sits on 250 sprawling acres of wide, open space peppered with brick and Tudor-style buildings in Castleview, a small, affluent suburb with a bucolic feel, thirty miles west of Boston. Castleview doesn't have a Wal-Mart or Target or any large retail presence. Instead, the town is dotted with small independent markets and surrounded by open land. Most of the white-collar professionals who inhabit the town take the MBTA Commuter Rail into Boston for work.

I drink in the panorama of colors displayed on the surrounding trees: the reds, yellows, oranges, and all shades in between. It's breathtaking, the last fall I'll ever experience at Saint Matthews. I shield my eyes from the sun's glare as I arrive in the parking lot, but I can't be certain I see what I think I see. As I get closer, he comes into focus, leaning up against my car, hands in the pockets of his well-fitted jeans, and a confident swagger to match.

I go on the attack as soon as I'm face-to-face with him. "What are you doing here? How did you know which car was mine? Are you stalking me?"

"It's after 3:00 o'clock, and school's out. You owe me an answer to my question from this morning. I have my ways of finding out stuff, and no, I'm not stalking you. Sweet ride by the way," he says, running his hands against the exterior of the car.

Dad bought me a midnight blue Audi R5 Cabriolet for my seventeenth birthday. It was a nice surprise, and I fell in love with it right away. I deactivate the alarm and nudge Christian with my hip. "Get out of my way."

He edges closer to me and leans in to whisper in my ear. "You know, babe, if you want to get physical, all you have to do is ask. I'd be happy to oblige."

"You disgust me."

He grabs my wrist as I open the driver side door. "We had a deal. So, what will it be? Are we going somewhere just the two of us, or do I have to accidentally on purpose mention the note to...who knows? My tongue might just slip at the wrong time."

"Why won't you let this go?" I snatch my wrist from his grip. "Look, Christian, I just can't, okay. I'm applying early action to Princeton, and the deadline is coming up fast; plus, I have my STEM Fellowship and my Debate Team Advisor gig."

"You're pulling the 'I'm too busy' excuse? Come on, Abbie; you can do better than that. Admit you're too scared to take a chance. You'd rather play it safe like you always do."

"Did you talk to Callie?" I ask, my tone suspicious.

"What does Callie have to do with this conversation?"

"I can't afford distractions right now, especially not you."

"What does that mean?"

"It means I'm not interested in dating anyone who hooks up with tons of girls, just for his amusement."

"Wow. That's harsh."

"Tell me I'm wrong."

His expression is bleak. Yet, the determined jut of his chin isn't lost on me. I reach for the door handle, but he stops me. "Can I call you? Just to talk, no pressure."

"I doubt you're that hard up for friends."

"I'm not looking for new friends."

"Then, what is this?"

"I want to spend time with you, in a non-friend kind of way."

He shoves his hands into his pockets. He looks down at the asphalt and shuffles his feet. Vulnerability is not a word I associate with Christian. I'm touched, even if I don't want to be. He's thrown down a challenge I'm not ready to answer.

"Look, don't get your hopes up, okay?" It's the quickest way to end the conversation without agreeing to anything.

He looks up at me. His eyes dance, their magnetic pull trying to drag me under. "You didn't say no."

"I have to go."

I toss my backpack in the passenger seat, shut the door, and then start the engine. As I join the line of luxury cars leaving the parking lot, I peek at my rearview mirror and catch him staring back at me.

"ARE YOU OKAY? You've barely said two words since you got home."

"I'm fine, Mom."

"Hmm," she says, pulling out the chair across from me. "You've been biting your nails, again."

I sit at the kitchen table, my first stop when I get home from school before heading upstairs to my room to get started on homework. It's a large, comfortable, eat-in kitchen with top-of-the-line cabinets and stainless steel appliances, tiled flooring, and a large island at its center. Mom's decorative skills give it a cozy feel: small potted plants along the window sills, curtains that scream country kitchen, and framed art depicting wholesome foods made the old-fashioned way.

She looks at me, concern written all over her smooth, girlish face.

"I thought my senior year would be easy. It isn't."

"How do you mean?"

"The stress of applying to college. Plus, I still have to keep up my grades."

Mom covers my hands with her tiny ones. "I know

it's hard, sweetie. You have a solid plan, though, and it will all be over soon. But are you sure college admission is the only thing on your mind?"

I should have known she wouldn't take my excuse at face value. Christian, Sidney, and the anonymous message are all running through my mind. I wish they would stop. It's getting crowded in there.

"Christian Wheeler keeps asking me for a date," I blurt out.

Mom leans back in her chair with a wicked grin on her face. "*The* Christian Wheeler? The one you trade insults with? The one you called a heartless, soulless Neanderthal who has no respect for women? The one who thinks—?"

"Okay, I get it," I say, throwing up my hands. "I said awful things about him. He deserved it, though."

"Is the feeling mutual? Do you want to go out with him, too?"

I frown at her. "My friends think I should. But come on, Mom. It's Christian."

"I know that. You've only been talking about him since junior year."

"Because he annoys me," I say. "One minute he's saying disgusting things to me, and the next he's all sincere like he'll die if he doesn't get a date with me. What's up with that?"

"He might be afraid you'll reject him."

I can't imagine Christian being afraid of any girl rejecting him. He dates only the most gorgeous girls at Saint Matthews, and when he's not at school, it's starlets and heiresses, according to Callie.

"I doubt that's the case. He just likes tormenting me."

"Are you sure that's all it is?"

"What else could it be?"

"That he likes you."

"I don't think so, Mom. I'm so not his type."

"What type is that?"

"You know what I mean."

She leans in closer to me. "No, I don't know what you mean. Tell me."

I can't believe she's behaving as if Christian asking me out is the most natural thing in the world, and I should have expected it. I didn't. The truth is, I'm not exactly ugly. I inherited mom's big, doe eyes framed by a set of double lashes, my best feature. At five-foot-eight and a solid D cup, I've heard guys refer to me as a closet hottie, whatever that means.

"Christian and I don't have a lot in common. He's only interested in casual hookups. Besides, he's been in trouble a lot."

"I see." Mom gives me a skeptical look. "Well, if you're sure...."

"What do you mean? Those are good reasons to stay away from him."

"I think you like him, but you're too stubborn to admit it. That's why you give him a hard time."

I stare at mom, my mouth open with shock. "You're supposed to be on my side."

"I am, sweetheart. Always. I just don't want you torturing yourself."

Three hours later, I abandon the homework desk and stretch. I pad over to my bed and sink into the plush comforter, enjoying the stillness for a few minutes. Soon, my brother, Miles, will bang on my bedroom door, announcing that dinner is ready. Mom makes a big deal about eating dinner as a family since she doesn't get to do it every night. She's usually at Shelby's Place, her five-star restaurant (voted one of Boston's best by *The Improper Bostonian*), returning home late from taping her popular show for the *Cooking Network* in New York, or working on another bestselling cookbook. Dad makes it home most nights, except when he travels on business.

My phone rings on the nightstand, and I reach for it. I don't recognize the number. I hesitate for a few seconds then decide to answer.

"Hello."

"Good evening, Ms. Cooper. I hope I haven't caught you at a bad time." The voice is male, one I don't quite recognize. I have to be cautious since people have been sending me strange notes lately.

"Who is this?"

"You've forgotten me already? That hurts my feelings, Abbie." Then he bursts out laughing.

"Christian! How did you get my number?"

"I get creative when I want something that's, shall we say, difficult to obtain."

"I'm going to kill Callie. Don't bother denying it. She gave you my number, didn't she?"

"Does it matter how I got it?"

"She can't give out my number without my permission. I'm going to wring her little neck."

"Callie is smart enough to know we should be getting to know each other."

"She thinks you're hot, and we should go out."

I don't know why that slipped off my tongue. Just because his phone voice reminds me of the rich, smooth organic maple syrup I have with my morning pancakes, doesn't mean I should lose my head.

"Do you agree with Callie?"

"I can't control what my friend says or thinks."

"That's not an answer."

I extend my legs until they touch the headboard. "It's the only one you'll get."

"Why can't you just admit that you like me?"

"Oh, my, what a massive ego we have. Still needs stroking after the endless parade of beauties who've fallen for your charms?"

"The only beauty I want falling for my charms is you, Abbie."

"Aww. I would say that's so sweet if you weren't full of it."

He belts out a hearty laugh. I can't help but smile. Good thing he can't see me. It would only encourage him.

"I like you, Abbie Cooper. I was right about you."

"Meaning?"

"You say what's on your mind. You don't care about being popular or showing off to get attention, and your academic record is fierce."

My bull-crap radar is usually sharp and accurate when it comes to guys. He just jammed it. I don't like that.

"Popularity contests are a waste of time. No one is going to care once we leave Saint Matthews and take on the real world. I have better things to do with my time."

"Like studying. Avoiding relationships. Hiding your feelings."

"I have plenty of relationships, thank you."

"You know I'm not talking about your brother."

"So what? I'm in no hurry."

"Who are you waiting for, Abbie? What if he never comes?"

That fastball hit me square in the face. I think back to Frances's comment at lunch, about Ty. He didn't want to *ruin our friendship*, so I'm permanently in the friend zone. I'm sure Christian's cousin Kerri was the reason nothing happened between us, not that I'm bitter or anything. Ty went off to Yale. I put my feelings on lockdown and haven't let them out since. It was the only way to preserve our friendship.

"I'm not waiting on anyone, okay?"

"So, is there a chance for us?"

"A chance for what, Christian?"

His breathing comes down the line. "Anything and everything."

Before I can respond, Miles bangs on my bedroom door. "Abbie, it's dinnertime."

I place my hand over the phone and yell back that I'll be right down. After Miles leaves, I speak into the phone. "I have to go, Christian."

"Think about what I said."

I'M TIRED, AND it's time to call it a night. I put in an extra two hours of studying after dinner and general goofing off with the family. I slip into my favorite pajamas and go through my bedtime routine. Afterward, I shut off the lamp and climb into bed.

Seconds after my head hits the pillow, my cell phone rings. Who could be calling me so late? I reach for the phone, pulling the plug out first. The screen says Blocked Number.

"Hello?"

"I know what you did. Hypocrite! Justice will be served. The Avenger."

I squeeze the phone so tightly that my fingers hurt. It's a girl on the line. If I had to guess, she's my age or a little older. She repeated the note I found in my locker, verbatim.

"Sidney, I'm going to kick your butt. This isn't funny anymore," I shout into the phone.

The caller hangs up.

CHAPTER 4

I GAZE AT my locker, fearing it will turn on me like some evil beast. I'm not requesting a new combination yet. Sidney won't get away with this. I don't care that her dad worked for the President and may know CIA agents who could make me disappear.

Christian isn't around this morning. Probably giving me some space to think about what he said. I take a deep breath and give myself a mental pep talk about not being a wimp. I shouldn't be afraid of my own locker.

I turn the combination and pull the door open with confidence. As if in slow motion, I exchange my books. Nothing looks out of the ordinary. My vision board is still intact—a collection of photos that help me stay inspired and focused on my goals. The biggest one in the bunch is Dr. Keith Black, one of the top neurosurgeons in the country. Next to him are pictures of Serena Williams and Malala Yousafzai. They're both fierce in my opinion.

I ignore the morning ritual going on around me: students on the way to class, the buzz of multiple conversations, and lockers banging shut. I'm too distracted. I can brush off a random note, but two things bother me. I was contacted on my personal cell phone. The caller knew what was written on the note found in my locker. She knows me. Sidney is the only *she* who fits the bill.

Someone taps me on the shoulder. I drop the book in my hand. It barely misses my toes.

"Abbie, what's wrong? Why are you jumpy?" Trevor Forrester picks up my giant calculus textbook from the floor and hands it to me. Trevor and I have English Lit together, and Frances takes advantage of that. I'm her lookout in case Trevor's ex-girlfriend, Brooke Westerly, tries anything funny.

"Thanks," I say, taking the book from him. "I'm fine. Just spaced out for a minute."

"Are you sure? You look worried."

He adjusts his clear, rimless glasses. With dirty-blond hair styled in a layered cut, sharp cheekbones, and a muscular build, Trevor has the hunky nerd look cornered.

"All good. Ready for another epic lecture by Dr. Campbell?"

"Arrggh. I swear if I have to dissect another didactic poetry piece, I'm going to hurt someone."

"I thought you lived for English Lit," I say, clicking my combination lock shut. "You know, so Brooke can drool all over you."

"Don't joke about that. I don't want Frances

breaking up with me over something stupid like Brooke causing trouble."

"She's part of Sidney's clique. They wear trouble like a badge of honor."

I slide into my usual seat, three rows away from the front of the classroom. Dr. Campbell sits at her desk, scribbling something on a notepad. We have about three minutes before class begins. I hear giggling one row over from me. Sidney and Brooke are whispering.

"You should just give up, Abbie," Brooke says.

They remind me of signs at the park that say don't feed the pigeons. If I say anything, it will unleash an avalanche of shallow and disparaging comments. Instead, I roll my eyes at them and let out an exaggerated sigh of disgust. I pull out my notebook from my bag and start scribbling. A couple of minutes later, someone taps me on the arm. Sidney.

"What do you want?" I ask.

"You should keep the hostility in check, Abbie. It makes you unattractive. Maybe that's why no one will date you."

I look past Sidney. Brooke and a couple of other girls crack up. Trevor drops his head on his desk in embarrassment over their antics.

"That's what you came over to tell me? Get a hobby and stop making a nuisance of yourself." I go back to my scribbling.

Sidney slinks back to her seat.

AFTER ENGLISH LIT, I head to the student lounge for an important meeting. This is my free period to do whatever I want. The lounge is empty except for one lone soul watching a program on the large, flat-screen TV at the front of the room. Leather armchairs are clustered in groups with a table at each center. I come here often to relax and chat with classmates who are boarding students. Equipped with Wi-Fi, a vending machine, and a pool table, the lounge also doubles as a study area.

Dahlia Sessions walks in, her gold bracelets making a racket as she shuts the door behind her. I secretly refer to her as a chocolate lollipop—tall and thin with a big head of unruly curls. Her parents are high-powered lawyers based in Atlanta, and she wants to follow their example. Dahlia and I aren't close the way I am with Frances and Callie, but we're on friendly terms. As a Resident Assistant, she's a good person to know.

She sits in the armchair across from me and blows a bubble with her chewing gum. She removes the sticky substance from her lips after it pops. "What's up, Abbie?"

"What, no small talk?"

"You didn't ask to meet me in the lounge for small talk."

"I need your help."

"With what?"

"Security footage."

Dahlia looks all around the lounge as if she expects people to pop out of nowhere to listen in on our conversation. Once she's satisfied it won't happen, she leans forward and whispers, "Are you crazy? Abbie Cooper is an uptight goody-two-shoes who freaks out if she's five minutes late for school. Who are you? What did you do with Abbie?"

Everyone at school thinks they have me figured out, with their cliché labels and simplistic assessment of who they think I am. They're dead wrong.

I whisper back, "I'm right here. I came to you because you're the only person who can help me."

She fiddles with the heart-shaped, gold pendant on her necklace. "What kind of trouble came looking for you?"

I haven't thought out every angle, only enough to persuade Dahlia to help me. My answers must be vague, yet specific, so she feels comfortable.

"I found something in my locker. I can't say what, but it's serious. I have to know how it got there."

"You want me to talk to Lance."

Lance Carter is Dahlia's boyfriend, and his Dad, Theo, runs school security. Lance is my insurance policy. I feel horrible for even thinking it. If we're caught, his father won't squeal on his own son, especially since Lance gets free tuition because his Dad works for the school. A random news item that turned out to be useful, thanks to Frances.

"Yes. Do you think he can get me a copy of the footage that records the hallways near the lockers?"

"I don't know," she says, fiddling with her necklace again. "That's a huge favor you're asking."

"I know it is. I wouldn't ask if it wasn't a big thing I'm dealing with."

That's it, my plan to catch the culprit. Security is serious at Saint Matthews. Ever since those school shootings in Boston last year, Kellogg spent a lot of money upgrading security. We're all well versed in lockdown drills, just in case a similar tragedy occurs at our school. He told the parents who objected to surveillance cameras that if they didn't like his methods, they could send their kids to another school. As far as I know, the cameras are confined to main areas like hallways, the perimeter outside of the school, and the main entrance.

"Please, Dahlia. Talk to Lance and see if he can get his Dad's keys to open the security office. I know the date, so it won't take long at all. I can hang around school until everyone leaves for the day."

"Why should Lance do this for you?"

"Because if I don't find out who left that stuff in my locker, and it escalates, it looks bad for Mr. Carter. He's supposed to be protecting us." I feel like a total douchebag for saying it aloud, but I need to convince Dahlia to help me.

She shrugs. "Okay, I'll ask him. But, if he gets in trouble for this—"

"He won't," I assure her. "I want to see what's on the tape between the time school ended the previous day and when I arrived at my locker the next morning. Lance is a tech genius. This should be easy for him."

"You better hope nothing goes wrong if he agrees to do this."

"Nothing will."

Dahlia picks up her bag and leaves. I remain in my seat for a while. If Sidney is behind the note and phone call, I'll confront her, and she'll deny it. The tape will incriminate her, and that will be the end of it. What if it's not Sidney, though? I haven't thought that far ahead. I don't have enemies. Sidney doesn't count. She's more like a turbo-charged nuisance right now. I try to do the right thing as much as I can. Except for that one time. I'm still ashamed, but everyone makes mistakes, right?

CHAPTER 5

A FTER I MOVE through the lunch line, I head to our usual table and have a seat. Frances gives me a puzzled look.

"What?" I ask, my senses on high alert.

"There's something different about you," she says.

"I haven't changed in twenty-four hours."

"Nothing crazy, just something," she insists.

Then Callie leans over and inspects my face. "Smile."

"No," I say and swipe her hand away. "Stop it, both of you. Especially you, Callie."

"What did I do?"

"You gave Christian my number without asking me first."

"I don't know what you're talking about." Her naughty grin says otherwise.

"You would have said no if Callie didn't handle the situation," Frances says. "You should be thanking her."

"He begged. It was so sad. I felt sorry for him," Callie explains. "And he was so sincere."

"How do you know he was sincere?"

"It's obvious he has it bad for you."

Frances agrees. "What did he say?"

"He wants me to give him a chance."

"Will you?" Callie asks.

"I don't know if he's the guy for me. He's dazzling and says all the right things, and he makes me weak in the knees. In the end, I wonder if it's all a game."

"You're doing it again," Callie says. "Overthinking. Just go with it and see what happens. We're out of here in seven months. You don't want to look back and wonder what could have been."

"I can't get past his reputation."

"Pfft, that's in the past," Callie says. "I don't see him chasing Sidney or anyone else. People change, Abbie."

"If you won't do it for yourself, do it for us," Frances pleads. "We want to stick it to Sidney. She'll have a coronary when she finds out she has zero chance of getting back together with him."

"Really? You want her to try and kill me the way she almost did Willa Schofield?"

"You're tough. You can take Sidney any place, anytime." As if to prove her point, Frances glances across the dining hall to where Sidney is sitting with her clique. Sidney makes eye contact with us. Frances smirks, and Sidney flips her the bird. Frances returns the gesture with a big old smile on her face.

"Don't get her started, Frances. Please. I don't need the drama."

"That's exactly what you need," Callie says.

"We don't have enough turmoil in our lives, between my mysterious stalker and Callie's parents' ongoing divorce battle?"

The split came as a shock to Callie and the rest of the world. Nicholas Furi is a famous movie director, with a bunch of mega blockbuster and Oscar-winning films to his credit. Callie's mom, model-turned-actress Penelope Bradshaw, met her Dad on a movie set, and it's been a fairytale romance, until now.

"Don't remind me," Callie says rolling her eyes.

"Sorry. You don't have to talk about it if you don't want to." I feel guilty for bringing up the sore subject.

"It's in my face all the time," she admits. "At the supermarket, on TV, online, here at school."

"Don't listen to the losers here at school," Frances says, leaning back in her seat.

Callie looks up from her plate. "What are they saying? I mean the stuff that I don't know. My parents won't tell me the truth. They give me the canned answer, the one I'm sure their publicists came up with. They still love each other and will remain friends, but they decided splitting up was in their best interest."

"What about your interests?" I ask.

"I'm eighteen. My interests are less complicated for them. I'll be away at college for the next four years, starting next year."

Her cobalt blue eyes shimmer, like the moon casting a glow on the ocean. Frances and I rally, taking her hands in ours. "You'll get through it, Callie. You have us, day and night. Right, Frances?"

"Duh," Frances says. She looks at me like I'm an imbecile who shouldn't even ask the question.

"My Dad called me this morning. He's filming in Budapest. He's already moved on, and the divorce isn't even final yet. I've decided not to speak to him for a while."

"How do you know?" I ask.

"I heard *her* in the background. I asked him who it was. He claimed it was his assistant director, trying to keep him on schedule for the day's shooting. Whatever."

"Maybe it was."

"Come on, Abbie. You can't be that naive. At 4:00 a.m. Budapest time, in his hotel room? She's just the first in a long line of rebound relationships to come."

We stay silent for a beat. I'm still holding her hand. I can feel the rage and disappointment pumping through her veins. Callie is a daddy's girl, like me. He's her superhero, and she just discovered he's a regular guy who was just pretending all along.

Callie lets go of our hands and wipes a tear before it escapes.

I try to lighten the mood with humor. "Okay, fine. I'll be your human pincushion again. You don't have to get all dramatic about it."

"Ha-ha," she says, amused. "Lucky for you, I have a couple of dresses I just sketched. You know what that means."

Callie is a talented designer and always has her sketchpad with her, although lately I haven't seen it much. Since I'm the tallest one in our group, all her design ideas are tested out on me. I'm always being poked and prodded. She's still working on pulling her portfolio together for application to Parsons and Fashion Institute of Technology in New York.

"Ooh, light bulb moment," she says, bobbing up and down in her chair. "How about I dress you for Evan Mueller's senior bash?"

"I didn't confirm I was going."

"You are going," Frances says, like an army general issuing orders.

"I have the perfect outfit in mind," Callie says.

Callie follows twenty different fashion and style blogs. I don't know how she keeps up with them all. I know whatever she has in mind, I'll find some reason to object. She's been trying to get me to raise my hemline ever since we met.

"I guess I'm going to Evan's party," I say, finally giving in.

CHAPTER 6

C ALLIE KEPT HER word. The outfit she picked for the party is laid out on my bed, and we've been debating for the past twenty minutes. Frances is in the bathroom, putting on her makeup. Callie was the first to get ready in a purple, bell-sleeved mini dress with a gold belt. Adorable.

"It's too short," I argue for the fourth time.

"With the matching tights, it will be fine. Stop being a killjoy. I wish I had legs that went on for days."

I glance at the outfit again. The chocolate suede mini skirt is cute, a nice contrast to the pale, yellow, form-fitting angora sweater she picked out. Callie has great taste. But I don't want to flash anyone, which is what will happen if I wear this skirt. Okay, I'm exaggerating. I've just never worn anything this short before, and it's making me crazy.

"Just put the outfit on already, Abbie," Frances says, in frustration. "Are we going to this party, or are we staying in your room all night?" She's done with her makeup, looking sleek and glamorous in a ruffle collared, white top and black slacks. Her long, thick hair hangs loose. She never questions Callie's choices for her.

"You just want to get there so you can make out with Trevor. Seriously, you two should just get an apartment," I say, teasing her.

"And send my parents to an early grave? I don't think so."

"Your Dad is worse than mine, and that's saying a lot."

Frances and her sister, Penny, are first generation Taiwanese-American. Her father, a trauma surgeon, founded a healthcare company that specializes in medical products and equipment to help improve surgical outcomes for patients. Her mom works for the Department of Environmental Protection for the State of New Jersey.

"That's why I haven't told my parents about me and Trevor."

Callie and I look at Frances in disbelief.

"You're kidding, right?" Callie says.

"They know that I like this boy named Trevor. They would go postal if they knew what Trevor and I get into."

"Frances, it's been six months, and you haven't told them he's your boyfriend?" I ask.

"What they don't know won't hurt them. All they want me to do is study. Besides, they're all the way in Jersey. What happens in Massachusetts, stays in Massachusetts," she concludes, winking at us.

"You're so wrong," Callie says laughing.

"Look, my parents see what they want to see. I let them."

The two of them eventually wear me down, and I decide to go with the outfit Callie picked. I added knee-high boots to the ensemble. Not bad.

I COME TO a stop in the long, winding cobblestone pathway leading to Evan's house and hand my car keys to one of the valet attendants. Callie, Frances, and I hop out and make our way toward the main entrance of the massive red brick colonial. Frances rings the doorbell, and the door opens instantly. Evan appears, sporting his famous rock star hair and a Led Zeppelin T-shirt.

"Ladies. Welcome to Casa de Mueller," he says, with a goofy grin. He opens the door wider to let us in. Music drifts from the sound system as we enter. "Abbie, you made it. Nice."

I thank him for inviting me, and he leads us into the foyer. A Steinway piano is to the left of us. Evan gives us instructions like a flight attendant before takeoff.

"There are two bathrooms on this floor. The kitchen and living room are through there," he says pointing to a narrow hallway off to the right. "There's food and booze in the kitchen. Help yourselves to anything you want. I'll catch you hotties later." He then disappears.

"Any bets on who gets plastered first?" Frances asks as we size up the living room area. The place is already thick with seniors drinking and socializing, a few swaying to the beat of the music. "I know there's a news story in there somewhere."

"Look who's coming this way," Callie says.

We follow her line of vision and land on a petite girl with flaming red hair, and an unlit cigarette between her fingers, squeezing her way through groups of people. Brooke Westerly, Sidney's underling. I sense the tension radiating off Frances. As if by telepathy, we each understand the threat and draw in closer to each other, forming a protective shield. Brooke stops in front of us, but her attention is focused on Callie.

"Total bummer about your parents splitting up. That's rough. I've been through it myself. If you ever want to talk, I'm here." She places her hand on Callie's shoulder. "We have to stick together, you know."

We all look at Brooke dumfounded. She takes the hint and scuttles off to fake friend someone else.

"What was that?" I ask. "Is Sidney recruiting for her clique?"

"Brooke the opportunist has been trying to be my friend since junior year. I gave her a bunch of hints, but so far, she hasn't picked up on any of them," Callie says.

"I hear she wants to be an actress," Frances says, using air quotes. "Even auditioned for a couple of TV pilots. No surprise she didn't make the cut since she has no talent. Well, that's not true. There are plenty of guys in the senior class who can testify to just how *talented* she is."

I arch my eyebrow. "Where do you get this stuff from? I never hear any of the juicy gossip first-hand."

"You don't give off the friendliest vibe," Callie says.

We arrive at the kitchen entrance and poke our

heads in. There's a spread fit for a banquet on the island in the center and all around the counter tops. It's only 9:00 p.m., and I already see a handful of people who would fail a Breathalyzer test.

"I'm plenty friendly," I say to Callie.

"We understand your intensity, Abbie, but other people don't get it," Frances says.

"Let's mingle," I say to the girls as if to prove I'm not an ogre. "Meet up in an hour to compare notes."

Frances goes off to find Trevor. Callie sees a fellow fashionista and takes off, too. I go back to the living room area and find a cozy spot against the wall next to a potted plant where I can observe everyone. I look across the room, and my heart skips a beat. There, next to the French doors with Sidney mere inches from his face, is Christian. His arms are folded, and his eyes wander aimlessly around the space. A few seconds pass with Sidney's mouth moving and Christian maintaining his bored stance.

Then Sidney places her palms on his chest. He removes them. She pouts. He looks up, and our eyes connect across the room. He smiles at me. Sidney turns around to see what changed his mood. Her eyes are hard as marbles, I imagine. I can't see too well because the lights are dimmed. The irritation on her face is unmistakable, though.

Christian opted for a black, crewneck sweater that stretches across his chest, revealing his perfectly sculpted form, and a pair of dark jeans. I can't blame Sidney for wanting to touch him. I bet he smells great, too. Still, she should keep her grubby little claws off him. Not that I'm jealous or anything. I leave them to sort out whatever issues they're having, elbowing my way through the throngs of people who've overflowed into the hallway from the living room.

Someone almost spills a drink on me. I run smack into Preston Harvey sporting a major Afro, looking like he was just struck dumb. Preston is into embracing his blackness in the face of what he calls almost *whiteout conditions* at Saint Matthews. He stares at me as if seeing me for the first time; his eyes fixated on my chest. I knew it! I told Callie this sweater was too tight. I snap my fingers to pull Preston out of his stupor.

"Abbie, my sister," he says, with a nervous chuckle. "Glad you came. You know we have to represent."

"Okay, Preston, duly noted. Excuse me."

"Hey, what's the hurry?" he asks, grabbing me by the arm. "Can't you give a brother a few minutes of your time?"

"I'm looking for Callie."

"Oh, last time I saw her, she was with our illustrious host. I don't think you need to worry about her. She's in great hands."

It's hard to miss the double entendre. I don't want to think about what kind of trouble Callie might get into. She and Evan have been flirting with each other since last year, but he had a girlfriend at the time. That's no longer an issue.

"So, what do you say we go somewhere quiet and get acquainted?" Preston asks.

There was a time I had a major crush on Preston and any attention from him would have been welcome. That was until he embarrassed me in front of the whole class. I never forgot the slight, and I refused to acknowledge his existence the rest of that school year. I only started coming around last month. He has some nerve hitting on me now.

"I have to go, Preston. See you around."

"Come on, Abbie."

"She said beat it, Preston."

We're both startled when Christian appears.

Preston throws his hands up in the air and backs up a few steps. "Sorry, man. I didn't know you were hitting that."

I'm stunned, unable to move a muscle. My brain is on pause as if it checked out to search for an appropriate response. The stinging sensation at the back of my eyes is about to erupt into a volcano of blistering tears. I look down for a second to see my hands trembling.

"You're a disgusting creep," I say. "How could you disrespect me this way? I thought you were better than that, Preston. Guess you can't teach a pig to be a gentleman."

He coughs and grabs at the collar of his shirt. Then he looks to his left and then his right, desperate for an escape route. I don't stick around for an apology. I know he won't issue one. All I want is to find a quiet spot to calm down and recover from the most grotesque insult ever hurled at me.

"Are you okay?" Christian asks. We sit next to each other in two accent chairs in a little alcove along the wall of the grand staircase.

"I will be."

"Preston is a jerk for saying what he did. Glad you told him off. He didn't have a single comeback. You're lethal."

I nudge him as if we've been friends forever. He flashes those perfect teeth at me, his eyes dancing under the dim light.

"You look supermodel fantastic," he says. "I couldn't believe it was you from across the living room."

I should say thank you and bask in the compliment. Instead, I kill the mood. "I saw you and Sidney earlier. She's probably wondering where you are."

"Sidney and I are not together," he says, his voice tight. "I've already told you that."

"Yet every time I turn around, there you are. Together." I cover my mouth quickly before any more embarrassing sentences pop out. Where did that come from?

A smile tugs at the corners of his mouth. "Are you jealous?"

"Of Sidney? Puh-lease." I have to set him straight before he gets any strange ideas.

"I'm flattered."

"Don't be. You're reading too much into it."

"You don't have to hide your feeling from me, Abbie."

"What are you talking about?"

Why does he have to make a big deal about everything? Okay, so I think he's beyond gorgeous.

Resplendent would be a more accurate description. I also spend too many of my waking hours thinking about him. None of it means anything. It's just a phase. It will pass.

"I really like you, Abbie. I think you like me too."

I look directly into his eyes, searching for anything that will confirm what I know about him so my heart will stop doing back flips every time he looks at me. Christian, the player, who has left a long list of girls sobbing in bathrooms or in their dorm rooms late into the night. The arrogant, self-involved bad boy who doesn't care what anyone thinks. The untamable, wild child who was expelled from two boarding schools for behavior most adults would find reprehensible.

I don't see any of that. I only see a vulnerable boy who likes a girl, and he's scared she won't like him back. Maybe Mom was right all along.

"I'm not saying that I like you, but I'm not saying I don't, either. What are you going to do about it?"

"This."

He lowers his head and moves his body closer to me. His lips connect with mine, soft and sensual, demanding nothing. My heart is pounding in my chest, and I can feel the blood roaring in my ears. Christian palms my face and pulls me closer to him. I don't resist. My bones have turned to liquid. He runs his lips over mine, taking his time, but I'm driven by my instincts. I open my mouth. When our tongues collide, I feel a lightning bolt go through me. I close my eyes, and a soft moan escapes my throat. His breathing is erratic and becomes more frenzied by the second. The kiss deepens, and our tongues engage in a powerful tango.

He vacates his chair and comes to kneel beside me. I shift my body, so it better aligns with his. My hands turn into tentacles, greedily clawing at him. I hear distant voices. I mentally shush them.

"Ahem. Excuse me."

The meddling voice pierces my subconscious. It's loud and irate. Christian hears it also. He lifts his head from my neck. His face is flushed. His expression vacillates between exhilaration and annoyance. He gets off his knees and returns to the chair. We both turn our attention to the unwelcome intruder: Sidney.

Sidney folds her arms as if waiting for us, the misbehaving children, to come to our senses. I don't know what I was thinking, making out in an open space like this. Guilt and shame consume me. It wasn't too long ago that I found the idea of going out with Christian distasteful. I had a catalog of reasons why I shouldn't, but I underestimated the attraction between us.

"What do you want, Sidney?" I ask. "Is the house on fire?"

"No, but someone should turn a hose on the two of you. You're such a hypocrite, Abbie. Pretending to be so innocent when—"

"Watch it, Sidney," Christian says, his tone menacing. "You wouldn't want anyone finding out about your vintage encyclopedia, would you? Lay off Abbie."

His words strike fear in Sidney. Her porcelain-like features take on a gloomy air. I've never seen her with an encyclopedia. It's obviously a code word for something else. If Sidney's involved, it has to be something nefarious. She frowns, tosses me a look of undisguised loathing, and then storms off.

"I should go," I say to Christian.

"Why?"

"The girls might be looking for me. We agreed to check in with each other."

He takes my hand in his and squeezes. "Are you nervous?"

"What?"

"The intensity. I feel it too."

I'm not sure how to respond, so I go with the truth. "I don't know what I'm doing."

"I'm scared too," he says.

I cast him a look of disbelief.

"It's true."

He reaches into his pocket with the other hand and pulls out his cell phone. He taps a few buttons and tells me to check my phone. I pull the phone from my purse. The text message from him is the yellow smiley face emoticon with a look of sheer terror.

Laughter escapes me. The corners of his eyes crinkle into a smile. He's not so scary. He's just a boy—a beautiful, infuriating, tenacious, curious boy who makes me uncomfortable.

"What are you so scared of anyway?" I ask.

"That you won't give me the chance to show you I'm not all bad. That you won't give me an opportunity to make you laugh, argue with you, spoil you, ask a million questions to learn what hurts you, makes you happy, scares you, what's important to you."

Every girl, no matter how sensible, can succumb to vanity. As wonderful as it feels to be chased, the cautious part of me, the part that needs everything to line up according to plan, still whispers: *be careful.*

"You made me laugh tonight. Getting me into an argument is easy. Just tell me about your favorite movies or singer, and I'll tell you why your taste in music and movies suck. When it comes to spoiling me, you already have serious competition. Between my family and friends, and the guy who works weekends at the French bakery downtown, you're going to have to up your game. The rest? Make me tell you."

"Okay," he says, leaning forward. "No surprises so far. But, I'm going down to the bakery this weekend to have a word with that guy."

"You can't do that. He'll stop adding freebies to my order. I'm especially fond of the Gâteau Saint Honoré and the Tarte Tatin."

He finds the scenario funny and says he'll file that in the back of his mind. I tell him I have to find Frances and Callie to make sure they're not getting into trouble, especially Callie. He makes me promise to text him when I find them, and we're ready to head home.

I NAVIGATE THROUGH the party to find the nearest bathroom to freshen up. The crowd is thick as if it swelled to hundreds of people in minutes. An idea occurs to me. Upstairs. Sleeping quarters in a house this large would have at least two bathrooms upstairs.

With a series of "excuse me" and "sorry", I make it up the stairs and find myself in a dimly lit hallway. Two couples lean up against the walls, making out.

"Bathroom?" I ask.

One of them points further down the hall to the right without interrupting his lip lock. I knock on a closed door and push my ears up against it, waiting for a response. I hear nothing. I turn the thick gold knob slowly and then peak inside. It's empty. I dash inside and lock the door behind me. Leaning up against it, I close my eyes and just breathe in and out. When I open my eyes, I notice how massive the bathroom is—a Jacuzzi, his and hers vanity sinks, thick rugs, a shower stall, and the scent of potpourri floating in the air.

I walk over to the large mirror with gold accents and glance at my reflection. I don't even recognize my own eyes, which now resemble two glistening, sable brown pools. Callie did my makeup, and the double quote of black mascara makes my already thick lashes even more dramatic. I didn't look too bad when I was hanging out with Christian, not that I care what he thinks of my appearance or anything. I prefer minimal makeup, if any at all, and little fuss when it comes to choosing my wardrobe. When Callie is around, though, all my efforts at keeping things simple disappear.

I fluff my hair and break out the lip-gloss from

my purse, then reapply. I sit on the toilet seat, let my shoulders sag, and do what I do best: overanalyze every situation.

Why did I enjoy Christian's kiss so much? Am I lying to myself about how I relate to him? Why does Sidney keep popping up, yet Christian insists they're not together? He makes me feel things I thought I would never feel for anyone else after Ty graduated and went off to Yale. Maybe it's time I grow up.

My pity party is interrupted when I hear the two-tone sound of a bell chiming—my text message ring tone. I open my purse and grab my phone in a flash, hoping it's Frances or Callie. I read the message, and my blood turns to ice.

BLOCKED NUMBER

Lying hypocrite! Stay away from him, or else. You've been warned.

CHAPTER 7

I BURST OUT of the bathroom, determined to have it out with Sidney. Why even bother to pretend the text is anonymous? She's crazy jealous, but with this new message, she's just flat out crazy. I amble down the staircase and turn left toward the hallway. I push my way through while scanning the faces of the partygoers, hoping to spot her. Nothing. I end up in the kitchen and notice the patio is lit, and a crowd has gathered.

Lounge chairs and small, colorful end tables are scattered throughout the space. Some partygoers relax in the chairs while others stand around drinking, conversing, or grooving to the music on the night air. A couple of seniors greet me when they spot me, and I offer a non-verbal acknowledgment.

I spot Sidney at the edge of the patio near the hedges— drink in hand, and conversing with Brooke and another senior I've seen around but don't know that well. I march over to them, clutching the phone with the threatening message.

I hold up the phone to Sidney's face. "Do you think this is funny?" I shout at her. "Just how twisted are you, Sidney?"

She gawks at me like I've gone mad. So do Brooke and their companion. I no longer hear the murmur of conversation around us. I turn around to see all eyes on us.

"We need to talk, Sidney," I say, lowering my voice and the phone. "This is getting absurd, and it ends now."

Sidney hasn't blinked once since I approached.

"What's going on?" Brooke asks.

"Sidney knows what she did," I say through gritted teeth. "I just want a moment alone with her to sort this out. Can you guys excuse us, please?"

They leave without protest.

"Does Christian know you're a full-on psycho?" Sidney asks, folding her arms. "Somebody should warn him."

"Are you going to deny you sent me that text?"

I flash back to the conversation with Frances about the things that Sidney is capable of. She almost killed someone, and her parents covered for her. I have to take the text seriously. It wasn't a subtle threat.

She scoffs. "I have no idea what you're rambling on about. If I wanted to say something to you, I wouldn't text you. I would tell you straight to your stupid face. Like, don't get your hopes up, thinking you have a chance with Christian. He's playing you for fun. When he gets bored, we'll be back together. You're a temporary distraction, like an irritating stomach virus that makes me puke but goes away in a few days."

We'll just see about that.

Her words inflame me. I wish I had superpowers right now that would allow me to wipe her off the face of the Earth. Instead, I force myself to remain composed and unaffected.

"Look, Christian and I like each other. I'm sorry if it upsets you. I don't get the impression that you were anything more than a casual hookup to him. If I thought for a minute that he was serious about you, I would get out of your way. I keep my business drama-free as much as possible. You know that about me, Sidney."

She looks bored as if nothing I've said interests her in the least. "Whatever, Abbie. Christian's family has a certain image to maintain, and that includes who he dates and brings home to Bedford Hills. Sorry if it upsets you, but you don't meet the criteria."

For the second time this evening, I'm speechless. Sidney flips her hair, looks me up and down as if I were a turd she discovered under her Charlotte Olympia pumps, then sashays her way over to a small group gathered around the fire pit.

I'M ON EMOTIONAL overload; a dense sponge wrung dry, not a drop of liquid left. It's getting late and time to leave the party.

The valet pulls up near the entrance with my car. Callie, Frances and I pile in. I send a quick text to Christian, letting him know we're leaving. We exit the Mueller's driveway and take the side street that will get us to Route 9 West. Frances sits next to me in the front passenger seat, and Callie is in the back, barely able to form a coherent sentence.

"Why are we leaving the party so early?" she asks. Her mouth sounds like it's filled with cotton balls.

"It's not that early," I respond. "Dad might blow a gasket if I miss curfew. I have thirty minutes to get you guys back to campus and get home. I'm not going to make it, just so you know."

Callie goes silent. Frances hasn't taken her eyes off me since we got in the car.

"Well?" she asks.

"What?" I can tell Frances is in news story mode.

"I'm waiting. Heard you and Sidney got in each other's faces, and you and Christian were caught making out. Callie and I figured we'd give you some space. What we really wanted was to find you so we could gang up on Sidney."

"I did need some space to think things through."

I break down the evening, starting with the insult from Preston, then the kiss, the text message that arrived soon afterward, and the confrontation with Sidney.

Silence envelopes the car, the sound of the engine eating up the miles the only reprieve from the uneasiness. Callie doesn't say anything about the fact that Christian and I kissed for the first time, even though she's our biggest cheerleader and to her, that's big news. I glance at her in the rearview mirror. She's staring out the window into the darkness, her face expressionless.

Frances doesn't have a snarky comeback about Preston insulting me or how dismissive Sidney was when I confronted her. Neither one of them tries to explain the text as a prank, no reassurances that it was just some idiot playing some silly games, or that the text was sent to the wrong person.

I hear rumbling in the distance. A deafening clap of thunder roars across the night sky, followed by lightning that sends shivers up my spine. I swerve from the left lane into the middle of the road. My passengers remain stoic. I hunch over in the driver seat, and my fingers clamp down on the steering with an iron grip. Beads of sweat break out on my forehead, but I'm powerless to do anything about it. I navigate back to the left lane, my gaze intense on the road ahead of me.

Thunder blasts through the night again. The sky opens, and a punishing downpour pummels the vehicle, lashing out at the windshield and windows. A whimper escapes my lips. I manage to get the windshield wipers going at maximum level.

"Pull over. I'll drive," Frances says.

"I got it," I squeak.

"Pull over, Abbie. This is your worst nightmare, getting caught in a thunderstorm."

"It's okay, Abbie," Callie says. "We'll spend the night at your house, drinking hot chocolate and gossiping about the party."

"And you have to tell us if Christian is a good kisser," Frances adds.

I can't help but smile, just a little. I'm terrified of thunder and lightning. It started when I was four. My parents would bribe me to crawl out from under my bed during a storm or make room for me in theirs. I'm embarrassed to say that I'm almost an adult, and I still haven't outgrown the fear.

The windshield is barely a match for the torrential rain. I make my way to the right lane and come to a stop. I put on the high beam. The nearest car is miles in front of us. On the count of three, Frances and I open the passenger and driver side doors simultaneously. We're drenched in seconds as we quickly make the switch. We're both shivering. Frances cranks up the heat even higher, and we take off. My phone rings. I reach for it in my purse resting on the console between the driver and passenger seat. It's my father. He must be worried about the late hour and the storm.

"Hi, Dad."

"Where are you? Are you girls okay? Are you close to home? Do you need me to come get you?"

"Dad, it's fine. Frances is driving. We'll be home soon. Please don't worry." I know he's pacing the living room floor. He'll then make his way to the family room and continue the pacing there, contemplating grabbing his keys and coming to get us, despite my reassurances. Mom is probably upstairs, pretending to be asleep since Dad is on duty tonight, but she won't fall asleep until I get home.

"It's nasty out there. I don't feel comfortable with you girls driving in this weather."

"We'll get home safely. I promise."

CHAPTER 8

W E ALL DRY off and change into pajamas. Three mugs of steaming hot chocolate were delivered to my room. After we warm up, all three of us sit on my bed yoga style.

"What are we going to do about the crazy text message?" Callie asks.

"I'm not sure. Sidney was too calm and uninterested when I confronted her. Either she's a sociopath or an excellent actress."

"She might be both," Frances says. "Although I haven't heard anything about her acting weirder or meaner than usual. I asked around, and, so far, nothing. It's still possible whoever sent the messages got the wrong person."

"I don't think so."

"How do you know?" Callie asks.

It was time to confess. "Last week, I got a call from a girl who quoted the note, word for word."

"Why didn't you tell us?" Callie asks, her eyes widening.

"You two have your own stuff going on. I didn't want to drag you into this."

"What else did this girl say?" Frances asks.

"Nothing. I said hello, she quoted the note and then hung up."

"Did it sound like Sidney at all?" Callie asks.

"I couldn't tell. I don't know what she sounds like over the phone. The caller could be in our age group, though."

"If this continues, you have to tell Dr. Kellogg," Frances says. "This stalking started on school property."

"I hope it doesn't come to that. I just wish I knew what the person wanted. Three separate incidents make it a grudge of some kind."

"But who besides Sidney has a beef with you?" Frances asks.

"That's the problem. She's the only one with means, motive, and opportunity."

My friends look at me like I'm a basket case. "I watch *Law and Order* reruns with my mother, okay?"

It's coming up on 1:00 a.m. We're physically drained and mentally exhausted. It's time to sleep. Callie has something else in mind, however.

"Don't think we forgot. Details, please."

"Forgot what?"

"The kiss," Callie says.

"It's late, and I'm tired," I say. "Can we talk about it tomorrow?"

Frances tosses a pillow at my head, and I duck.

Callie picks one up, too, and aims for my face. I put my hands up in surrender. "Okay, okay, I'll talk. You don't need to suffocate me."

I describe how the chemistry between Christian and I took me by surprise. That the idea of us as a couple doesn't seem so improbable anymore because he's attentive, funny, and genuinely wants to get to know me. How scared I am that falling for him could lead to disaster, if I don't guard my heart.

"What's the real reason you're so scared to be with Christian, Abbie?" Callie asks.

"It's simple," Frances quips. "Abbie is afraid she could end up looking like a fool if things don't work out between them. We know how much she's a control freak. Christian's true intentions are unknown right now, the X in a romantic algebraic equation."

I couldn't have explained it any better. She nailed it.

"Yeah, what Frances said," I say, nodding at Callie.

Callie moves her head from side to side, working out the kinks in her neck. The sound of her bones popping creeps me out every time she does it.

"What happened to the Abbie who wouldn't back down when a psycho was trying to get rid of her mother?" she asks. "Now, you're scared of a boy? Come on."

Two years ago, a deranged lunatic who wanted revenge for reasons that made sense only in her mind framed my mother for murder. Mom spent three months in jail until we figured out who was behind it. In the end, the nutcase had killed three people including her psychiatrist, who had suspected she knew more about Mom's case than she was saying.

"It's complicated, Callie. When I'm around Christian, it's as if I'm on an exhilarating rollercoaster ride. When I come down from the high, I have my doubts."

Frances rolls her eyes at me and flops down on the bed. Callie stares at me like a helpless cat.

"Christian is making it up as he goes," Callie says.

"What?"

"I have to hear this," Frances says. She pops back up into a sitting position.

"He's clueless when it comes to you, Abbie," Callie states. "We attend some of the same parties outside of school, mostly during the summer. Girls swarm around him like bees. I've seen Hollywood starlets throw themselves at my father, hoping to be cast in his next movie. Christian has him beat. These girls know how influential the Wheelers are and how many digits are attached to their family fortune. Eleven, in case you're wondering."

"I wasn't, but thanks for sharing. I still don't see what any of this has to do with me."

"In plain English," a frustrated Frances says, "Christian doesn't chase girls. They chase him. You changed the game on him, and now his playbook is useless. He needs a whole new strategy to deal with you."

"Frances is right," Callie says. "All his life, people have been catering to Christian because of his family name. It's sad to say, but he's been taught that they don't care about him, that they only want what the Wheeler name can do for them. That includes the girls who want to 'date' him. I think the fact that you blew him off for so long is a game changer for him."

"I'm just a regular girl, Callie. I'm not here to be a game changer for anyone but myself, for now. I don't have magical powers."

"That's the best part. Your powers move like the wind," Frances says, gesturing with her hands. "Mysterious and invisible. Christian doesn't know what hit him."

"That was beautiful," I say. "You're going to be a great reporter. They may as well hand over your Pulitzer Prize right now."

She grins and pretends to punch me in the arm.

We talk into the wee hours of the morning, but now, sleep won't come until my curiosity is satisfied. I finally get up the courage to ask the girls what has Sidney so afraid.

"Have either of you seen Sidney with a vintage encyclopedia? Christian mentioned it after she caught us kissing and went ballistic. There was fear in her eyes. I don't think he was talking about a real encyclopedia, though."

Frances sits still. Callie stares off into space, her expression grim.

"What is it?" I ask.

"The encyclopedia is real," Callie confirms. "The one she owns is special for a reason. It has a hidden compartment. I'm surprised Christian said anything. He must like really like you to put Sidney on blast like that."

"I'm officially confused. Why does Sidney's encyclopedia need a hidden compartment?"

"Because of what's in it," Frances replies.

My eyes roam back and forth between them. "So, what's in it?"

Callie looks straight at me. "Cocaine."

CHAPTER 9

I T'S MONDAY MORNING. I stand at my locker replaying the events of the weekend in my head, again. What should I do with the secret I learned about Sidney? Is it a gift, a way to force her to leave me alone and stop threatening me? No way. I shake off the idea as soon as it occurs to me because I would never betray my friends' confidence for a temporary victory.

My phone chimes, alerting me to a new text message. I grab it from the side pocket of my bag.

BLOCKED NUMBER

Liar! Hypocrite! Poser!

I should have known Sidney wouldn't relent. She's always hated me, but this is a new level of meanness, even for her. Is this all about Christian? And what about the strange note and the phone call?

I exhale slowly, and then turn my attention to opening my locker. Dahlia is walking toward me, her stride purposeful. My heart rate skyrockets as I anticipate some massive failure in my quest to get my hands on video surveillance that would prove Sidney's been to my locker and is behind the threats. I start turning the combination on the lock.

"Is it true that you lost it at Evan Mueller's party?" she asks, leaning up against the locker right next to mine.

I don't answer at first. I keep turning the combination. I hear giggles as students walk by. Jessica Wallace, a plump blonde with a permanent smirk, one-third of Sidney's clique, laughs under her breath as she passes by.

"So sad," she says and then takes off shaking her head.

"That was weird," I say to no one in particular.

"Everyone's talking about it," Dahlia says. "What happened at the party?"

I pop the lock. "Everyone's talking about what?"

"How you went cray cray at the senior bash. Sidney started a rumor that you sent yourself a threatening text and then yelled at her in front of everyone. She claims it was a pitiful move to get attention from Christian."

My thoughts are a jumbled mess. What does Sidney hope to gain by starting the rumor? Was she high when she came up with the idea?

"There's a picture, too," Dahlia says.

That statement grabs my attention. "What picture?"

She whips out her phone from her bag and scrolls. She hands it to me, and I have a look. It's a shot of me, yelling at Sidney and holding up my phone so she could read the text. Everyone on the patio that night witnessed the whole thing. Anyone could have snapped the photo. My face isn't very clear because my back is to the camera, but there's no mistaking it's me.

I cover my face, mortified by the image.

"So, it's true?" Dahlia's tone is a blend of surprise and accusation.

I remove my hands from my face. "Not exactly. I did get a threatening text, and I did yell at her, but not for the reason she says."

She edges closer to me and whispers, "Does it have anything to do with what we talked about the other day? The stuff you asked for?"

I shake my head.

She takes a step back. "Oh. So, it's a huge deal, then?"

"Yes. I wouldn't have asked you to help me if it wasn't. And by the way, do you know when Lance will have the footage?"

"He's working on it. It's not as easy as it sounds. He has to find out where his Dad keeps the pass key for the office and get it back before anyone realizes it went missing in the first place. I told you, this is a big favor you're asking."

"Okay, Okay. I don't mean to be impatient."

"What if it's not Sidney?"

"It has to be her. There's no one else."

"But what if it's not?"

"Who else would it be? Sidney hates me because I don't take crap from her."

Dahlia sighs loudly. "That's messed up."

"It's Sidney."

"Yeah."

Dahlia takes off, and I swap the remaining books for class. I look to my left and then freeze. Lance Carter and Christian are both heading my way. I have to think fast. I need to hear what Lance has to say, but I don't want Christian asking me questions I'm not ready to answer. I back away from the locker as if I'm meeting them halfway. Lance is ahead by a few steps. I have seconds to say something to him. I casually plant myself in his path.

"What's up, Mama?" he asks in his booming voice.

"Nothing much, Lance," I say, then I whisper with lightning-speed, "Meet me in the chapel during lunch." I smoothly step out of his path.

Lance doesn't miss a beat and continues walking as if we didn't just agree to a secret meeting.

Christian takes his usual spot next to my locker. His hair hasn't completely dried from his morning shower. I catch a whiff of his cologne drifting through the air. He's casual chic in a long-sleeved Lacoste Polo shirt, jeans, and a scarf.

"Why was Lance all over you?"

My best defense is to play dumb. The first-period crowd has thinned out, so we're virtually alone in the hallway. I shut my locker and grab my bag. He walks with me to my calculus class.

"He was just saying hi."

"You whispered something to him."

"I don't know what you're talking about."

"Do you like him? Because I'm not afraid of the competition."

I slow down the pace and look at him. "There is no competition, Christian. Lance has a girlfriend. I like Dahlia. I wouldn't go after her man."

"Cool. We have unfinished business."

"We do?"

"We were interrupted at the party."

"A good thing. People saw us making out. It's all over school."

"Let them talk. I hope it doesn't bother you."

"I try not to let it bother me."

I brace myself for what's coming next. The rumor Sidney spread about why I yelled at her and the accompanying photo floating around. He doesn't bring it up at all. He just scored major points with me.

We arrive outside my AP calculus class, and it's time for him to head to his class across the hall. "Can we meet after school? At Joe's Pizzeria?"

"Um...I—"

"Don't say no, Abbie. Please."

That does me in. It would be cruel to say no after such a heartfelt plea. I swallow hard. "Sure. I can meet you there."

"Great. See you then."

MY HEART THUNDERS in my chest as I bustle down the main hallway, heading to the chapel. I barely paid attention to anything in my morning classes. Mr.

Winters, my AP calculus teacher, caught me staring out the window and wanted to know if I cared to share with the class what was so fascinating outside. Trevor caught up with me afterward and asked if I was okay, whether I was still flustered about the incident with Sidney. He told me to ignore her, that she fights dirty, and I shouldn't come down to her level. Good advice, although Sidney is determined to get me to do just that.

I enter Westford Chapel, an intimate, interfaith structure with gorgeous architectural detailing and beautiful stained glass windows that illuminate the chapel when sunlight seeps through. Two angels on the back walls, one on either side of the organ pipes, look down as if passing judgment on all who enter. The pews are on opposite sides of the aisle, so worshipers face each other when service is in session.

Lance is already seated in the first row, playing a game on his smartphone. With a dark roast coffee complexion and a perfectly round shaved head, he reminds me of that giant poster my father has in his man cave of basketball superstar Michael Jordan. Ironically, Lance is six-foot-three and gets annoyed when people assume he's a basketball player. He's not.

"Thanks for meeting me," I say, sliding next to him.

"Anytime, Mama," he says, revealing a toothy grin.

"Dahlia told you everything?"

"Yeah, she did. You're lucky I like you. Dahlia said you're freaked out, so I'll do it tonight."

This is a surprise, despite my earlier whining about

how long it was taking. Relief washes over me, but I feel trepidation battling its way into my consciousness. "How are you going to get the pass key?"

"The less you know, the better. I'll save the footage on a flash drive, and you can watch it on your laptop."

I give Lance the dates to narrow his search and reduce the amount of time it will take to find the video. We agree to meet again in the chapel tomorrow when he will turn over the flash drive. I give him my cell phone number just in case he needs to get in touch beforehand. We head out of the chapel together.

"So, Christian Wheeler, huh? Stranger things have happened, I guess. Is it true?"

"What are you talking about?"

"Answering a question with a question. I see you, Mama, trying to act coy. It's cool if you and Christian are on the down low."

"Christian and I aren't anything, yet."

"The dude had smoke coming out of his ears just because I said hi to you. I'll say that's something."

"Lance, Christian was behind you. You didn't see anything of the kind."

"I felt his eyes on me. I was in for a serious beat down if I didn't get out of there."

We both crack up as we leave the chapel. By this time tomorrow, I'll have my answers.

CHAPTER 10

I PULL OUT of the parking lot on my way to Joe's Pizzeria to meet up with Christian. It's a cold fall afternoon, the first week of November. A light breeze rustles the trees, adding to the collection of leaves already on the ground. Thanksgiving, one of my favorite holidays, second only to Christmas, will soon be here. It also means I only have a month left to submit my remaining college applications. No pressure at all.

Traffic slows down as I get closer to downtown, an enclave made up of small shops, a farmer's market, the Town Hall, a couple of churches, and the library not too far off. Castleview came into existence in the 1600s and was first settled in the 1700s, primarily as a farming community. Today, despite modern amenities and its affluent status (voted as one of the best places to live in America), most of the town is still rural. It's quite normal to see cows grazing on wide, open land.

I stroll into Joe's Pizzeria and spot Christian right away at a booth. The afterschool hangout is already packed with kids from Saint Matthews and Castleview High School. The joint is lined with booths and tables that seat two to four, covered in red-and-white-checkered tablecloths. A series of black-and-white photographs depicting the 1950s dot the walls. The smell of pizza pies coming from the brick oven competes with the scent of Pine-Sol. They must have just washed the floors.

"Hey, you," I say, sliding into the seat across from him.

A dazzling smile lights up his face. I would have fainted if I weren't already seated.

"Glad you agreed to come. I thought you were going to say no."

"The thought crossed my mind."

"I'm not so scary, Abbie."

"You're not?"

"You shouldn't listen to rumors."

"What rumors, in particular, are you referring to, Christian?" I'm feeling puckish at the moment, and he's not about to get off easy.

He blushes, his face turning crimson red. "I won't lie to you. I've dated a fair number of girls."

"Don't be modest. I hear you've dated much more than a fair number."

"Wow, you don't hold anything back," he says, removing his scarf and placing it on the seat next to him.

"No."

"Except when it comes to me."

"I have to be cautious, Christian. I've never been on a bad boy's radar before."

"You might like it," he says, leaning in closer, so our faces are only inches apart. "You're exactly what this bad boy needs. Are you up for the challenge?"

His eyes gleam under the lantern suspended above our table. I'm mesmerized. I know I'm supposed to say something clever, but my thoughts have deserted me. The spell is broken when someone close to our table clears her throat. We ease back into our seats. Frances and Callie are grinning at us.

"What are you guys doing here?" It's the first thing to tumble out of my mouth.

"The same thing you're doing here," Frances says.

Callie winks at me as if to say *good for you*.

"Okay. We're all here to eat greasy, fattening food," I say. "You know how much I hate exercising."

Everyone chuckles. "Well, we're off to stuff our faces," Callie says, pulling Frances along. Frances makes the *call me* sign with her hands.

Christian and I both leave our seats and head to the counter to order pizza and drinks. Once we're back at the booth, he grabs the crushed red pepper shaker from the table and douses his pizza with it.

"You like spicy food?"

He looks up from his task and his lips part. "I love all things spicy."

I shift uncomfortably in my seat. Part of me is drawn to his openness, like a moth to a flame. The other part wants to run because he's breaking down my barriers. I can't afford to be laid bare.

"What else do you love, besides spicy food?" I take a bite of my pizza.

"Music, old western movies, and painting. I get some skiing done in the cold weather."

I stop mid-chew. "Get out of here. I didn't know you paint. You'll have to show me your work one of these days."

"Maybe."

"Why maybe?"

"If you behave, maybe I'll show you my work."

"Who says I want to behave?"

That's what hanging out with Christian does to me. I say strange things. I can tell I shocked him. I shocked me, too.

"Well, then, I can't wait for you to misbehave."

"Is that all you think about?" I ask, shaking my head.

"Hey, you're the one with the dirty mind. I was talking about my art. If you want to put another spin on things, that's on you."

"Well, if it isn't sad, pitiful Abbie. Enjoy it while it lasts. You know Christian is just slumming it, right?" Sidney opens her mouth and sticks her finger in. She makes a gagging sound as if she's about to throw up. Her minions, Brooke and Jessica are stuck by her side, with matching sneers on their faces. Why, oh why can't Sidney just disappear into a black hole, and never come out?

"Welcome to slumming it, Christian," I say, looking directly at him. "You're in for one heck of a ride."

Sidney's jaw drops. Jessica and Brooke just stand there looking like the insipid creatures they are. I look

Sidney up and down with contempt, wave her off with indifference, and return to eating my pizza.

She storms off, and her underlings follow suit.

"What did you ever see in her?" I ask Christian in between bites. "Her obsession with you is unhealthy."

"It was just one of those things."

"That was rude. I shouldn't have asked. It's none of my business."

"It's okay, Abbie. You can ask me anything."

"Would you like another drink? I can get you one."

"No, thanks."

He reaches across the table for my hand. He begins to stroke the back of it. Electricity pulses through me. He leans forward, intent on kissing me. It takes a herculean effort on my part to resist.

"What subjects inspire your work? Do you use oil or water-based paint?"

"Water-based." He breaks eye contact with me, and his shoulders droop. I move a small piece of pizza around the plate in a circular pattern. He sips his drink. The chatter of conversation around us is a welcome distraction from the awkward moment.

I stop fidgeting with my food and wipe my hands with a napkin. Without looking at him, I reach for his hand and interlock our fingers. He looks up at me with a questioning gaze, and then leans in again. I meet him halfway, and our lips lock.

"You two shouldn't be allowed in public together."

We're interrupted for the third time since we arrived.

"Hi, Trevor," I say after Christian and I separate and try to get our breathing under control.

"Abbie, I didn't think you had it in you. Bad girl," he says with a mischievous glint in his eyes.

"What's up, Trevor?" Christian asks.

"You're the man, bro."

"Why did you say that to him?" I ask Trevor.

"It's nothing," Christian says.

"Abbie, I'll see you tomorrow. Catch you later, bro," he says to Christian.

"I have to get home," I say. "Mom's not going to be happy that I'm stuffed and won't have dinner."

"You're so lucky to have a celebrity chef as a mother. She can make you anything you want."

"Yeah, well it's not good for my hips. I can't stay away from her cooking, especially her desserts."

"Your hips look just fine to me," he says. "I like a girl who eats like a normal person."

"Are you saying I'm fat?" I ask, teasing him.

"No. You're nowhere near fat. In fact, I thought you might be too skinny for a girl your height."

"Nice save."

We both laugh at the absurdity of the discussion.

"What about your mother? What is she like?"

His lips form a grim line.

"Did I say something wrong?"

"Not at all."

"Then why did you just flip?"

"I don't like to discuss my family."

"Why not?" It sounds odd to me. Even people who hate their families have something to say about them.

His eyes focus on the half-eaten pizza slice left on his plate. I don't know what brought on the sudden change to a simple question people often ask.

"Sorry, I asked. I won't do it again."

"You didn't do anything wrong."

"You said I could ask you anything."

"You can. It's just that when it comes to my family, well, it's complicated."

"I understand complicated. I wasn't trying to be nosy. Okay, I was. I just want to know what kind of woman you call 'Mom.' What you were like as a kid. That's what normal people talk about when they're trying to get to know someone. I don't want anything from you, Christian. I only want to know what makes you who you are. The same questions you asked me at Evan's party."

He hangs his head slightly, embarrassed by his behavior. He looks up at me. "Being Mrs. Alan Wheeler is a full-time job. She doesn't have time for much else."

"I don't understand."

"She's always busy with her charity work, traveling and hosting duties. You know, being a socialite."

"Oh. I see. Was it always that way?"

"Since I was born. I know she loves me. I was just never her number one priority. That was the nanny's job."

My heart hurts for him, learning that he didn't have his mom's constant attention. "What about your dad?"

"He wants me to be his clone."

"Meaning what?"

"Alan Wheeler 2.0. He wants me to work at Levitron-Blair one day, handle business the way he does, do exactly as he says."

Levitron-Blair is the second largest media conglomerate in the world, owner of dozens of media brands and subsidiaries including: TV networks, radio stations, film production companies, theme parks and video game companies.

"But you don't want that?"

"I'm not sure. I don't like that my future is all planned out according to someone else's ideas. On the other hand, it's my legacy."

"Being an only son sucks, huh?"

"Yeah," he says, nodding. "That's exactly how I feel. Sometimes I wish I had an older brother to take the pressure off."

"You'll figure it out. If you decide to work for the company, don't get stuck being president of some division. You want to be CEO and Chairman of the Board with enough shares to cement your power. That way, you can run things the way you want with little interference from other board members. And your dad, he can take a permanent vacation."

"Wow," he says," suddenly sitting straight up. "How do you know so much about business?"

"My Dad. When he was next in line to be CEO of Orphion Technologies, I picked up a few things from dinner table conversations and eavesdropping."

"You're the coolest girl I've ever hung out with," he says, like Congress just made it a new law.

"Because I threw some business jargon at you, stuff you already know?"

"No. It's because you're smart, unpretentious, and gorgeous—a triple threat."

"Is that how you make girls feel special? Lovely words gift-wrapped in your charisma?"

Someone should put a leash on my mouth. Sometimes I wish I were a regular girl. A regular girl would be inwardly thrilled and outwardly feign modesty. Me? I practically insulted the guy.

"That came out all wrong. I have trust issues. You make me nervous. Okay, I'm just going to leave now. That would be best."

He cocks his head to one side. "I think I'll add adorable and captivating to the list."

I slump back in my seat. "You're not mad that I said those things?"

"Why should I be? It's what makes you Abbie. It's why you're awesome. Don't change for anyone."

"I never planned on it."

We leave the pizzeria and head to my car. It's dark out and much colder than when I first arrived. I pop the locks with the remote control, and he opens the driver side door for me. Once safely inside, I hit the power button to wind down the window. He pokes his head in and kisses me. "I'll see you tomorrow."

DINNER IS SERVED: grilled steaks, vegetable salad, and mashed potatoes. A pitcher of sweet tea rests in the center of the table. Mom likes to infuse her cooking with southern classics, an ode to her Louisiana roots. I admit that I'm still stuffed from eating pizza, but she doesn't mind. I intend to eat the salad anyway to balance out my junk food binge. Dad made it home just in time. Mahalia, the family golden retriever, is at Mile's feet, her usual mealtime spot. She's the only dog I know who hates dog food. She eats what we eat.

"How was the date?" Miles asks.

"What date?"

"Mom said you went out on a date."

Miles is a thirty-year-old man in the body of a thirteen-year-old boy. He has no filter. His protruding ears catch everything, all sorts of conversations, whether they're meant for his consumption or not. That's when the uncomfortable questions start. He gets away with it because he's so darn cute with those dimples.

I shoot Mom an accusing glance, and she looks away for a second or two.

"I never said it was a real date. Miles just assumed because you went out with a boy that it was a date," she says, in her defense.

"So, it wasn't a date?" Dad chimes in. He covers his mouth to hide his amusement.

"It was just pizza, people. Stop making a big deal out of it."

"So, that means you like him, right?" Miles isn't satisfied with my answer.

Mahalia puts her paw over her face. She's used to Miles always in my business. Both my parents are staring at me, waiting for my response.

"Well, do you?" Dad asks.

"Mom, make them stop," I say, and then I cram salad into my mouth.

She shrugs. I won't get any help from her, so I put my fork down and swallow my food. It's time to say it aloud.

"Yes, I like him. A lot. Are you happy now?"

"When do we get to meet him?" Dad asks.

"Dad, stop. We're just getting to know each other."

"If he wants to date my daughter, we have to meet him. Those are the rules," he says.

"You'll scare him off. I don't even know if I'll go out with him again."

I really want to, but I'm not about to acknowledge that fact.

"Invite him over for dinner, a casual get-together. If you never go out with him again, no harm done."

I'm sure that will go over well with Christian, the guy who's used to girls chasing him.

"He can come over for Thanksgiving too," Miles adds.

"That's three weeks away, and I don't know what will happen between now and then. Besides, Christian may go home to his family for Thanksgiving."

"You'll never know unless you ask, now will you?" he says, licking mashed potatoes off his fork.

Mom and Dad chuckle under their breath like this is the funniest thing they've heard all week. I just shake my head and tell them how wrong they are for making fun of me.

The dinner table banter is interrupted by a text message alert. My eyes dart to the island in the middle of the kitchen. Dad looks at me.

"Tell that boy to hold his horses," he says with a half-grin. "There's plenty of time for the two of you to get acquainted."

I don't respond right away because I need time to think. It's not Christian, and it's definitely not Frances or Callie. I know this because a dark, thick cloud just rolled in and decided it was going to hang with me for a while. I reach for the pitcher of sweet tea and pour myself a glass, downing it in one long gulp. I was texting Christian when I entered the kitchen earlier, and casually placed the phone on the island when I was done, without giving it a second thought.

I get up from the table and walk toward the island to retrieve my phone. I peer down at it without touching it.

BLOCKED NUMBER

Cheater! Soon everyone will know what you did.

Justice will be served. The Avenger

I wrap my arms around my mid-section and pretend those terrifying words aren't carved into my brain. A million explanations are battling to be heard, but only one comes through loud and clear: *Sidney knows.*

"Abbie, what's wrong?" my father asks.

I look up from the phone to see all eyes trained in my direction.

"Um...it's nothing, Dad. I promised one of the juniors on the debate team I would help her with her rebuttal statement for the upcoming debate against Ravenwood Academy. I'll head upstairs now to call her back, and then get started on homework."

That explanation seems to satisfy him, and everyone gets back to dinner. As I walk away from the kitchen, Mom's statement stops me in my tracks.

"A package came in the mail for you today. I forgot to mention it earlier. It doesn't say who it's from, though. Strange."

That's surprising news. I haven't ordered anything lately.

"Where is the package?" I ask Mom. "I'll grab it on my way upstairs."

I sit in the middle of my bed with a padded, manila envelope in hand. Nothing unusual about it, the same kind I've seen dozens of times. My name and address are typewritten on a white label. There's no return address, but the post office stamp indicates it was mailed from Ridgefield, Connecticut. My Grandma Naomi lives in Ridgefield, but she would never send me something without her personalized return address label.

Fear stabs at me, ferocious and unrelenting. I have a sinking feeling that if I open this envelope, my life will never be the same.

PART TWO

TRAPPED

CHAPTER 11

I STAND ROOTED to the spot in front of my locker. It looks harmless, just a place to store my things, made of metal and red paint. I shouldn't worry. Except, there's a monster in my bag, an envelope I'm afraid to open. It all started with my locker. Then came the late night phone call and the threatening texts. There must be a connection.

A tap on the shoulder jolts me out of my daydreaming. I turn around to find a wide-eyed Christian gazing at me. "I didn't mean to startle you. What's wrong, babe?"

I swallow hard and calm myself. I'm happy to see him. He called me babe. I like it. However, the only thought dominating my mind right now is the fact that he's one more person I have to lie to until this whole situation is resolved.

"Nothing's wrong. Sometimes I get carried away with my own thoughts, and I don't even know what planet I'm on."

He beams at me. "It happens to me too. When I'm painting."

"Painting must take a lot of concentration. And tuning out the world," I say, opening my locker. My stomach is in knots. If I see any strange notes, I'm going to pretend I don't and come back for it later.

"Yes, but I'd much rather concentrate on you."

I don't see any mysterious pieces of paper lurking in the locker, waiting to get me. I pull out my AP biology textbook and then drop it in my backpack. "Oh. What do you mean?"

"Thinking about where we should go for our next date."

"I didn't know there was going to be a next date." I look over my shoulder at him.

He runs a hand through his hair. "I don't mean to overstep. I thought we had a great time the other night."

I close my locker and feel the laughter bubbling up inside me, but I don't want him to see that I'm about to burst out laughing. I sling my backpack over my shoulders. He blinks at me, nonplussed, an adorable lost puppy.

I whisper in his ear before I take off, "I was just giving you a hard time. You're invited to dinner at my house Thursday evening. My parents insist."

I march toward my class, down the hall, and to the left, with quick strides.

"Abbie, wait up!" he yells.

I keep moving, chuckling to myself.

He catches up with me. "Is this another joke? Like before?"

"What do you think?"

"I believe you 're serious this time. What did you tell your parents about me?"

"Are you scared?"

"No. I mean, yes."

"Why?"

"I don't do the meet the parents thing."

"Don't freak out. No one is going to handcuff you to me for the rest of your life. My father has rules about how his only daughter should be treated. He has to meet any guy I spend time with, especially since my experience with dating and relationships is limited. He's an overprotective father. That's all."

"Oh." Then his eyes go big as if a wild idea just occurred to him. "Oh. You mean…"

"What?"

"So, it's true?"

"Is what true?"

"The rumors."

"What are you asking me?"

He whispers in my ear. "Your lack of experience. Is that real?"

I can't help it. A perfect opportunity to tease him presents itself.

"What do you think?" I whisper back. "Did the rumor mill finally get something right, or is what you heard just another piece of lame gossip?"

I SIT IN the first row of the chapel, switching my cell phone from one hand to the other. Any minute now, Lance is going to walk through the door and show me the footage. Within seconds, as if we're communicating via telepathy, he walks in, his expression unreadable.

Adrenaline surges through me. My breathing is rapid and shallow.

"Did you find it?" I ask.

He reaches into his pocket, pulls out a flash drive, and then hands it to me. "See for yourself."

Something about his tone sounds alarm bells in the back of my head, but I'm too busy pulling my laptop from my bag to give it much thought. Lance sits next to me while I boot up my computer. After it spurs to life and I enter my password, I stick the flash drive into the USB port and wait.

"I queued it to the afternoon before you got the note so you could see if anything happened during the night," he says.

A black-and-white image of the bank of lockers appears on the screen. The hallway is empty. I fast forward until I see people scattered around the area, going about their business. They all pass near my locker without giving it a second glance. I perk up when I see a figure heading toward me, but my excitement turns to disappointment when I pause the image. It's me. I go through the motions of opening the locker and swapping books.

"There has to be something on here," I complain.

Lance remains quiet. I don't know how much time passes as I fast forward through the tape, what must be the overnight recording. Nothing. Zip. Zero. Empty halls. As exciting as watching grass grow. I fast forward to the next morning, the morning I discovered the note. Again, similar images: kids going about their daily routine. I pause when I come into the frame. I see Christian show up. I can tell his mouth is moving. I swap the books, and we leave my locker together.

I'm numb. I stare straight ahead, and the rapid, shallow breathing returns. I'm not crazy. I don't care what the footage is missing. I may be paranoid, but that doesn't mean the threat isn't real.

"I don't understand," I say, turning to Lance. "How is it possible? How could someone open my locker and place something in there without being captured on camera?"

"Look, Mama, I don't know anything about what you found in your locker, but I can tell you there is no way anybody could open any of these lockers without being seen. The cameras are set like that on purpose. You know security is no joke around here."

"You don't believe me, do you?"

"I only saw what's on the tape."

"What if someone knows the angle of the cameras and how to avoid them?"

"Doesn't matter. They would still be recorded."

I power down my laptop and thank Lance for helping me. He gets up to leave, and so do I. As we go our separate ways, he stops and turns to me. "If someone really put that note in your locker, they would need to have access to the security office, disable the cameras, drop the note, and turn the cameras back on when they were done. There are no gaps in the timer, no footage unaccounted for. I'm sorry. I did all I could."

CHAPTER 12

M Y NERVES ARE on edge as I enter the empty house. I head straight to my bedroom, slam the door shut and toss my bag on the bed. The envelope I've been too afraid to open might explain why there was nothing on the surveillance tape. I rummage through the bag until it's found. I sit at the edge of the bed, my heartbeat erratic. I rip the envelope open and push my hand inside, pulling up a piece of paper folded in half. When I unfold the paper and see a photo of a familiar face staring back at me, dizziness overtakes me.

The one horrible mistake I made my entire life has come back to haunt me. Someone captured it for eternity. I thought I buried it long ago but based on the photo, not deep enough. Someone dug it up. The image depicts me sitting in a chair, my eyes glazed and unfocused, a powdery substance on the table in front of me. A tiny, clear plastic bag sits next to the substance. My hands are wobbly as I replace the photo in the envelope and then pick up the note.

Thought you got away with it, didn't you? Hypocrite.
Now that I have your attention, are you ready to play?
Justice will be served.
The Avenger

Yes, The Avenger has my attention. I know what will happen if I don't play this game—a game in which I'm already handicapped. I don't know the rules, but I know there will be consequences to breaking them. I'd be expelled from Saint Matthews immediately, my transcript invalidated. No college in the country will accept me, let alone the Ivy League with an image like that floating around. My reputation, all the hard work I've put in, meaningless. My parents shamed. My friends humiliated and saddled with the same labels as me: *cheater, addict, loser.*

Only none of it is true. I made a mistake that lasted all of two weeks. I cracked under the pressure of my mother's murder charge and what it was doing to our family. I was a naïve fifteen-year-old. I convinced myself it was a short-term solution, and that I would stop as soon as things got back to normal at school. I couldn't afford to let my grades tank. I hid it from everyone—or so I thought.

I made the decision to quit when my baby brother had to drag me out of bed one morning because I couldn't get up for school on my own. One of the side effects was insomnia. With the increased heart rate, energy depletion, and crashes that came when the drugs wore off, the risks were too high. I stopped using that same day and never once looked back.

My cell phone rings, and I retrieve it from my bag. Blocked number, just like the text messages. My nightmare is only beginning. I answer the call but let her speak first.

"Did you get my package?"

"What do you want?"

"Be patient, Abbie. You'll find out soon."

"Who are you? Where did you get that picture?"

"Quit with the questions. It's annoying. For now, you don't need to know who I am. Only that I own you, and you'll do exactly as I say."

"How do I know the picture isn't fake? Anyone can use Photoshop these days."

"You know the picture is real, so let's not kid each other. However, I'll humor you this once. You'll get another note in your locker. Study what's in it. After that, it's my move."

"I'll just request a new locker combination."

Silence comes down the line. She never thought of that possibility.

"You do that, and I'll expose you for the fraud that you are. Kellogg will not hesitate to kick you out of Saint Matthews if he were to accidentally come across that photo. Do not test me. You've been warned."

"Why are you doing this?"

"Stop whining. That annoys me too. Bye, Abbie."

She hangs up. I gather the note and the photo and

stuff them back into the envelope. I slide the envelope under the mattress. When I'm done, I assume the fetal position and fall into an abyss of numbness.

CHAPTER 13

MY BRAIN IS about to short circuit. It can't contain any more thoughts about the fallout if the photo were to be circulated or who this girl is and what she wants from me. School let out a half hour ago, and I'm on my bedroom floor, writhing in agony. Christian threatened to come over this morning when I told him I was skipping school because I was sick.

The scent of jasmine oil floats in the air, part of my Zen routine, but even that has lost its appeal. My tear ducts have called it quits, not a single tear left. It's that time of the month. Some girls call it having their period. I haven't yet found a word that adequately describes my torment.

Someone knocks on the door. Mom must have changed her mind about leaving me alone.

"Go away," I squeak. I'm too weak and hoarse from crying for my voice to be heard, but I try anyway. "Go away, please."

The knocking gets louder. I don't have the energy to fight her, so I just lie there, bracing myself for her impending freakout. She usually calls Dad to help get me onto the bed because she can't do it by herself. He isn't home right now. I know Kindergartners bigger than Mom.

"Cooper, are you in there?"

I screw my eyes shut. The pain must be causing me to hallucinate. I haven't seen him in two years, although we've kept in touch through email, calls, and text messages. My heart knows it's him, though. Besides, he's the only person in the world who calls me by my last name. "Cooper, are you okay in there?"

He can't see me like this. I want to get off the floor, but my body isn't cooperating. I stretch my legs out, but my stomach protests. More cramping. I whimper like an injured puppy.

The door opens in slow motion and in walks Ty Whistler Rambally—the boy who knows all my secrets, things I haven't told my girlfriends or anyone else. He's the one who made me feel strong and fearless when Mom was away from us, in jail. The one I thought would be my first, but that turned out to be a joke, on me.

"Over here," I say, like a flower wilting in the summer heat.

He looks down and finds me between the bed and the sofa. Yes, I have a sofa in my bedroom. It's ivory. I was going for an elegant, classy look.

"Cooper, what's wrong? Why are you on the floor?" He kneels over me, panic in his eyes. "Are you hurt?"

"Nothing to worry about. What are you doing here?" I try to sit up again and fail.

He slides one arm under my legs and supports my back with the other. "I'm taking you to the bed."

"I'm fine. You don't have to do that."

"You're not fine, and I'm not leaving you on the floor. End of argument."

I don't get the chance to continue my whining because he just scoops me up and plops me down in the middle of the bed like it was nothing. Like he just reached out and picked a leaf from a low-hanging tree branch. He leans in, both arms dipping into the mattress.

"Tell me why you were on the floor, and don't say it's nothing."

The boy (now almost twenty) I've been in love with since freshman year of high school went off to Yale and came back with double shots of smooth, chocolate hotness. Everything about him is blatantly masculine: the way his clothes fit, the scent of him, his liquid brown eyes with green flecks that connote he knows things he shouldn't. Naughty things. I shouldn't think of him this way, not now, not ever again. He chose someone else, and I got friend-zoned. For most girls, that would suck. For me, it worked out. Ty would do anything I ask of him.

"It's better to stay out of that storm. Shouldn't you be on campus?"

He sits on the edge of the bed, inches from me. "After you called me last night, I had to come see you right away. I didn't have classes today, and it's a quick, two-hour drive. You're in pain. What's wrong, Cooper?"

I keep my hands firmly on my belly. I know him well enough to know he won't let this go.

"It's that time of the month."

"Is it always this bad?"

"Yes. Now, can we talk about something else, please?"

"No, we can't. What does your doctor say?"

"Are you serious? You drove all the way from New Haven to discuss my period?" I can't believe I just asked him that. Someone should just shoot me now.

"It's important."

"Since when?"

"Since I walked in here and found you on the floor."

I grimace as another wave of cramps attack. Ty disappears into the bathroom. I hear water running and have no clue what he's up to. He returns with a small white towel and comes around the edge of the bed again.

"Tell me if this is too hot." He rests the towel on my arm.

"It's fine. What's it for?"

"Take your hands off your abdomen."

"What? No."

"Cooper, if you don't do it, I'll do it for you."

"I don't like being bossed around."

He chuckles. "I remember. You like to be the one doing the bossing around."

"And don't you forget it."

I remove my hands from my sore midsection. He lifts up my top, and I shiver from the brief contact.

"There," he says, placing the warm towel over my stomach. "That should help soothe the cramps."

The warm towel is soothing, but I have to get rid of him. I'm about to throw up. My vomit all over his sweater is not a look he would go for.

"Thank you. Can you do me one last favor? Ask Mom for a cup of mint tea. She already made some this morning. Just zap it in the microwave for thirty seconds."

"I'll be right back."

Once he's out the door, I bolt from the bed and make it to the bathroom just in time to puke my guts out. When it's over, I sit on the cold marble floor and lean up against the tub for support. I should start feeling better soon.

I drag myself off the floor and then rinse my mouth with Listerine. After I make it to the bed, I sit up with my legs tucked under me, using the pillows to prop me up. Ty walks in, balancing a teacup and saucer. He places it on the nightstand next to the bed.

"How are you feeling?"

"Better."

"What did the doctor say about the cramping?" He perches next to me and blows out a series of short breaths.

"She wants me to take birth control pills. I won't."

"Why not?"

"Because…because…I just don't want to. They have side effects and—"

"Almost every drug has side effects. The birth control pills will help with the cramps and control the bleeding so you'll have lighter periods."

"Yes, Dr. Rambally."

He smiles. "Not yet. Two more years at Yale, and four years of Harvard Medical School."

Ty wants to be a cardiothoracic surgeon and has his career planned out, like me. He actually has a chart. As the only child of two successful surgeons, the pressure he feels can be overwhelming, even though he doesn't talk about it much.

His mother, Jenny, a former Miss Bahamas, is one of the top Reproductive Endocrinologists and Fertility Specialists in the country and lectures all over the world. His dad, Bobby, a Guyanese Indian, who loves cricket, is a well-known plastic surgeon.

"So, you've already settled on Harvard for medical school?"

"Yep. What about you? Where are you applying?"

"Duke, Brown, Princeton, Yale, and Johns-Hopkins. I also have Cornell in the mix."

He perks up. "I didn't know you were applying to Yale. That's great."

"It would be silly not to consider Yale, especially because of their track record in medicine."

"I'll save all my notes for you, give you the lowdown on the professors."

"I would have to get in first and decide to attend. Your lecture notes would give me an unfair advantage over the incoming freshman class."

"I don't care. I want my girl to have every advantage possible. You deserve it."

"Thanks."

Ty scoots off the bed and paces the length of the room. He stops in front of my homework desk, rocking the chair back and forth. "Can I see the picture? It could have been faked."

"At first, I thought it might be. But deep down, I know it's the real thing."

I crawl to the edge of the bed and stick my hand under the mattress, pulling out the envelope. Ty gives me a look as if I'm some peculiar creature.

"What? It's a great hiding spot. Can you imagine if my brother walked in here and found it? Or my parents?"

"I'm not judging," he says with a lopsided grin.

I place the photo in his outstretched hand. He stares at it for what seems like forever before handing it back to me.

"This is bad. If this photo gets out, the damage could be irreparable."

"I know."

"It looks like you're about to snort cocaine."

I cringe at his observation. "I crushed the pills into powder. Sometimes, I would put it in orange juice or food."

"Do you have any idea when it was taken?"

"That was two years ago, and I've tried hard to forget that I ever took Adderall. I was too scared to take the pills at home, so I would get to school a few minutes early, head to the student lounge, and take it there."

"There's no mistaking it's you in the photo.

Whoever took it must have been highly motivated. It was snapped without you knowing."

"I must have been careless that day."

"It's the spiral. When it starts to get out of control, you get careless. Why didn't you tell me you were struggling?"

"I was ashamed. I was already leaning on you way too hard because of my mom's legal problems. I couldn't dump that on you too. I couldn't tell you that Dr. Kellogg called me into his office and said in that nice way of his that I had to get my act together or I was out of Saint Matthews, for good. I had fallen behind with most of my schoolwork because I didn't care. Nothing mattered besides getting Mom out of jail."

Ty starts pacing again, muttering to himself.

"Did you tell anyone at all about this? I don't understand how the person who took the pic knew you were taking Adderall in the first place—and that the student lounge was your spot. We have to find Kyle Davidson. He's the only one who can answer those questions."

"I never told anyone. Not even my girlfriends. It's illegal Ty, what I did. Purchasing a drug like that without a prescription is a felony. The funny thing is, Kyle purchased my supply for me because I didn't want to go to the place where people bought it and be seen. That didn't work out, did it?"

He comes to stand in front of the bed. "Stop beating yourself up. You made a mistake. You trusted someone you thought had as much to lose as you did."

"I'm still not ready to throw the blame at him. I just

don't see him snitching on me, especially since he was known in certain circles as the go-to guy. He wouldn't implicate himself."

"And you have no idea why this person is blackmailing you?"

"No."

I let Ty in on my Sidney suspicions, the texts, the note, and the failure of the surveillance footage to provide any proof of who's behind the scheme.

"Why you? The way I figure it, if she knew you were taking Adderall, she would know about the others too."

"I wondered the same thing. She could be blackmailing a bunch of people for all we know, but I don't believe that's the case."

His eyes darken. "What makes you say that?"

"Adderall exits the system fast, ten to twelve hours maximum, depending on how you take it: slow release or the faster route. Even if she knows all who were using, that was two years ago. She can't prove a thing."

"Except when it comes to you. That photo is a gold mine for her plans, whatever they are."

"A noose around my neck. With every call, every threat, every message, it gets tighter and tighter."

He plops down next to me on the bed. Neither one of us says anything. My actions amount to a volcano no one knew existed until the day it erupts. Callie, Frances, and Christian are still at Saint Matthews. They will be the ones burned by the ashes. My parents will be angry and disappointed, but they'll find a way to deal with it.

I don't have answers, but I feel relieved that I've shared the secret with Ty.

His jaw is set tight. Part of me feels guilty for dumping my problems on him, again. I can't stand the tension in him, so I change the subject to distract him.

"So how's you love life? Do you have a girlfriend?"

"What?"

"You heard me."

"Come on, Cooper," he says, and then he scurries off the bed.

"What?" I ask innocently. "It's nothing to be ashamed of, Ty. You're a smart, handsome college sophomore at a huge university with lots of beautiful, intelligent women. Don't tell me you haven't sampled the candy. I won't believe you."

"We shouldn't be having this conversation."

"We should. We've discussed my period and a mysterious stalker since you've been here. Spill your guts. Who are you seeing? Are you using protection every time? You can't be too careful these days."

"Stop it, Cooper!"

He stands next to the dresser across from the bed, stiff as a board. I won't relent.

"Your mother deals with the female reproductive system for a living, and you're going to be a doctor one day. Please tell me you're not afraid to talk about s-e-x."

"That's not it. I just don't think it's appropriate to discuss with you."

"Oh," I say, offended. "I didn't realize we were only

sort of friends. Spell it out for me like I'm a simpleton so I don't get confused in the future."

I know I sound mean. Blame it on hormones or the anger that rears its head because someone is out to get me. Whatever.

"You know that's not true," he says, edging closer to the bed. "You're still my best friend."

"Then stop treating me like a kid. If you're going to behave this way, I suggest you tell me what the rules of this friendship are. A list of topics that are safe to discuss and the ones that are off limits. I thought we could talk about anything."

"I'm sorry. I know you're not a kid. It's just awkward talking to you about it."

"Because?"

"Okay, I was seeing someone, but not anymore. It was only for a couple of months."

"Tell me about her."

He tells me about Vanessa Miller, a BioMedical Engineering major from Brooklyn. Her family is Jamaican, and they bonded over having West Indian parents who push them hard. Soon, the very thing they had in common got in the way. They were both ambitious and quickly realized it wasn't going to work.

"Now, did that kill you?"

He blushes. "I guess not."

"Your turn."

"For what?"

"Not fair. You have to talk about who you're dating.

Last time I checked, you weren't, but things could have changed. Did they?"

I think of Christian. How he's chipping away at my inhibitions and doubt. How he's a great kisser and a smooth talker, and I don't have to censor myself when I'm around him. How he makes my hands clammy, and my heart beat faster.

"Look at that smile. You *are* seeing someone," Ty says as if accusing me of some grave crime. "You've been holding out on me, Cooper. This is big news. Who is he?"

"Christian Wheeler."

I notice his hands twitch and his nostrils flare. "Oh, wow. Wow. That's great. Surprising, but great."

"What's wrong with Christian?"

"Nothing. I just didn't think you would go for someone like him."

"Someone like him? Care to explain?"

"Entitled, arrogant, treats women like disposable toys."

"Tell me how you feel, Ty."

"I'm just saying I thought you would go for someone more wholesome, safe, and kind. Someone who would treat you like a princess and not another name to be entered onto some list of conquests."

"You mean someone like you?"

He fiddles with the sleeves of his sweater. "Christian could hurt you, badly. If that happens, it will upset me for a long time."

I touch his forearm. "I can handle myself. There's a lot more to him than rumors. This is unexpected for me too, Ty. Christian goes after what he wants, no hesitation, and no ambivalence. With him, I don't have to wonder where I stand because he holds nothing back. He's funny and charming. He makes me feel like no one else compares to me."

"You and how many others?"

"Don't be like that, Ty. I'm not stupid. Just be happy for me that I have fun with someone I really like."

"Watch yourself. I don't want to have to punch him in the face."

"What am I going to do with you?"

"I mean it. I'll hurt him if he hurts you."

"It won't come to that."

CHAPTER 14

I RETURN TO school the next day, on edge. The Avenger said something would be waiting for me, proof that the photo wasn't fake. It's been forty-eight hours since we had that conversation. The bell will ring in ten minutes. The hallway is bustling with the usual morning routine. I snake my way through the crowd. I have to make it to my locker, grab the note before Christian shows up, and make it to class on time.

My heart beats faster. Is my stress showing? I remove a lock of hair from my face and tuck it behind my ears. My text message ringtone goes off. I shouldn't check to see who it's from, but I'm wound up and can't help it.

BLOCKED NUMBER

Does Christian know you're a drug addict? Someone should warn him.

Justice will be served.

The Avenger

"Hey, Abbie."

I spin around too fast and catch a major case of whiplash. I massage my aching neck.

"Hey, Trevor, what's up?" I say, dropping the phone into my pocket.

"Are you okay?" he asks, falling into step with me. "You look terrible. Your eyes, they're all wild and crazy."

"What? I'm all right, Trevor," I say in my brightest voice. "You sure know how to make a girl feel good about herself."

"Sorry. It's just that you seemed out of it a moment ago, and you were out yesterday. You never skip school."

"I was sick yesterday, but I'm fine now."

"Good. Because you're not going to like what I have to say."

"What is it?"

I can't handle any more bad news. Trevor is right. I am stressed out. My future is at stake, and Sidney holds the key. Competition (both national and international) to get into the Ivies is intense, as in over 27,000 applications to Princeton last year alone. Based on results of my online research, Princeton only admits a paltry seven percent of applicants. Yale is even lower at a measly six percent, and Harvard admits five percent. All Sidney has to do is send my name along with that photo. They won't even bother to consider my application. Even worse? It could have a viral effect. She could decide to send that picture to every school on my list. It's no secret where I'm applying. My guidance counselor and teachers won't shut up about it.

"Sidney is acting out again," Trevor says with a sigh.

"What has she done now?"

"She's been telling people that you and Lance are hooking up. She saw the two of you coming out of the chapel and that you looked cozy. I'm telling you because Christian is going to hear about it too."

"I can't deal with this right now," I wail. "Sometimes I wish she would just die."

The words are already out, and I can't take them back. The horror on Trevor's face is all the proof I need that I'm close to a breakdown.

"I didn't mean that, Trevor. I just want her to stop aggravating me. It's her new favorite sport, and it's getting to me."

"Sidney has always been a troublemaker. Her jealousy is off the charts. She can't stand it that Christian likes you and ignores her like an ugly baby."

I laugh at his joke. "I didn't know you and Lance were friends," he says.

"Looking out for your bro, Christian? Want to make sure he doesn't get played?"

His eyes blink rapidly. "No. You're not that kind of girl."

"Lance and I say hello when we see each other. We were at the chapel at the same time and left at the same time. I'm not the only student who goes there to pray or just to have some quiet time for reflection. Sidney is behaving like her usual hateful self. Besides, Lance has a girlfriend."

We arrive at my locker and Christian is waiting for me, looking like he just came from a GQ photo shoot. Seeing him makes me feel better. However, I must get rid of both he and Trevor in case there's a message from Sidney/The Avenger, as she promised. Trevor and Christian greet each other. Christian gives him a look. Trevor takes the hint and says he'll see me in a few minutes for English Lit.

Christian leans in and plants a wet, lingering kiss on my cheek. I giggle like the teenage girl that I am. He does things to me.

"How are you feeling this morning? I'm still mad at you. You wouldn't let me come over and make you feel all better."

"Is this our first fight?"

"Yes. But we're still on for tonight, right?"

I turn the combination for my locker, my back to him. "Oh, that dinner thing is tonight?"

"Stop playing around. I know you didn't forget."

I turn around to look at him after the lock pops. "I like seeing your face when I give you a hard time. Your expression is priceless."

"So I amuse you, huh?" he asks and snakes his hand around my waist, pulling me close.

"You do more than that."

That's it. After school, I'm heading to the mall to purchase some kind of gag or mouth restraint thingy.

"Sweet," he murmurs and then kisses me. A slow, unhurried kiss, like we are the only two people on the planet. As if the very essence of time belongs to us. Once it's over, I realize I have three minutes to make it to class on time.

"I'm going to be late for class. See you tonight?"

"I can walk you to class."

"That's okay. I'm going to end up sprinting all the way there."

After he leaves, I open the locker and push a couple of books aside. It may be in the textbook that's furthest to the right, on the top shelf of the locker. I'm spot on. My hands are sweaty as I reach for the book. Another piece of folded white paper sticks out from it, just like the first note. Butterflies roil in my stomach. I place the textbook back in its spot but don't bother to close the locker. I open the message and begin to read.

The Users.

My name is first on the list, separate from the others, in bigger letters with a circle around it. The list is long, requiring three columns. Three names pop out at me besides mine. Kyle Davidson, Kerri Wheeler's ex before she set her sights on Ty. Pete Cora and Aaron Bailey (no relation to Sidney) who were friends with Ty, and his teammates on the school's championship crew team.

I go down the rest of the list, column by column. I recognize several other names, people I've sat next to in class over the past four years, others who were a year or two ahead of me. Some of them are kids of rock stars, high profile politicians, CEOs, pastors of mega churches, and foreign diplomats.

I sit on the floor with my back against the locker, alone with my thoughts. Getting to class on time doesn't seem that important anymore. Then my phone rings, breaking through my melancholy. I reach for it in my pocket. Same as always, blocked number.

"Hello."

"Did you get the list?"

"What list? Who is this?"

"Don't play games with me, Abbie."

"What do you want? A gold star?"

"You're crabby right now. That annoys me."

"As far as I can tell, everything annoys you. I wish breathing annoyed you, too, so you would stop."

"Funny. The list is no joke. I think you know that, don't you?"

"Now what?"

"Let the games begin. Don't disappoint me. I know you're up for the challenge. Looking forward to it."

"What are you talking about?"

She hangs up. I stare at my phone, thinking she'll call back. She doesn't.

I drag myself to class, and the only thing that saves me is the fact that Dr. Campbell is running late. She's never late, but whatever. Trevor mouths the words, *are you okay* as I trudge to my seat. I nod. After I sit and place my backpack on the floor, I notice a piece of notebook paper folded in half on my desk. I open it and read it.

Whore!

My heart rate accelerates and nausea rises up in my throat. I place my hand over my mouth, afraid I'll puke all over my desk. I look up to see Sidney standing beside me.

"What have you got there, Abbie? A love note from your new boyfriend, Lance?"

She's like the one cockroach that would survive a nuclear blast. There's just no getting rid of her. I remove my hand from my mouth and hold up the note so she can see it. I speak loud enough to be heard by the class of twelve.

"Someone called me a whore. It takes one to know one, doesn't it, Sid? You're miles ahead of me, but who's counting?"

All our classmates look in our direction, stunned and curious. That includes Trevor, who just shakes his head.

"You make me sick," she says. "Don't get too cocky. You're due for a takedown."

I ignore her, and she walks back to her seat, confident she won this round.

CHAPTER 15

C ALLIE STARES AT her lunch tray. Frances has been twirling the same lock of hair since we sat down and hasn't touched her food, either.

"So," I say, stabbing my grilled chicken with the fork, "I've been doing some snooping about the note in my locker and the phone calls."

Callie leans in, and Frances stops twirling her hair. "Without telling us?" she asks. "Abbie, we're best friends. You can't go all vigilante on us."

"Yeah," Callie says. "We used to tell each other everything."

"Don't keep us in suspense," Frances says. "I'm dying over here."

I blow out a puff of air from my cheeks. "I asked Lance to get me surveillance tapes so I could see who put the note in my locker. We got nothing. It makes it look as if I made up the whole thing."

"I don't get it," Frances says. "How is it possible to get into your locker without being caught on camera?"

"That's the confusing part."

"What did Lance say?" Callie asks.

I explain to the girls the only scenario under which someone could avoid the cameras; the way Lance explained it to me. They would have to turn off the cameras and turn them back on again after leaving the note.

"That's even worse," Frances blurts out.

"What do you mean?" I ask.

"If someone can do that to you, we're all in trouble."

"It must be an inside job then," Callie says.

"Which brings us back to Sidney," Frances says. "She's the kind of girl who could convince," she says, using air quotes, "some poor guy in the security office to do something like that."

While I agree with the girls, something jabs at me. The more I think about it, the scarier it feels. It's what Sidney said at the party: *If I wanted to say something to you, I wouldn't text you. I would tell you right to your stupid face.*

Sidney's right. She has always been vocal in her contempt for me and makes certain I know how she feels every opportunity she gets. As if I could ever forget. The Avenger is mean-spirited and relentless but thrives on secrecy. She gets off on the power the mystery affords her. That doesn't sound like Sidney. The realization I could be wrong hits home. I reach for the bottled water on my lunch tray and chug it down.

"What just happened?" Frances asks.

I explain my theory.

"Sidney likes playing games," Callie says. "Remember last year when she tapped Madison Wilder to be part of her clique and made her do all that crazy, embarrassing stuff to prove her loyalty? Stuff that could have gotten Madison expelled if she was ever caught?"

Madison was so desperate to fit in with Sidney's group that she would have shot her own mother if Sidney asked her to. Sidney went so far as to pretend to be a hot senior guy (stock photo) from Blake Hall School, who was interested in Madison, and convinced her to send him naked pictures of herself. What did Sidney do? She sent the pictures to all her friends, and soon, those photos of Madison popped up on the smartphone screens of half the school. Madison couldn't live down the shame and transferred out of Saint Matthews soon after.

"You may be right Callie," I say. "Sidney has never met an evil scheme she didn't like."

"What if The Avenger is two people instead of one," Frances says, twirling her hair again.

Callie and I look at each other, then say in unison, "what?"

Frances leans in. "Think about it. Sidney could have an accomplice, and I'm not talking about Brooke or Jessica. It could be somebody we don't know. Somebody she could feed information about you, Abbie."

I feel a headache coming on, fast and frantic. It would explain how The Avenger knows where my locker is located, my home address, and my cell phone number.

If Sidney manipulated someone at the security office so the note could be planted in my locker, it would be easy enough to go through the school's computer and pull up my information. Would the school tell us if there was a breach or is Sidney's blackmail accomplice a computer genius? And what about her latest text? *Does Christian know you're a drug addict? Someone should warn him.* It was similar to what she said to me at Evan's party, if Christian knew I was a full-on psycho, and someone should warn him. If it looks like Sidney and sounds like Sidney...

"The stalking won't stop anytime soon," I say. "It will get worse before it gets better."

"Stop scaring us, Abbie," Callie whispers.

I shore up the courage to tell them why this is happening to me, and how it could have consequences for them.

"I cheated. A long time ago, and this girl, whoever she is, found out."

Callie stares off in the direction of the cafeteria exit. Frances resumes twirling the same lock of hair, that's now a knotted mess. My breath hitches. I tell them how I was almost thrown out of Saint Matthews. How I took Adderall so I could study for long hours without getting tired to get back on track.

"That's what the note in the locker was about. She has a photograph of me. Using. And a list of all the students at this school who bought and used over the past two years."

Frances stops her hair twirling. Callie grabs on to my arm. My skin tingles with embarrassment. I want to run away from the table, anything not to have to endure the humiliation of my friends finding out that I'm a cheater.

Frances backs her chair away from the table, and so does Callie. They both stand up.

"Where…where are you going?" I stammer.

They each step away from the chairs. Are they leaving? My thoughts are fuzzy, and I can't think straight. Maybe I deserve this after I kept it from them for so long.

I'm dragged out of my misery when I feel a pair of soothing arms around my neck. Callie. I struggle to remain composed, and it's a losing battle. Frances sits next to me and strokes my forearm. I breathe a sigh of relief. My girls are rallying as usual.

"You're planning to hack Sidney's email account, aren't you?" Callie surmises.

"Yep. You can bet your trust fund on it," I say.

"When?" Callie asks.

"How soon can you convince Brooke to give up Sidney's email address?"

"Would tonight be fast enough?"

"Can't do it tonight. Christian is coming over for dinner," I remind her.

"Right. Tomorrow after school then."

"I have that online newspaper internship interview," Frances interjects.

"We can give you the details afterward," Callie says.

"Why so glum?" Trevor, who just pulled up a seat across from us, startles us. He has a different lunch period than we do.

I rub my nose a couple of times, and Callie goes back to her seat. So does Frances.

He tilts his head to the side. "You guys okay? It looked seriously intense when I walked in."

"It's nothing," Frances says, cozying up to her man. She drops a kiss on his lips and reassures him. "Abbie was just having a moment."

"About what?"

"It's Abbie. Take a guess."

"Ah, I get it. Application deadlines. Don't sweat it, Abbie; you'll do fine."

"See, even Trevor knows," Frances says. "Lighten up, Abbie. It's going to be okay."

I catch her hidden meaning. "Thanks for calming me down." I turn my attention to Trevor. "What are you doing here? I thought you had the lunch period after ours."

"Skipped out of French class early today on account of my 'upset stomach.' What's the use? I'll never be conversational, let alone fluent in French. And there's no way my father is going to pay for my Paris trip, so forget it."

Frances kisses him on the cheek. "It's okay, Trev. We don't have to go."

"Hold on a minute," I say, making the timeout sign with my hands. "What's this I'm hearing?"

"Trevor and I were going to Paris for spring break," Frances says. She has a big old grin on her face as she looks up at him, adoration in her eyes. "I was going to pick out my gown for the Platinum Ball while we were over there. I didn't want to say anything until the plans were finalized."

"But the parents have been stingy lately," Trevor says with a scowl. "Dad said he would only pay for the trip if I aced French class this term. I'm sick of listening to his lectures about responsibility and how I have to start earning my way. He never cared before. I mean, what's the big deal all of a sudden?"

I've never seen Trevor get this worked up about anything. It's obvious the Paris trip meant a lot to him, and he hated to disappoint Frances. She won't care. All three of us will end up shopping together for our gowns anyway. The ball is the social event of the year, and the planning committee, headed by Sidney (eew) goes all out.

Trevor stands up to leave. "Hey, Abbie, take it easy on my bro this evening, will you?"

I throw him my most sincere smile. "Are you implying that I'm difficult?"

Callie and Frances look away. Frances starts to whistle a tune, and Callie drums her fingers on the table. I know they think I'm difficult at times.

"I'm just saying this is a big deal for him, and he doesn't want to screw it up," Trevor says. "He's been studying up on Mr. Cooper's business exploits so they can have things to talk about."

I say the first thing that pops into my head. "Get out of here."

"I will."

Before he leaves, he plants another kiss on Frances.

"Gross," I say, mocking them.

"Get a room," Callie says, joining in the fun.

"I'm going to have to bleach my eyeballs," I say, as they continue to ignore us.

Callie hits Trevor in the back of the head with a piece of bread from her lunch tray. That gets his attention.

"All right, I'm leaving. Oh, I almost forgot: You may not have to worry about Sidney anymore, Abbie."

The girls and I look at each other. "What do you mean?"

"She's moved on to a new victim, er, I mean, new boyfriend, so you don't have to worry she'll get in your face about Christian anymore. Well, see you later."

"Trevor Forrester, get back here right now and explain yourself," Frances says.

He backs up and takes a seat again.

"You never told me about this."

"Just found out in French class. Jeff Lazenby's sister, Courtney, overheard Sidney on the phone. She's been getting flowers and gifts. She even has a new phone just to talk to the new boyfriend. I don't think he goes to Saint Matthews. Well, gotta run."

After Trevor disappears, all three of us say in unison what we've been thinking, as if the circuits in our brains are somehow linked. "Totally suspicious."

"That new phone is a burner phone to talk to whoever is helping her, and the flowers and gifts are a cover," I say.

The girls concur.

"Interesting how Trevor just happened to overhear that newsflash in French class," Frances says.

"Obviously, it was for his benefit," Callie says. "They knew it would get back to us."

"Sidney is smarter than we thought," I say. "This isn't going to be easy."

"She's not the mastermind," Frances says. "She's devious, but she doesn't have the cunning and imagination it takes to pull off stalking you like this. Text messages that disappear after you read them, untraceable phone calls, notes that magically appear in your locker? The Avenger is a phantom. Sidney likes attention too much to be the brains behind the operation."

"We can't take our eyes off her."

"The hack should tell us more," Callie says.

"Let's keep our expectations low. My computer skills aren't that advanced."

"You're a STEM fellow," Callie reminds me.

"On the science side. I took computer classes, but I'm no expert. I just want to see if I can crack her email."

"Be careful," Frances warns.

"Of course. I'll use a VPN code so my IP address won't be easily tracked."

Lunch is almost over, and the girls tease me about the upcoming dinner with Christian.

"What are you wearing?" Callie asks. "I hope it's something short and sexy."

I roll my eyes. "My wardrobe is going to be rated G. This dinner was my Dad's idea, remember?"

"Text as soon as it's over," Frances, the twenty-four hour newshound, says. "I don't care how late it is."

"Tomorrow is Friday, and I'm going to cut class," Callie says. "Around 7:00 a.m., I'll come down with a raging case of the flu, so I'll be up late waiting for the report from you also."

CHAPTER 16

A FTER SCHOOL LETS out, I drive home like a maniac. I rush up the stairs, anxious to get to my bedroom. I slam the door shut, pull the phone from my bag, and give a voice command to the phone. He answers on the second ring.

"It's not good, Ty."

"What happened?"

I repeat the brief conversation I had with The Avenger. Then I get to the list. "There are three columns worth of names on the list, close to fifty names, including people in your graduating class, like Pete and Aaron. Kyle Davidson is on there too. And my name, obviously."

"Read me all the names."

I drop the phone on the bed and tear through my backpack for the list. I kept it hidden in one of the inner pockets. Once I pull out the paper, I pick up the phone again, placing it in between my ears and shoulder blades, while I unfold the sheet.

What the heck? I stare at the blank sheet, trying to

make sense of what just happened. I remember many of the names on the list. I remember my name at the top in big letters with the circle around it. I did not imagine the list. I didn't displace it. There is only one inner pocket in my bag, and I was careful that the list was the only document in that space. My bag has been with me all day long. Ty is asking if I'm still here, his voice breaking through my panic.

"The names are gone," I inform him.

"What are you talking about? How could they disappear?"

"I don't know, Ty but they did. I just pulled the list from my bag. I have the sheet on which the names were written, but it's blank. Don't you think that's odd? I wouldn't believe it if I didn't see it with my own eyes."

"It's not impossible. I believe you."

"How come?"

"She wrote the names in invisible ink. After a while, anything written in that ink disappears."

"Invisible ink? I thought that was a myth."

"It exists. Researchers came out with a new version a few years ago using nanoparticles. Once the paper is exposed to light, the written text disappears in hours."

I plop down on the sofa and tuck my legs under me. "I hate not knowing what's coming at me next."

"Don't worry, Cooper. I'll track down Kyle Davidson and see if he knows anything that can help. I'll find Pete and Aaron too. I'll handle it, okay?"

I STAND IN my large walk-in closet and scratch my head, trying to decide what to wear. I want everything to be perfect for tonight, not that I'm trying to impress Christian or anything. My outfit must strike the right balance: classy, but not uptight boring; flirty, but not slutty; elegant yet accessible. I go through the closet, and I'm not satisfied. I grab a bunch of clothes and toss them on the bed for better inspection.

After an hour of aggravation and dismissing anything that looks promising, I decide to keep it simple and chic. I settle on a pair of black skinny jeans and Brian Atwood ankle boots. I choose a ruched V-neck top Callie insisted I had to purchase in this weird color called Marsala. She swore to me it's one of the hottest trends this fall—a red-brownish color she says is sophisticated yet earthy, like me.

My hair is going to take a while, so it's best to keep that simple, too. I'll complete the ensemble with a scarf and a pair of sterling silver, disc earrings with bezel-set diamond details.

I hear Christian's voice drifting from the kitchen. I thought my parents would have parked him in the family room or living room. I stand in the doorway, observing for a moment. He stands next to mom at the kitchen island, pointing to a dish and asking questions. He looks stylish in a cashmere pullover sweater, with a navy blue and white gingham dress shirt underneath. Don't get me started on the jeans. With a perfect view of his backside, all I can do is inwardly sigh.

They turn around at the same time. The sigh wasn't so silent after all. His eyes go wide and then crinkle at the corners. He walks over to the kitchen counter and picks up a gigantic bouquet of peach roses, my favorite. If I weren't busy checking him out, I would have noticed the flowers right away. He walks toward me and hands me the bouquet. I thank him.

"We didn't hear you," Mom says. "Christian and I were getting acquainted. Turns out he knows a lot about food."

"Christian knows a lot about many things," I tease.

Mom shakes her head and begins to slice oranges. Christian kisses me on the cheek.

"Wow," he says and steps back to get a good look at me.

"Right back at you," I say. "Don't let it go to your head, though. We don't want it to get any bigger than it already is."

"You see how mean she is to me, Mrs. Cooper?" he says, looking in Mom's direction.

"I can't help you, Christian. That's what you signed up for."

"Where are Dad and Miles?" I ask.

"Setting the dining room table. I better check on them."

"Mom, we need a vase for the flowers."

She takes the flowers from me, and with impeccable efficiency, she finds the perfect vase and fills it with water.

"This will make a great centerpiece for the dinner table," she says and then scuttles off to make sure the table is set to her specifications.

"How did it go?" I ask, turning to Christian. "The introductions, I mean."

"Your parents are cool. Your mom is a sweet lady. I like her."

"And my dad?"

"Mr. Cooper is intense."

I give him a sad face. "I promise you'll leave here alive. Beyond that, I can't say what will happen. Just don't at look him directly. His laser eyes will slice you in half."

"Okay," he says, his voice shaky.

I look away from him to have a laugh at his expense. He peeks down at my face. I pretend I wasn't making fun of him.

"You're not a very nice girlfriend. You're supposed to be reassuring me that your dad will like me. Instead, I'm breaking out in hives, and you think it's funny."

Silence. He said the G word. It catches us both off-guard. Uncertainty flares in his eyes. He looks downward, a lock of hair falling over his eyes. I palm his face with both hands, and he looks up at me.

I have to be sure I heard him correctly, so I ask, "What did you just say?"

"You know what I said. Is that a problem?"

"No. Aren't we moving too fast, though?"

"Is that how you feel?"

"Yes. No. I've never had a boyfriend before. How much time are we supposed to spend getting to know each other before we enter girlfriend/boyfriend territory?"

He gives a look as if I'm kidding him.

"Sorry. I overanalyze everything."

"I notice that about you. Abbie, we've known each other for two years. We've been fighting our attraction to each other for at least a year."

"So, that's what you call the insults and put downs. Attraction?"

"Well, yeah. You're a great sparring partner. I hope it never stops."

"I thought you liked your girls easy."

Damn! I did it again. Not knowing when to shut up and just go with the flow.

"I'll give you a tour of the house now." I flee the kitchen, not even looking back to see if Christian is following me. I bump into Mom in the hallway, bringing my grand escape to a halt.

"What's the hurry?" she asks.

"No hurry. I was about to give Christian the tour before dinner."

As if to corroborate my story, he appears right next to me.

"Dinner will be served in thirty minutes," Mom informs us.

After Mom leaves, I go on the defensive. "I didn't mean to insult you back there. I don't know what came over me. Words have a way of escaping my mouth, whether or not I want them to. I'm starting to worry about my bedside manner when I become a doctor."

"I never thought it was going to be easy with you,

Abbie. I knew you were amazing the first time I saw you. I had just transferred to Saint Matthews. We were at general assembly one morning, and you had this look on your face like you were ready to take on the world, yet there was an unhappy air about you. Anastasia Cruz was still here. The way she, Callie, and Frances rallied around you made me want to learn more about the girl who could inspire such fierce loyalty from her friends."

"I was dying inside during that time," I confess. "My world was imploding. If I didn't have my friends, things may have turned out differently for me."

"Whenever I saw you in the hallway, there was no way I could tell. The news reports and kids whispering about your mother's case were the only signs that anything was wrong in your world. I started asking about you, and everyone said the same thing. 'Abbie Cooper, she's a little weird, but she's a good person. And, don't mess with her because she'll rip you a new one.'"

"And you still wanted a chance with me, even after that warning?"

"You barely knew I existed back then. Someone else was on your mind."

"What do you mean?"

"You had it bad for Ty Rambally. All the kids at school were saying that you hated my cousin Kerri because she was dating Ty, and Kerri hated you because you and Ty were close."

"Is that what Kerri told you?"

He nods. That seems like a century ago.

"I was just a kid back then. My mother taught me that Ty didn't have to be my everything, and that, sometimes, the thing you want most isn't necessarily what's right for you."

"I really like your mom."

"She's great," I say.

"Glad I decided to bide my time."

"What?"

"Ty wasn't going to be around much longer. Once he and Kerri graduated, it was time to put my plan into action."

"What plan?" We both lean up against the wall.

"I would come by your locker and say things I knew would offend you, on purpose."

"Are you serious?"

"If I had asked you for a date during that time, you would have laughed in my face."

"You got me. I would have."

"I figured antagonizing you was the only way to get you to talk to me. I looked forward to it every day. The weekends couldn't go by fast enough."

"Wow, your life must have been really boring."

"You left me no choice. Plus, it wasn't just about talking to you."

"No? What else?"

"I couldn't wait to see what outfit you would wear every day. If I missed you at your locker for some reason or didn't see you around, I would have Gabe and Trevor tell me what you wore that day."

I don't know what brought on the need for confession.

It has my attention. I'm flattered and horrified at the same time. "You had spies?"

"Sympathizers, babe, not spies."

"Trevor is so dead," I say, my voice breezy. "He didn't say a word to me."

"He's the man. He knows how to keep a secret."

"As long as he's not keeping anything from Frances."

"He wouldn't do that."

"He'll answer to me if he hurts her."

"I'll be sure to pass on the message, but you don't have to worry about him."

"We better get going on that tour."

He asks a bunch of questions about family photos and artwork that interests him. He even wants to know about my favorite room in the house. It's the sunroom. I like to curl up with a good book on lazy sunny days. It's heated, so even in the winter, I can hang out there.

We enter the dining room, and everyone is already seated, waiting for us. Mom placed the bouquet Christian brought as the centerpiece like she promised. Tall candles burn at either end of the table.

Mom and Dad sit at opposite ends, Christian across from me, and Miles next to me. Mahalia is waiting for him to overfeed her. After Mom says grace, our mealtime ritual, everyone digs in. Salad, pumpkin soup, salmon for the main course, and coconut cake for dessert. My mouth is already watering.

"How do you like Saint Matthews, Christian?" my dad asks. "I hear you transferred from another school."

Christian licks his lips, his posture rigid. "It's working out well for me, Mr. Cooper. There's a lot of pressure to excel. Everyone is scrambling to make good grades and get into good colleges. Well, maybe except Abbie. That stuff comes to her naturally."

I tug at my scarf. Next thing I know, I'm biting my fingernails at the dinner table. Mom gives me an irritated glare, and my hand drops to my side. I won't get into dogcatcher school let alone college if I don't stop The Avenger from blackmailing me. I still have no clue why she's doing it or what she wants. I just know it's going to be bad. I shiver.

"Are you cold?" Dad asks.

"No. I'm not cold."

Everyone's attention is now focused on me.

"Are you sure?" he presses. "What's bothering you, sweetheart?"

"Dad, nothing is wrong. Let's not spend dinner talking about me. Did you know that Christian paints?"

I shouldn't have put Christian on the spot like that, but Dad was about to start interrogating me.

"Tell us about your work," Mom says to Christian.

"I paint whatever inspires me. It changes all the time, so I never know what I'm going to work on from one painting to the next."

"What's your favorite piece so far?" Mom asks.

He says nothing, pondering the question. Then he looks straight at me. "I haven't created it yet."

My hand is halfway to my mouth when I feel Mom's

eyes on me. I quickly grab my spoon and scoop up the last of my soup.

"I think you should showcase a few of your pieces as part of the art exhibit at school," I say to him.

"My work is not for exhibition. Just for me. I never show it to anyone."

"Why not?" Miles, asks. "Do they suck?"

"Miles, stop it," Mom hisses. "Apologize."

"Really?" I say to him in my sternest voice.

"What?" Miles asks, offended. "I didn't do anything wrong. I just want to know why he's putting all this effort into painting if nobody is going to see. It's weird."

"It's okay, Miles," Christian says. "You asked an excellent question. For me, it's a way to express myself without worrying about judgment. I can paint whatever I want and not think about whether or not it's good. It's about how I feel at the moment when I'm creating it."

"I get it," Miles says. "It's like recording time."

"Exactly," Christian says.

The good feelings don't last. Dad's next question ends that party. "Why were you expelled from two boarding schools, Christian?"

Everyone freezes. I want to crawl across the table and tell Christian he doesn't have to answer the question, and it will be okay. He slumps in his chair as if already defeated.

I close my eyes and will him not to back down. Dad will think he's a wimp, and I don't want that.

I open my eyes when he begins to speak.

"I've made a lot of mistakes I regret, Mr. Cooper. I did dumb stuff because I wasn't thinking in a mature way. I mostly did it to aggravate my parents. Tired cliché, I know. If you're worried about Abbie, I would never do anything to cause her pain or make her look bad."

Right. Because that's my job—bringing shame to my family and friends by illegally obtaining a central nervous system stimulant.

"You're young. You're supposed to do dumb stuff. The key is to learn from those mistakes and prevent others from falling into the same trap."

Whew. That was close. Dad is being reasonable.

That didn't last long either. "Why were you railing against your parents? I understand teenagers like to push boundaries and spread their wings, but getting kicked out of two schools is being irresponsible on purpose."

Crud. He's on the warpath.

"Jason, take it easy," Mom says.

Christian fidgets with the sleeves of his sweater.

I have to say something. My father's not playing fair. "Dad, Christian already explained he made mistakes. Nobody is immune from screwing up. He's just a kid. He has his whole life ahead of him to correct his mistakes and make some new ones. How would you feel if someone called you out on every faux pas or misstep you ever made?"

My heart is beating so fast that I think everyone can hear it. I've never challenged my father before. Not ever.

I can't look at him. Christian focuses all his attention on the flames from the candles on the table. We're all waiting for what comes next. Last year, I was grounded for entering the kitchen one morning and not speaking to Dad. I was in a bad mood. He didn't care. He said that he wouldn't tolerate being disrespected in his own house.

"You're right, sweetheart. I shouldn't have come down so hard on him. Christian, please accept my apology."

I look across the table, and Christian's eyes flash with admiration. "I understand, Mr. Cooper. You're just protecting your daughter."

By the time dessert rolls around, the mood is much lighter. Christian impresses Dad with his business knowledge. Mom asks about his college choices, which include The University of Pennsylvania (although he doesn't think he will get in), University of Virginia (his mom's alma mater), New York University, and University of Texas, Austin (my dad's alma mater). Christian scored some major points with that one.

"Mrs. Cooper, do you miss being a scientist at all?" Christian asks.

"Sometimes, but once I discovered my passion, I never looked back. There's no need to be so formal, Christian. You can call me Shelby."

Mom has a Ph.D. in Computational Biology and used to run her own lab as Director of Bioinformatics for a biotech company in Cambridge. When everything was falling apart, she resigned her post and never looked back, as she says.

"When is your next cookbook coming out?" Christian asks.

"Next year. I'm working hard to make it the best one yet."

PART THREE

HACKED!

CHAPTER 17

I FINALLY MAKE it to my room and discover three missed calls from Callie. Dinner was an overall success, despite the rough beginning. Christian got a check mark in the like column from Mom. Dad, it's hard to say. I don't think he'll be taking selfies with Christian any time soon. I go through my bedtime routine. When I'm done, I perch myself on the bed and call her back.

"So, how was it?" she asks, bubbling with excitement.

I give her the highlights and lowlights of the evening. She can share the details with Frances later.

"Are you guys official now?"

"He did call me his girlfriend. I freaked. But we worked it out."

I remove the phone from my ears to save my eardrums from the tone-deaf-inducing scream coming from her.

"Are you done now?"

"Yes. Now, on to a more serious topic."

"Let's hear it."

"I got the email address."

"Fantastic. I'll wait up another hour or so before I try. What is it?"

Callie rattles off Sidney's email address. It was smart to call with the information. I don't want any evidence on my phone.

"Was it hard to get the email from Brooke?"

"Nope. She was flattered that I used actual words to communicate with her instead of my usual blank stare."

"Thanks, I owe you. And Dahlia."

"What are friends for? Good luck. I'm going to text Frances and tell her you and Christian are officially a couple. That should ruin the rest of the school year for Sidney."

After I hang up from Callie, I pull out my laptop, prop myself against a pillow, and get to work. I connect to the network and plug in the unique VPN code. Once it's successful, I log on to her email service provider site and click on mail. Her username is the email address, but the password will be harder. I can make three attempts before she's alerted. My fingers hover over the keyboard as the cursor blinks in the password box. I try to think like Sidney. My brain screams in protest and spits out a better idea. I know how to get Sidney to hand over her email password.

CHAPTER 18

I SPRINT ACROSS the parking lot, heading for the main road that leads to the entrance of Saint Matthews. I'm invigorated this morning. I barely feel the cold wind nipping at me. Two weeks to go before Thanksgiving. I plan to send out my remaining applications by then, roughly a month before the January 1 deadline. Can't wait to bust Sidney and put an end to this stupid game.

I hear the faint sounds of footsteps behind me. Not the usual footsteps of fellow day students heading up the hill to the main road leading to school. The fight or flight reflex kicks in. Flight. I quicken my pace. I don't look back. The main road is in front of me. I look left and right. No cars. I cross the street at full speed. I have to make it on to the school grounds before I stop running. I'm curious too. I have to see the face of the person chasing me and find out what he or she wants.

When I arrive at the main gates, the footsteps fade. Only then do I turn around.

"What do you want? Why are you chasing me? Who are you?" I lob the questions at him, barely breathing between each one.

He holds up both hands, indicating he's not a threat. Non-threatening people don't go around chasing teenage girls out of school parking lots, so I'm not about to breathe easy. My chaser looks to be in his early thirties, or maybe he's in his twenties. His long hair is pulled back in a ponytail, and his outfit is simple: jeans, a T-shirt, and a black leather jacket. I have to remember those details just in case he's shady and I have to report him or something.

"I didn't mean to scare you. Are you a student here?"

"What do you want? If you don't tell me, I'll scream."

"No need for that. Nicholas Furi's daughter goes to this school, right?" He removes a piece of paper from his jacket pocket. "Callie Furi. She's a student here?"

Of all the students leaving the parking lot, he picks me. Why? I school my features into what I hope is a look of utter confusion. Freaking paparazzi. I can't believe they're lurking around the area. How many of them are there staking out the school? Poor Callie. Her parents' messy divorce isn't leaving tabloid hell anytime soon.

"There are over four hundred students at this school. Excuse me."

I start sprinting again. I burst through the entrance of the main building and hurry down the hallway to Ms. Spencer's office, our director of communications. She can coordinate with security. Then I remember the staff members don't come in until 8:30 a.m. I whip out my phone and text Callie while walking down the hall to the bank of senior lockers.

ME:

Stalkerazzi alert. They're here.

CALLIE:

Are u serious? OMG. This sucks wind.

ME:

They're not sure they have the right school. Looking for confirmation. You have to see Ms. Spencer about it. Meet me at my locker.

CALLIE:

k

When I arrive at my locker, my day takes a nosedive. Sidney is waiting for me. I moan in frustration.

I turn my back to her and zip through the combination lock, which she already knows. I have yet to find out how that happened.

"You think you won, don't you?"

Callie will be here in a few minutes, so the fastest way to get rid of Sidney is to speak to her. I can't imagine a more intolerable task at 7:30 in the morning.

"Won? Was there a contest going on?"

"I don't know what kind of voodoo you worked on him, but this isn't over."

"I meant it when I said you should get a hobby. Your

attitude was just annoying at first. Now, it's working my last nerve. Besides, I heard you have a new boyfriend. Did he get tired of you already? Can't blame him."

Her face turns furious, raging clouds ready to burst into a rainstorm. "You'll pay for that."

"Get your nose out of my business. I'm sure you have other uses for it, like snorting."

She gets up in my face. "What did you say to me?"

"Your hearing is perfect."

Her shoulders slump, and she takes a step back. "It's so easy for you, isn't it? You don't have to try that hard. Perfect family, perfect grades, perfect friends, perfect figure, and now the perfect boyfriend. You really have it made, Abbie. Soon, you'll go off to the perfect college and do it all over again. Or not."

"What are you saying?"

"I'm saying one of these days, your luck will run out."

Was that an admission of guilt, or am I grasping at straws?

"Don't bet on it, Sidney."

Where is Callie? I want Sidney to leave.

"I'm just telling you the way it is."

"The world according to Sidney. There's a scary thought. By the way, why are you so miserable all the time?"

"You don't know anything about me," she says, her green eyes glistening with moisture. "So, shut your stupid mouth."

I must have touched a nerve. I look past Sidney to see Callie hurrying toward me. Thank goodness. When she gets closer, she does a double take. She doesn't hide the hostility in her voice. "Sidney."

"Callie."

Then Sidney takes off without another word.

"What was that about?" Callie asks.

"I don't know. She's messed up."

"Duh."

My phone goes off. It's another text.

CHRISTIAN:

Sorry babe. Can't walk you to class this morning. Got a call with my mom and then heading to first period. See you later, though.

I text him back a string of smiley-face emoticons. He responds with a series of red roses. The tune to some sappy love song pops into my head, but I don't recall the name.

"Earth to Abbie," Callie says.

"Um, yeah, the Stalkerazzi."

I fill her in on my run-in with the creepy guy before school. We agree that the school should be alerted.

"How did it go last night?"

"It didn't."

"You couldn't crack her password?"

"I didn't try. I have a better idea."

"What?"

"Will tell you at lunch."

MORNING CLASSES FLY by in a blur. All I could think about was how to get ahead of The Avenger, a.k.a.

Sidney, before she makes some outrageous demand. I had moments of doubt, where I questioned if what I'm about to do is the right thing, the moral thing.

Callie and Frances are already seated in the dining hall. As much as I like food, I'm always late to lunch. Strange.

"Dish," Frances says. "What's this new plan you have to trap Sidney?"

"Can I get some food first? If that's okay with you, Ms. Newshound."

"Okay, hurry up."

I return from the lunch line and place my tray on the table. "Guys, I don't feel good about this plan. I have to keep talking myself into it."

"Explain it to us, and we'll tell you if it's a good plan or not," Callie says.

"Keylogger software."

She scratches her head. "I don't understand your nerd speak."

"I can remotely access Sidney's computer by sending her an email. Once she clicks on it, the software launches and operates in stealth mode. It records every keystroke she makes and logs it. I then login to a special server to retrieve the information. All she has to do is access her email using her password, just once, and I got it."

"I like it," Frances says, impressed.

"Genius," Callie says.

"You guys don't think there's anything wrong with this?"

They look at each other and then at me. "No," they say in unison.

"How do you get her to open an email from you?" Callie asks. "She hates you."

"I can set it up so it looks like the email is coming from someone she hangs out with."

"Brooke?" Frances asks.

"Or Jessica, her other minion. Should I be doing this? It's a gross invasion of privacy and illegal."

"Will you get caught?"

"No. She won't even know the software is running on her computer. Once I prove she's behind the photo and the stalking, I can shut it down."

"So, what's the problem?" Frances asks.

"I don't know. Sidney brings out the worst in me."

"She's doing you a favor, Abbie."

"How do you figure, Frances?"

"She's forcing you to fight dirty. Stop being the good girl already. Do you think she felt bad when she got that photo and started threatening to expose you? You have a lot to lose, and Sidney knows that. If she shows that picture to anybody, you're one hundred percent toast. Extra burnt."

She's one hundred percent right. If I hesitate, it could speed up my demise.

"Okay. I'll do it. What are you two doing for Thanksgiving?" I ask, trying to distance myself from the devious plan I just concocted.

"That's coming up fast, isn't it?" Callie asks. "Haven't

thought about it much. Not sure where home is anymore. Both my parents moved out of the house in Malibu."

"Why don't you guys both spend Thanksgiving with my family? It's the last time we'll all be together before graduation. We can Skype with Anastasia. It will be like old times."

"Your parents won't mind?" Callie asks.

"My parents adore the two of you. Mom will be thrilled. You know how she makes a big spectacle when it comes to the holidays."

"You got yourself a deal then," Frances says. "Penny's Asian tour is wrapping up, and my parents expect me to be home. Oh well, they'll understand."

"Are you sure?" I ask. "If you have to go home, you have to go home."

"Don't worry about it. I'm not leaving you and Callie to have all the fun. I want in. I'll talk to my mom today."

"We could have even more fun with two additional guests," I say with a mischievous grin.

They look at me, puzzled.

"Trevor and Christian."

"Woohoo," Callie says. "Good times.

CHAPTER 19

W HEN THE BELL rings, signaling the end of the school day and AP Biology, I grab everything not nailed down to my desk and stuff it into my bag. Mr. Curry, our teacher, pretends he doesn't hear the bell and continues to lecture. Everyone ignores him and packs their belongings, ready to jet out of here. When he says class dismissed, we trip all over each other in a mad dash for the door. I move off to the side after I exit the class. The text message alert from my phone gets my attention. It must be Christian. I know he's waiting for me at my locker so he can walk me to my car.

When I whip out the phone and read the text, I stumble backward into the wall.

BLOCKED NUMBER:

$50k. Will call with instructions.

BLOCKED NUMBER:

You know what happens if you don't cooperate.
U get everything you deserve. NOTHING!!!

A swift kick to the gut would have been less painful. I stay stuck to the wall for a moment, afraid I'll fall to pieces if I don't use it for support. This is what it was all about? Money? It doesn't make any sense. A big, fat dose of irony slaps me across the face. I have the funds. The only problem is I can't touch that account until I'm eighteen, which doesn't happen for another few months. I suspect The Avenger will come up with some ridiculous deadline I can't possibly meet.

I pull up the call log on my phone, and tap the screen. He answers after three rings.

"Cooper, I was going to wait until you got home from school to call. I don't have good news," Ty says. "I did some digging. Kyle Davidson dropped out of UCLA, and no one has seen or heard from him since. I spoke to both Aaron and Pete, and they have no idea who would compile a list of the kids who were using Adderall. They're not proud of it, either, and didn't want to talk about it much."

"I have bigger problems, Ty. Call me in twenty minutes. I should be home by then."

"What's wrong? What's going on?"

"Money. Lots of it."

"You're not making any sense."

"I'll forward you a text. Talk to you in twenty minutes."

I hang up and then try to forward him The Avenger's extortion text message, but it's gone. I stare at the screen for a few seconds, and then scroll up. Nothing. Did I accidentally delete it? Was it there at all? Yes. It was real. The amount of money she asked for is permanently emblazoned in my mind. I start to bite my fingernails and realize it's not a good idea. I need to stay focused. Why is this happening? Even the first text I received, warning me to stay away from Christian while I was at Evan Mueller's party, has disappeared. All of her texts have disappeared. I'll have to restore my text messages from the cloud backup when I get home. They have to be there.

I put on a cheerful face for Christian when I meet him at my locker. We walk to the parking lot in companionable silence. He opens the driver side door for me after I unlock the car. Once inside the front passenger seat, he gets chatty.

"What's wrong, babe? You can talk to me."

I stick the key in the ignition and start the car. The temperature barely made it to forty degrees today. I crank up the heat.

"I'm having a bad day. I can handle it."

He strokes my hair. "Tell me about it."

"It's not worth discussing. There are more important things we could talk about."

"Like what?"

"Thanksgiving. You're invited. Sorry for the short notice. Frances and Callie are coming too."

"To experience Mrs. Cooper's Thanksgiving dinner instead of watching it on TV? That's a treat. I would love to come. Under one condition."

"What's that?"

He moistens his lips with his tongue.

"I promise I won't flip out, whatever it is."

"I've been trying to work up the courage to ask you this for a while now. I started thinking about it after we had what was officially our first date at Joe's Pizzeria."

I squeeze his hand. "Just say it."

"Would you like to see my paintings?"

I squeal with delight and reach over to hug him. "Are you kidding? Yes, I would love to see your artwork. I knew it. You have a few stashed away in your dorm room, don't you? Oh, I can't wait."

"Um, they're not in my dorm room."

"Oh. Then how will I see them?"

"Where I keep them. Home, at Bedford Hills."

"Huh?"

A million thoughts run through my mind. What does it mean? Would my parents allow me to go? Did he run this by his parents?

"Abbie? Will you come? Please. Don't leave me hanging off a cliff."

"When?"

"New Year's Eve. My parents throw a huge charity ball every year. The timing is perfect. My dad will be home because it's the holidays."

"Are your parents okay with this?"

"Yes. They think it means I'm finally growing up."

"In that case, I'd love to."

"Seal with a kiss?"

"How can I refuse such an offer?"

Somewhere between the kissing, and heavy breathing, I hear ringing. It gets louder. It's my cell phone. I already hate whoever's calling. I'm in no hurry to pick up. Christian eases back in his seat. Then the fog clears from my mind. *Ty.* I told him to call me. I should have been home by now.

"Aren't you going to check to see who called?"

"No."

"Why not?"

"I'll call back later."

We make out some more, but I cut it short. I tell Christian I have to catch Mom at home to ask her about Bedford Hills before she goes back to the restaurant. It's better if I don't waste any time asking.

BOTH MOM AND Miles are home. I make a quick apology and race to my bedroom where I dump my bag on the floor and don't bother to take off my coat. I flop down on the bed and call Ty.

"Sorry," I say when he picks up. "I got held up at school."

"With school or with Christian?"

His question takes me by surprise. "Why would you ask me that?"

"Have you told him what's going on?"

Guilt creeps up on me. Christian is part of my life now, and he has a right to know that his association with me is a trap that could spring at any time. I will tell him. I just have to figure out when and how.

"The Avenger wants $50,000. She says she will call with instructions."

"So, all of this was to extort money from you. Why?"

"That's what I don't understand. Sidney, she has plenty of money of her own."

"That is a mystery. What can I do to help?"

"You can loan me the money. I can't access the trust my parents set up for me for another few months. I can pay you back once I turn eighteen."

"Do you think that's a good idea? Paying, I mean."

"I don't know. I'm stalling until I can come up with a permanent solution." I give Ty the rundown on my plan to remotely access Sidney's computer.

"What about the text messages you promised to send me? I never got them."

"That's because they disappeared. I planned to retrieve them from my cloud backup until I realized she's using an app that sets a time limit on how long I can view the message."

Ty lets out a low whistle. "You're dealing with a pro."

"That's why Sidney's computer is a critical part of my plan. It might also reveal the identity of her accomplice. She's making sure her calls to me can't be traced."

"I'll get you the money. Call me the minute you have instructions. And you don't have to pay me back."

"Thank you. Wait, what?"

"I'll do anything for you, Cooper. You know that."

"Ty, that's a lot of money."

"It is, but I'm good for it. My parents were generous, and I play the stock market in my free time. It's worked out well. For the most part."

"I didn't know you played the stock market. When did you start doing that?"

"Last year. Don't worry about it; I want to do this for you. Consider it a gift."

I know to argue with him would be pointless, so I give up.

After I hang up from Ty, my phone lights up: blocked number. That didn't take long at all. Less than an hour from the time the text demanding money appeared. I click the green answer button, slide off the bed, and then walk toward the window. I pull the curtains aside and observe Mrs. Wilson, our neighbor from across the street pulling into her garage.

"You're out of your mind," I say. "I can't come up with $50,000."

"Boohoo. Poor Abbie. Aren't you dating a billionaire's son? I'm sure you can convince him to part with a few dollars?"

"You really are a sicko, you know that?"

"Wait a minute. He doesn't know you broke the law, does he? Hmm. We have ourselves a conundrum. Oh well, your problem. As long as you solve it by Black Friday."

"That's next week. Are you nuts?"

"You'll make the drop at Taylor Books in Framingham," she continues, ignoring my protest. "These are one-time only instructions, so listen up. The money has to be in unmarked bills, nothing larger than a twenty. Put it in a plain, brown shopping bag— the kind with two handles. After you pack the money in the bag, add a plain, black scarf on top of it. Got it so far?"

"Yes." My tone is flat and void of emotion.

"When you get to the store, an identical bag with the black scarf on top will be waiting for you. Make the swap. The other bag will have a bunch of shoeboxes in it. You don't want to walk into the store with a bag and walk out empty-handed. You have to appear like you've been shopping all day and decided to drop by the bookstore."

I listen to the rest of the instructions in a trance. Black Friday is one of the busiest shopping days of the year. It doesn't matter that this is supposed to go down at 9:30 p.m., thirty minutes before closing. How can I ensure that a customer won't find the bag and call the store manager—or worse, store cameras capture the whole thing?

She says something about the magazine section, a bench, and armchairs. But my brain is focused on one thing and one thing only.

"I want something in exchange. The photo. Fair is fair."

"Oh, Abbie. Do you really think you have any bargaining power here? Don't make me laugh."

"You're desperate for money for whatever reason, so yes, I have bargaining power. I don't want the picture getting out, and you need $50,000. If you want your money, I need the photo in exchange—and the drive on which it's saved."

She says nothing, pondering my counter-offer.

"Okay, Abbie," she says finally. "I'll play ball for now."

"How can I trust you? How do I know you won't double-cross me?"

"You'll just have to wait and see, won't you?"

"Call me back when you're sure about whether or not I can trust you," I snap. "Until then, you get everything you deserve. Nothing."

I hang up on her. Tears prickle at the corners of my eyes. I don't know what came over me, why I hung up on her. Will she end this once she gets the money? I don't know. It could be the beginning of something far worse.

Shoving the negative thoughts aside, I leave the window and pad over to my homework desk. I pull out the chair and sit. It's time to get to work, so I boot up my computer and set up Keylogger. After I hit the send button on an email to Sidney from "Brooke Westerly," I receive a new text message.

BLOCKED NUMBER:

You shouldn't have hung up on me.

Another text follows. A letter.

BLOCKED NUMBER:

Mr. Christopher Reston

Director of Undergraduate Admissions

Princeton University

110 West College

Princeton, NJ 08544

Dear Mr. Reston:

I wanted to bring to your attention an issue that has the potential to taint the reputation of the university if it's not addressed right away. Abigail L. Cooper, an applicant from Saint Matthews Academy in Castleview, MA, has cheated to gain an unfair academic advantage—mainly use of the drug Adderall. Attached you will find photographic evidence of Ms. Cooper's blatant disregard for the rules of fairness, school policies, not to mention the law. I'm sure you're aware, Mr. Reston that the use of Adderall without a prescription is a felony. As one of the gatekeepers of this fine institution, I trust that you will make the right decision with the information provided to you.

Sincerely,

A concerned citizen

CHAPTER 20

I READ THE letter, repeatedly, in slow motion. Every time I do, the burning sensation tearing through my stomach intensifies tenfold, bringing me one step closer to total collapse. Sweat percolates at the tip of my nose and upper lip. My heart skips several beats. I force myself to inhale air. The letter is no hoax. Christopher Reston worked as Assistant Director of Admissions for five years. He was promoted to Director when his predecessor left last year to work for the Tuck Business School at Dartmouth. I still have the press release in my Princeton application file.

Any residual guilt I had left about spying on Sidney has vanished. She's out to ruin me, and now, my options are limited: let her succeed or destroy her first.

LATER THAT NIGHT, after my Dad goes to his study and Miles is shuttled off to bed, my mother and I sit at the kitchen table for a serious conversation over hot chamomile tea. I tell her Christian invited me to his home for New Year's Eve.

She takes a sip of tea and with deliberate slowness puts the cup down on the coaster. "How do you feel about that?"

"I'm happy that he asked. But I get the feeling you're not."

"That's not it at all, sweetie. It comes down to more practical, parental concerns, like the fact that you're still a minor. Your father and I don't know the Wheelers. It's an out of state trip, and—"

"And what?"

"I don't want you getting into a situation you can't control or one you might regret."

"Is that your way of telling me don't come around here with no babies?"

She makes a face at me, and then chuckles. "It's my job to advise you of all consequences."

"It's not even like that between Christian and me."

"How long do you think that will last? Is it something you're ready for?"

"He's not pressuring me if that's what you mean."

"Good."

"You don't have to worry, Mom. I'm responsible. Haven't I proven that repeatedly? I'll be eighteen in a matter of weeks. I can be resourceful if anything weird pops up, which it won't."

"What about Christian's parents? Are they okay with this?"

"He says they are."

"I'll have to discuss this with your father."

"I know you do. But I want to hear how *you* feel about it."

Dad will say no, and I need Mom to work him over. She can get him to agree to anything.

"I understand. I was a teenager once. I know it's important to you. My main concerns are your happiness and safety."

"I invited Christian over for Thanksgiving. Sorry, I didn't ask first."

She picks up her cup of tea with both hands and holds it to her lips, not quite touching. "Well played, daughter. Well played."

CHAPTER 21

I FIRE OFF a text to Lance Carter on my way to the student lounge.

ME:

Need your help again. Nothing crazy, I promise.

LANCE:

Can't.

ME:

Why not?

LANCE:

Too risky.

ME:

Not this time.

When I enter the lounge and grab a seat, he still hasn't responded. I unload all my paperwork and spread them out on the table in front of me. A few students are on their laptops, and others are playing foosball. I pick up a pen and begin the tedious process of reviewing my essay for Duke, line-by-line, looking for errors or sentences that need clarity. My cell phone alerts me that I have a new text message. I pick up the phone in a hurry and read the text.

LANCE:

Where are u?

ME:

Student lounge.

LANCE:

Be there in a few.

I'm relieved that he's come around. I continue with my essay, but I can barely concentrate. In less than five minutes, he plops down in the seat across from me.

"So, Mama, what's cooking?"

"Voice analysis."

"I'm listening."

"Some random girl is harassing me over the phone. It has to do with that locker situation. She calls me at odd times. I want to compare her voice to the person I think is doing it."

"Easy."

"There's only one problem. I don't have the voice sample from subject B yet, the girl I think is behind it."

"How soon can you get the sample?"

"A couple of days. I need the analysis done before Thanksgiving."

"You're squeezing me, Mama."

"Please, Lance. I really need this."

"I'll see what I can do. Email me the audio file for subject A. You have to work fast on subject B."

"I'm on it."

After Lance takes off, I lean back in the seat, contemplating the best way to bait Sidney into a verbal smack down so I can record her voice. The answers don't come easy, so I wrap up my essay editing and head to the girls' bathroom.

I HEAR INCESSANT sniffling in one of the stalls, followed by the sound of retching and finally puke hitting the water in the toilet bowl.

"Are you okay in there?"

"Shut up," she yells. "Mind your own business."

Sidney. She doesn't sound right, but she told me to buzz off. I pull out my phone before she exits the stall. I tap the voice memo icon, hit the red record button, and then slip the phone back into my bag just in time. She flushes the toilet and comes out of the stall seconds later, looking like a troll. I gasp at her appearance. Sidney takes pride in her upkeep, and nothing less than perfectly coiffed hair, flawless makeup, and a killer wardrobe will do. The girl standing before me with defiance radiating off her is a hot mess. Her hair looks like a flock of birds decided to make it their permanent home. Her pupils are dilated and bloodshot. She swipes her finger under her nose.

"Should I call someone?"

"What part of mind your own business don't you understand?"

"I just thought… well, it sounds like you need help."

"Not from you. Now, go away and stay out of my face, you stupid cow."

I back up slowly.

She splashes water on her face.

"That really hurt my feelings, Sidney. Was it necessary to go there?"

She gives me the finger over her shoulder.

I turn on my heels and exit the bathroom. I wonder how long Sidney can keep this up.

PART FOUR

THE DROP

CHAPTER 22

O UR HOUSE IS filled to the brim with laughter and chaos. It's the day before Thanksgiving. Just for the next forty-eight hours, I'd like to forget about my problems. Before the break, I texted Lance and told him I couldn't come up with the voice sample before our agreed timeline. I just couldn't do it. What I saw in the bathroom did something to me. School let out at noon today. Christian, Miles, and Trevor are in the family room, playing video games. I've never heard such trash talk in my life. Dad is on his way home.

Every inch of available counter space in the kitchen is taken up with fruit, vegetables, meats, and baking ingredients. The girls and I are helping Mom with various tasks in preparation for the big meal.

"Why don't you kids go relax? You've helped me a lot. I think I'm all set for now."

"Mom, are you sure? There's a lot of work still left, and you need to relax, too."

"I will. Later, with a glass of wine and your dad to help me unwind."

"Mom, stop it. You're embarrassing me."

Frances and Callie giggle. Then the doorbell rings. We look at each other.

"I wonder who that could be?" Mom asks. She leaves to answer the door.

Frances and Callie gather around me.

"How are you going to handle this?" Frances whispers.

"Improvising. I have no idea how I'm going to move fifty grand from his car without arousing suspicion. Remember, act surprised."

Ty appears in the kitchen in a fleece pullover and a smile as bright as a Light Bulb.

"Surprise," he says.

"Ty, what are you doing here?" Frances asks, sounding sincere.

"I wanted to see the Coopers before I catch my flight out of Logan."

He walks over to where I'm standing and pulls me into a hug. Mom chooses that moment to return to the kitchen, with Christian at her side. His semi frown makes me feel all kinds of guilty. Frances clears her throat while looking in their direction. Ty lets go of me, and then turns around. He says hello to Christian and Christian nods back.

"Abbie, can I borrow you for a minute?" Christian asks.

Ty wants to say something. Instead, he remains quiet with his hands fidgeting at his sides. As I follow Christian out of the kitchen, Frances asks Ty what he's been up to these days.

We're in the library on the main floor of the house. A large, mahogany bookcase is the main attraction. Luxurious carpeting, a brown leather sofa, and a variety of photos and paintings on the wall give the room a cozy feeling.

Christian leans up against the bookcase, arms folded with me facing him. "Did you know he was coming?"

"No, I didn't. It's a brief visit. He's on his way to Logan."

"This is way awkward."

"Why? Ty is a friend."

"A friend who's in love with you. I saw the way he looked at you."

"Are you serious?"

"Yes."

"There's no reason to be insecure about Ty. Whatever I felt for him, that's in the past. We care about each other, but nothing romantic is going on."

"Have you told him about us?"

"Yes."

"How did he react?"

"He was happy for us."

For the first time since the conversation started, he relaxes. "Are you sure this is just a surprise visit on his way out?"

"What do you mean?"

"I don't know. Something about this visit is weird. Most people scramble to hit the road the day before Thanksgiving, as early as they can. Yet, he took time out to come see you. He could have called or texted. He could have planned a visit. Instead, he takes a detour on one of the busiest travel days of the year."

I can't dispute his logic. All I can do is alleviate his suspicions. Before I get the chance to come up with something plausible, he jams his hands into his pockets and starts pacing.

"And there's also the way Callie and Frances were looking at him and me. I feel like the four of you are in on something, and I'm left out in the rain like some unwanted fool."

"No, baby, that's not true at all." I lift his arms and place them around my waist. "Please don't feel that way. What you saw was just the girls being nervous. They know how I used to feel about Ty, and it was just weird for them, seeing the two of you in the same room."

"You can trust me with anything," he says, pressing his forehead against mine. "I want you to come to me if you're in trouble or hurting. I want you to be happy."

I'm such a fraud. I have a great guy who's been straight with me, and all I do is lie to him. As if that wasn't bad enough, I went behind his back and made a deal with someone he considers his competition. I don't like me right now. I'll find a way to get over it, though.

"You do make me happy," I assure him. "And I trust you."

"Good. I have a confession to make," he adds.

"What is it?"

"You're not the only one with trust issues."

"Oh?" Even though Callie told me the same thing that night after Evan's party, there's something special about Christian telling me in his own words.

"All my life I've been trained not to trust anyone."

"Because of your family?"

"Yes. My parents transferred their jaded attitude to me. No one could just like me for me. It's all about the Wheeler name and money."

"That makes life challenging."

"It's not when I'm with you."

That phony feeling is rearing its ugly head again. I kick it to some faraway place. I kiss Christian, and at that moment, I know I will break his heart.

TY IS ABOUT to leave to catch his flight, and I've spent all of two minutes with him. We head out to his car to chat, but not before I remind Callie in front of everyone that she left her bag with some sample dresses and her sketchbook in my car and that I would bring it once I'm done talking to Ty.

Once we're both inside the car, he cranks up the heat to keep us warm.

"How is Christian about me showing up?"

"Suspicious. I had to reassure him."

"Can I ask you something?"

"Sure."

"You may never want to speak to me again after I ask you."

"We're always honest with each other."

"I'm glad you came to me for help, but why did you ask me and not him? Why won't you tell him the truth?"

I sigh and dig deep inside. I've backed myself into a complicated corner, and under the scrutiny of Ty's question, I don't know if my reasons will stand up. I give it a shot anyway.

"Our relationship is new. I want it to be just that: a new, exciting relationship full of possibilities. We're still getting to know each other. It's not the time to bring in something this heavy, although the window is closing. Besides, it would be inappropriate to ask him for the money, although I'm sure he wouldn't hesitate to help me. With you and me, it's different."

"So, you're hiding who you are from him, all of you?"

"Everybody has secrets, Ty. This is not an easy thing for me. I struggle with it. And maybe I'm selfish."

He drums on the steering wheel. "Why do you say that?"

"Christian doesn't trust people because of his upbringing. He has opened up to me, and he's going to dump me when he finds out I've been keeping secrets from him. He thinks I'm the perfect girlfriend, wonderful and amazing. Call me vain, but I want to ride that wave for as long as I can. He invited me to Bedford Hills."

"Oh. I didn't know you guys were that serious. Aren't you moving too fast?"

"What's too fast?" I ask, shrugging.

"I know you."

"I'm not fifteen anymore."

"I know. I screwed up."

"What does that mean?"

"Sometimes, I wonder if…" He struggles to find the words. "Never mind." He puts the car in reverse.

"What were you going to say, Ty? It's not like you to hold back."

"Maybe I've changed."

We sit in silence, the sound of the heat blasting from the vents keeping us company.

"Be careful tomorrow, Cooper. Call me if you run into trouble. And think about telling Christian the truth."

"I should tell him when we get to Bedford Hills."

"However this turns out, I got your back. I always will."

"Thanks, Ty. Now get out of here before you miss your flight. Your mom will say it's my fault."

"My mom loves you."

"Does she?"

"Yes."

"If you say so."

After Ty pulls out of the driveway, I enter the house and start up the stairs with the bag. I'm one step up when I hear Christian say, "Let me carry that."

I freeze in place, then turn around to face him. He comes to stand next to me and extends his hand.

"I got it. It's just Callie's stuff. I'm taking it up to my bedroom."

"Still, I don't want you carrying anything up the stairs."

"It's nothing at all. Besides, I don't think my parents will be happy if they see you anywhere near my bedroom."

"I'm willing to risk getting caught. That bag looks heavy."

"I'm not that fragile."

"I know, but still."

I almost tell him everything right then, so the guilt will stop choking me. Then I remind myself that I have a plan.

"You spoil me enough. I can make it to my room without any major disaster. Give me a minute. I'll be right back, and you can tell me all about the plans for our trip."

"Your parents haven't given a firm answer yet."

"They'll come around."

Next thing I know, he takes the bag from me and lifts it. "What does Callie have in this thing? Are you sure it's just clothing?"

The hairs on my arms stand at attention. "Um... that's what she said. She's sensitive about her stuff, so please don't open it."

"Hey, Wheeler, get down here so I can kick your butt in *Assassin's Creed*," Trevor says. "Oh, and Mr. Cooper is home. Stay strong, bro."

I didn't know I was holding my breath until Trevor appeared and saved me from disaster. "You heard Trevor," I say to Christian. "A butt kicking awaits you. What's going on with you and my father anyway?"

"That's between Mr. Cooper, and me," he answers, coyly.

IT'S A FEW minutes after midnight, and the house is quiet. I hit the submit button on the last of my college applications. A sense of relief embraces me like a warm blanket. I don't have to worry about the January 1 deadline anymore, and I can enjoy my holiday season. At least that's the story I'm telling myself. I sense a presence behind me and turn around. Dad enters the family room.

"I thought you were already in bed," I say to him.

"I had calls to make to a few foreign clients," he says. He plops down on the sofa and motions for me to join him.

Ever since Dad quit his job as chief financial officer of Orphion Technologies, he's been helping companies all over the world access new markets and beef up their profits.

"Is everything okay, Dad? You look frazzled."

"Your old man is all right. Working on an acquisition that turned out to be more involved than I anticipated."

"You work too much."

"You're no slouch either. You've been working hard on your applications."

"I just submitted the remaining ones."

"Great. In a couple of weeks, Princeton's early action decision will come in. I'll save a bottle of our best champagne for the occasion, so your mother and I can celebrate."

I look away from him. It's suddenly too warm in the room. My dad's innocent comment floods me with doubt and fear. With the threat from The Avenger hanging over my head, I worry about my college plans.

"What's the matter, sweetheart? Are you nervous about Princeton? I'm not. You'll get in. No doubt in my mind."

I turn my head toward him. "You're my dad; you're supposed to say that."

"I wouldn't say it if it weren't true. I'm proud of you, Abbie. Not just because you're a brilliant student, but also because you're an all-around A plus.

"Does that mean you'll let me go to Bedford Hills?"

I didn't mean to put him on the spot, but I have to know. Besides, I don't want to think about The Avenger right now. It's not good for my mental state.

"Christian is a charming and persuasive young man."

"Is that a yes?" I ask. I can feel the excitement bubbling up from my chest.

"Look, sweetheart, it's not something I endorse—"

"I know you're worried, Dad."

"Let me finish. I can't stop you from growing up. However, I'd rather know what's going on instead of you lying to my face and sneaking around behind my back."

"Dad, I've never done that before," I say, offended.

"You've never had a boyfriend before," he says, looking me dead in the eyes. "I was once a victim of raging teenage hormones. They can be as intoxicating as any drug."

I recline further into the sofa, mortified. Dad hit the nail on the head. When I'm with Christian, I do feel those hormones raging out of control, and I have to work overtime to keep them from gobbling me up.

"I know it's hard for you. Letting go. I'll be out of high school in five months and on my own at college three months after that."

He squeezes my hand and stares straight ahead.

"Dad, it's going to be okay. You can't protect me from life. You and mom have done a great job. It's up to me now. I have to find my own way."

"You'll understand one day when you have children of your own. I have a few conditions," he says, turning to me.

"What are they?"

"You check in twice a day as long as you're out there. You install a companion app on your phone. You take enough cash and a credit card with you. These are non-negotiable demands."

"Yes, sir."

"I spoke to Alan Wheeler."

"You did?"

"We've met on a couple of occasions, introduced by a mutual friend."

"Dad, you never said you knew him."

"I didn't need to. Whether Christian was his son or someone else's, my feelings wouldn't change. I let him know that I will hold him personally responsible if anything happens to you."

That's classic Jason Cooper: straightforward, thorough, and unflinching.

"I love you, Daddy," I say, hugging him.

"Love you too, sweetheart. Now, go to bed. That's non-negotiable."

CHAPTER 23

F RANCES AND CALLIE squeal like toddlers in the candy aisle and jump up and down on my bed. Thanksgiving day has arrived, and I just gave them the news that my parents agreed to let me go to Bedford Hills.

"Oh, my goodness, there's so much to do," Callie says, out of breath. They've both stopped jumping and join me on the sofa.

"It's only for a few days. We leave December 27th. I have to buy a plane ticket right away."

"You won't be needing that ticket," Callie says.

"I am not sitting in a car for eight hours. No way. I'm flying."

"We know," Frances says with a goofy grin on her face.

"What is it with the two of you this morning?"

"Nothing. We're just excited for you," Frances says.

"The Wheeler's New Year's Eve Party is epic," Callie says. "There's going to be a lot of press there."

"And please don't do that thing you always do," Frances says.

"What thing?"

"That face you make," Callie says. "When someone or something offends you."

189

"I don't know what you mean."

"The party is going to be filled with huge egos, people who think everyone should suck up to them. I can see you giving them the look and dismissing them like they're idiots who shouldn't be allowed to breathe."

"In other words, you want me to be anything but myself."

"Exactly," Frances says. "You're going to have to smile a lot, even when you don't want to."

"A lot of attention is going to be focused on you because you're Christian's girlfriend," Callie says. "Also, you need to watch out for vindictive exes and wannabes."

I rub my temples. This trip has taken on a new tone. I was looking forward to meeting Christian's parents and spending time with him in the home where he grew up. He was going to show me his paintings, and we would spend every moment together, laughing and having a lovely time. Now, I'm not so sure.

"What if I screw this up? You know I say the first thing that pops into my head. What if someone provokes me and I insult him or her?"

Twenty minutes later, my cheeks ache from practicing my fake smile in the mirror with Frances and Callie hovering like two fairy godmothers. I've been to a couple of galas and countless charity events with my parents, and I never felt this kind of pressure. We spend the next half hour discussing my wardrobe for the ball, Frances's upcoming newspaper internship in January, and Callie's portfolio for fashion school. None of it can disguise our collective fears about tomorrow. The drop.

"We can't let you go alone," Frances says. "Drop us at school in the morning so we can pick up my car. Callie and I will follow you."

"What if The Avenger is watching to see if I'm being followed?" I ask. "That's what makes me nervous. She has to be around to collect the money."

"So we should get there at least a half hour before you do, and hopefully ahead of The Avenger," Callie says. "We won't be too close, just hanging around the area in case you need us."

Anything could go wrong. I have this nightmare where someone chases me out of the store with the bag in tow, yelling that I forgot it, causing a scene. What if the cameras in the store capture my face? What if there are too many people around, and I can't make the swap because someone will see it and call the store manager?

"I have to wear something that won't draw attention. No bright colors, no makeup, my hair up in a ponytail and covered with a dark baseball cap with no logos."

"And keep your head down without making it look like you're doing it on purpose," Frances adds.

"What's our backup plan in case something does go wrong?" Callie asks.

"Turn on the waterworks and threaten to sue the store for harassing a minor?"

"That doesn't sound like a good plan," Frances says.

"It's either that or confess everything to my parents. It's not an option I want to consider."

"Have you found anything from the logs since you put that software on Sidney's computer?" Callie asks.

"Give me a minute."

I leave the sofa and boot up my computer at the desk. I access the site that contains the logs of Sidney's computer activities and punch in my username and password. The screen comes alive, populated with data.

I do a quick scan, first looking for email activities. Sidney did not disappoint. She logged into her email account from her computer twice since I installed the software. I can also see which apps she opened. Even more intriguing is the fact that she opened her photos app.

"She was looking at pictures," I yell to the girls. They both appear at my side in seconds.

"Let's see what's going on," Callie says.

I open the folder and start clicking on random pictures with the girls leaning over my shoulder. A ton of selfies with Sidney and her minions at various places, Sidney chugging down a bottle of what looks like vodka, Sidney in a cocktail dress at some party with three other girls I don't recognize.

"Boring stuff," Frances says.

"I know. So far, I don't see any encrypted folders on her hard drive, so this is it for photos."

"There could be one for video," Callie says.

"I haven't checked yet. Let's get through these pictures first."

"There are hundreds of them," Frances observes.

"I'll do a search for my name although I don't think

Sidney would be dumb enough to label anything with my name. It's worth a shot, though."

I type my name into the search bar at the top right hand of the screen and wait. I get a "no results" response. After trying my name in variations of first and last name with no results, I'm convinced the photo I'm searching for is elsewhere or labeled with a name I won't recognize on her computer. A deep-seated disappointment flows through me after an exhaustive search yields nothing. Does it mean Sidney is not involved in the blackmail, or her accomplice has all the files?

Before I check for videos, I do another scan of the other applications she used. I check the Word files, but only an essay for English class pops up.

"This sucks," Callie says.

"She does everything on her phone like we all do. We still haven't looked at video files yet, and her email might give us something."

I click on the QuickTime file. A hotel bathroom appears on the screen. Sidney leans over the sink, wearing only black panties and matching bra. The person behind the camera says something.

"Hey, baby, watcha doing?"

She looks into the camera. On the bathroom sink is a white powdery substance.

"What does it look like I'm doing, stupid? Get that camera away from me," she says.

Her eyes are glazed over, her face gaunt and dirty. Blood drips from her nose. She swipes her finger across her nose. "I'll be right out okay, baby. We're going to have fun. I promise."

Sidney returns to her task. We don't need the camera to tell us what's going on, so I fast forward through that scene. In the next frame, she comes out of the bathroom and dives onto the king sized bed. The camera must have been set up to record the two of them. A guy we assume was recording the earlier bathroom scene starts to kiss her. We can't see his face, but he has long black stringy hair and a tattoo of an eagle on his shoulder blades.

"I think we can figure out the rest," I say to the girls.

Callie and Frances make it back to the sofa. I power down my computer and join them.

"I don't think I can do this anymore," I tell them.

"What do you mean?" Callie asks.

"I have to shut down the Keylogger software. I didn't sign up for this. I'll have to find another way."

"I don't understand why she would store that video on her computer without a password," Frances says. "It's just reckless."

"That's Sidney," Callie says.

"I'll check her email; then I'm shutting down the whole thing."

"What if the evidence you're looking for shows up afterward?" Frances asks. "With the drop tomorrow, somebody may contact her or she may contact someone."

"They would call her phone," I say.

"Look what we found on her computer. You never know."

Loud banging on the bedroom door startles us. "Abbie, Callie, Frances, breakfast is ready," Miles yells.

"We're coming," I shout back.

I WALK DOWN the stairway, holding on to the railing so I won't trip on my heels. I hear a voice beneath the stairs. I slow my descent. As I get closer, I recognize Trevor's voice.

"Come on, Cole. I told you I'm good for it. Get off my back already."

He pauses, listening to his brother. He removes his glasses with his free hand, blows on the lenses, and then returns them to his face.

"Have I ever let you down? I always come through. Just going through a dry spell right now, but it will all work out."

A pause.

"Don't worry about it. And please don't tell Dad we spoke."

Another pause from Trevor.

"No, Cole, I want to major in Anthropology. I don't want to be tied to a desk in some stuffy office, no matter how nice it is. So I won't be joining the firm after college."

I don't know if I should alert him to my presence or not. That conversation is intense.

I clear my throat, and he looks up as I descend the stairs.

"Talk to you later," he says to his brother, and then he hangs up.

"Is everything okay, Trevor?" I ask.

"Wow. Christian's eyeballs are going to fall out when he sees you in that dress."

I reach the bottom of the stairs and face him. "Thanks for saying that. Are you okay, though?"

"Oh, the call. That was nothing. I'm fine."

"Are you sure?"

"Yes. Working on something for Frances. Don't tell her. I want it to be a surprise."

"Okay, I won't say a word."

When I arrive in the dining room, my brother yells, "It's about time. Let's eat."

I receive enthusiastic thumbs up from my girls about my wardrobe choice. Trevor wasn't kidding. Christian's eyes are stuck on me. I take the seat next to him.

"Sorry, everyone. I didn't mean to take so long. As my brother said, let's eat."

Mom created a feast. The table is loaded with grilled sweet potatoes sprinkled with brown sugar, butter, and nutmeg, homemade macaroni and cheese, bread rolls, dried fruit and sausage stuffing, lasagna, creamy mashed potatoes with chives, butternut squash, and pineapple cranberry sauce. A giant roasted turkey with all the trimmings is at the center of the table. She still found space for the perfect table linens, plates, and flowers. A smaller table in the back of the dining room is loaded with the best desserts ever: cheesecake, apple pie, sweet potato pie, Crème Brulée, and coconut cake, all homemade. I think Shelby Cooper figured out how to squeeze more than twenty-four hours out of a day.

After a brief prayer of thanks led by Dad, we all dig in. The atmosphere is festive with lots of ribbing and teasing. Trevor holds hands with Frances, and they look like a couple in love. I chase away thoughts of what I heard on the stairs.

"Mrs. Cooper, this is the most delicious Thanksgiving dinner I've had in my entire life," Christian says.

"Here, here," we all agree and toast her with our glasses.

"To the best chef in the business, the most incredible mother, and best wife any man could ask for," my dad says and plants a big, wet kiss on mom's cheek.

She giggles like a teenager.

"Thank you, Mrs. Cooper, for adopting us, too," Callie says.

"You made being away from our families bearable," Frances adds.

"I'll miss you all come graduation," Mom says.

A melancholy mood sweeps over the room. We all recognize that this moment, this Thanksgiving, will be the end of an era. For four years, this has been a second home to my friends—and Mom, their surrogate mother. Now, we're about to all scatter like leaves in the wind.

After dinner and dessert, everyone assembles in the family room to relax and watch a movie. I take off to my room for a few minutes. I tell them to start without me. I boot up my computer again. I want to see if anything on Sidney's email will help. I punch in the username and password I retrieved from the logs. It works, and her email inbox opens up. I scroll through what appears to be mostly junk mail offers from various retailers. I look closely at those because I might find the receipts for any unusual purchases made online. Nothing jumps out at me. I scroll down further and see an email from Patty Bailey, her mother. I open it, and a brief message appears.

Sidney,

Why won't you return my calls? We need to talk. Your father's worried, and so am I. Please call.

Love,

Mom

Yes, her mother should be worried. I do a search for Patty Bailey to see if there are any more messages. I find two. One of them includes the string. From what I can put together, Sidney is angry with her parents. What's interesting is the reason why. Sidney accuses her mom of being a horrible mother, not caring about her, and being just a stupid cow who should leave her alone. She doesn't say anything about her father. All her rage is directed at her mother.

In another message, Sidney tells her to stop pretending to care; she's eighteen now and an adult. Her mother's denials of Sidney's accusations are strong throughout the email. Patty tells her they can work through *this* as a family and how worried they are about her. Sidney isn't having any of it.

I'm beginning to have sympathy for Sidney. My

friends and I thought she was messed up because she was a spoiled, entitled brat. In other words, she was like ninety-nine percent of the student population at our school. However, when I think of the video, her condition when I found her in the girls' bathroom, her overall behavior, and now these emails, I sense that something is terribly wrong.

How does it tie in with The Avenger and her blackmail scheme? Is Sidney acting out because of her troubles and focused on me because I'm already someone she hates?

I go through the inbox, but nothing else stands out. I check her outbox and see only the messages between her and her mother. I go all the way back to the date when the note first appeared in my locker, and there's nothing. I search one more time. The only thing that piques my interest this time around is an email from a Dr. Heather Willis.

Sidney,

Below is the address we discussed during our last session. Remember, you don't have to share anything if you're not comfortable, but I think being in a room with others who've had similar experiences will be helpful. Don't forget to keep writing in your journal.

Dr. Willis

Whatever Sidney is angry with her mother about is so painful she needs to see a psychiatrist. I still don't know what it has to do with me. Did I make a terrible mistake or is Sidney a much cleverer adversary than I thought? The answers may lie in her journal.

CHAPTER 24

Black Friday 9:00 p.m.

I PULL INTO Shoppers World off Route 9 in Framingham. I score a parking spot close to the cluster of stores that include Starbucks, Old Navy, and Taylor Books, the place of the drop. I text the girls to let them know I've arrived at the bookstore. They tell me they're hanging out at a fast food joint on Route 30, a five-minute drive from me. I take a visual sweep of my surroundings, looking for anyone suspicious. My hands are clammy. I wipe them on my dark jeans, several times.

At 9:15 p.m., I take a deep breath, calm my nerves, and exit the car with the big brown paper bag with the handles and a plain, black scarf on top. I walk at a steady pace, careful not to appear nervous or in a hurry. I enter the store, and I'm greeted by the smell of new books and an extensive display of fiction bestsellers. Customers are scattered in every section of the store. I mentally remind myself not to let my eyes wander. Look straight ahead. The cameras are embedded in the ceiling.

I stroll past the eReader Center, toys, games, and the teen section. I stop in the diet and nutrition aisle and pretend to browse.

"Can I help you find something?" I feel my leg muscles tightening, my body ready to make a run for it but I don't. A store employee is assessing me with a forced smile. She is an older lady, perhaps in her fifties with glasses perched on her nose, and barely-there lips.

"No, ma'am. Just comparing these diet books."

The woman backs up a little and presses her glasses further down her nose. She takes a good look at me. I mentally scold myself. The diet section? Really?

"It's for a friend," I explain.

She raises an eyebrow.

"You know what, she can come look at the books herself. I'll probably get yelled at for picking the wrong one, anyway."

Another fake smile.

"Excuse me." I ease past the skeptic. I can feel her eyes on me as I head to the back of the store, my heart hammering in my chest. I must be giving off that nervous vibe. There was no reason for her to be suspicious of me. I look back to see if she's still staring at me. She is. I have to drop the money before she calls store security. I'm on her radar. Soon, she will start following me around the shop.

What if someone already moved the decoy bag? What if people witness the exchange? It's now or never. I glance backward again. Ms. Skeptical has her head down, looking at some paperwork in the customer service center. I duck into the next aisle and ease my way to the opening where the newsstand and magazines are. Two people are browsing through the magazines, their backs to me.

Decision time. Do I swap the bags while their backs are turned or wait until they leave? The risk in that strategy is that more customers might show up in the area, increasing the odds that one of them may take the bag to the front of the store and explain to the staff that someone forgot it.

My body is suddenly freezing. My hands are shaking so badly I'm afraid I'll drop the bag. One of the browsers turns around. Her eyes land on me, then the bag on the bench. "Is this your bag?"

"Um…yeah. My friend is in the ladies' room, and she sent me over to get it."

"Okay."

She won't leave. She just stands there, waiting for me to make a move.

"Are you going to pick up your friend's bag or just stare at it?"

I want to yell at her and tell her that it's none of her freaking business. Instead, I take tentative steps toward the bench with the bag identical to the one growing heavier by the second in my hand. I pick up the decoy bag loaded with empty shoeboxes and the same black scarf on top. I turn around and take a slow, tense walk down the aisle of biographies. I stop in the middle, drop both bags on the floor, and pretend to browse again.

Painful seconds tick by. She's still here. The other customer browsing the section has left. The store will close soon. My plan is to wait out Ms. Nosy. Another minute goes by. I can't stand it. I'm sweating profusely. I want to take off the baseball cap, but I can't. I walk casually to the end of the aisle and take a book off the shelf. I scan through the pages, unable to absorb any of the content. I then peek around the corner. She's gone.

I exchange the bags and duck back to the biography aisle, careful to keep my head down, and then slowly backtrack through the store. The double doors are only a few feet away from me. I'm moments from a clean getaway when I hear someone call out.

"Miss, Miss, you forgot something."

That's it. They're going to haul me off to jail. They're going to call the cops if they opened the bag and saw the money. If I make a run for it, it makes me look guilty, and they'll definitely call the police. My only chance of walking away unscathed is to turn around slowly. Damn it. Miss Nosy again.

"Yes?" I say, my voice as sweet as honey.

"You forgot this," she says, holding up the scarf. "You dropped it on the way out."

What did she do, follow me and pick up the scarf the minute it dropped? I remind myself to look at the positive side of things. She thinks it belongs to the empty shoebox bag I'm carrying.

"Thank you."

I take the scarf from her and rocket out of the store.

I don't stop until I reach my car, and then burn rubber out of the parking lot. Once I'm safely on Route 9, and certain no one is following me, I pull my phone out of my jacket pocket. I give a voice command to call Frances.

I let her know the drop was made.

"I have an idea," she says.

"What?"

"Callie and I should drive to the store to see if anyone walks out with the bag."

"Whoa. That wasn't part of the plan. I don't want you guys caught in the middle of this. She could be dangerous. She could have another accomplice. There are too many unknowns, Frances. It's a good idea but too risky."

"Okay. We'll meet you at the house then."

I know she'll go against my advice. I don't have the energy to argue further.

I make a second call, to Ty, and I leave him a message.

"WE GOT THERE too late," Frances says. "It was ten minutes before closing when we got to the store, and mostly employees were still around. The bag was gone."

"She must have been watching me from somewhere," I say.

Callie concurs.

We're on the sofa in my bedroom, recounting the evening's events. I'm relieved that the drop was made, but this story is far from over.

"It has to be somebody familiar with this area," Frances says. "What if she was in the store the whole time?"

Goosebumps appear on my arms, and I shudder. I think back to the store employee who looked at me with suspicion, and the woman who chased me to return the scarf I dropped.

"What's wrong, Abbie? Callie asks.

I tell them about the two ladies at the store. The only problem is I don't know either one of them. The store employee was older. Sidney hates anyone over thirty. The younger lady, the one who just happened to be at the spot where I was supposed to make the exchange, seemed to be just a customer. But was she?

"That is odd," Frances says.

"The younger lady could have been there to pick up the cash. Which means, The Avenger was afraid I would recognize her face."

"Which brings us back to Sidney," Frances says.

"Right."

My cell phone rings, putting an end to our supposition. I scurry off the sofa and grab the phone off the bed. It's better to stand when I answer. I don't say a word when I accept the call.

"You're competent after all," she says, her tone scornful. "I knew this game would be fun."

"You got what you wanted. Now it's your turn to hold up your end of the deal. You know what I want from you."

"I'm not ready to quit this game, not when things are just starting to heat up."

"What are you talking about?"

"Your next assignment."

"We had a deal," I shriek, anger rising like bile in my throat. "You promised the photo in exchange for the money. I followed your instructions. Now, it's time to step up. Are you going to add 'filthy liar' to your list of crimes, too? Extortion is a crime. You do know that, right?"

"Did you really think I would make it that easy?" she asks. "This was only a test. You passed. Congratulations."

"You can't do this." My voice gets louder as my panic mounts. I pace the room. The girls follow the conversation from the sofa, disbelief in their eyes.

"I wasn't the one snorting Adderall, Abbie. Why should you get away with it? How is that fair?"

I have to get through to her, somehow. "So you want to even the score? Who made you the moral police? Without me propping up your extortion scheme, you have nothing, you hear me. Nothing. You know what, send the picture to the Easter Bunny or whomever. I don't care. I'll survive the fallout. I'm that desperate to get rid of you."

I hang up on her, and then make my way to the bed where I collapse.

Frances and Callie join me, looking as if they have serious concerns about my mental state.

"I'm sorry, Abbie. Are you okay?" Frances asks. "Why did you do that?"

"Do what?"

"Hang up on her. Now, you're in for it. You don't know what she's going to do next."

"Maybe you guys should stay away from me for a while until this whole thing blows over."

"So you're just giving up?" Callie asks.

"I don't want my friends to become targets. I know you can handle yourselves, but if she sends the photo around, people are going to assume you guys did drugs, too, because we're close. You have to think about how that could affect the remainder of your time Saint Matthews, and possibly your college plans."

"After everything we've been through together, do you think we'd let someone do this to us?" Frances asks. "Break up our friendship? We can't go out like that, Abbie."

"She's right," Callie says. "We know you said those things to her because you're frustrated and angry, but you can't give in."

"Sidney's diary might hold some clues," I say.

I let the girls in on Sidney's other secret, the email I discovered from her psychiatrist, and the struggle with her parents. I don't give them a chance to dwell on that tidbit for long, though.

In five months, we'll go our separate ways. If I'm not careful, the remaining weeks and months will fly by, and I will have missed out on precious moments that could form a lifelong bond between us.

"How's your dad, Callie?" I ask. Still not talking to him?"

She makes a face and mutters a curse word that would make a truck driver blush. "He's sad that I didn't make it home for Thanksgiving. He and Mom love me very much; the divorce has nothing to do with me, blah, blah, blah."

"You don't think he misses you?" Frances asks.

"Sure he does. Like he misses a hole in the head. That's why I'm getting my own apartment in New York after graduation."

Frances and I look at her, troubled by her admission.

"Callie, you can't do that," I say.

"Why not?"

"New York is great, but crazy too. At least on a college campus, there's a community. It's better than you living all alone."

"It will work out," Callie assures us. "I'll have easy access to school and the garment district. My dad owns a townhouse in Lenox Hill. I'll pop by occasionally if I ever start speaking to him again. Mom can come visit me whenever she wants. Plus, the both of you will be on the East Coast, so we'll still be close to each other."

"I'm not a hundred percent sure," Frances says. "I also applied to Columbia and BU, but I'm picking Northwestern if I get in."

"What about you and Trevor?" I ask. The Thanksgiving conversation I overheard comes to the forefront of my mind.

Frances shrugs. "Trevor and I are realists."

"Are you guys okay?" I probe. "I overheard Trevor on the phone with Cole over Thanksgiving, and it sounded serious. He said he's working on a surprise for you, but I shouldn't tell you."

"I don't know," Frances says. "He's been distracted lately."

"You think something is up?" Callie asks.

"He's bummed out about his parents. His dad took away most of his credit cards since he's paying the bills. He also raised the age Trevor can inherit his trust fund from eighteen to twenty-one, and even then, he only gets half of it. The remainder kicks in when he turns twenty-five."

"What did Trevor do to piss off his father?" Callie asks.

"He wrecked two sports cars over the summer, and his dad compares him to his brother all the time. He thinks Cole is responsible and ambitious, and Trevor isn't. He wants Trevor to be more like Cole."

"I thought Trevor didn't want to join the agency," I say. "I heard him tell Cole he wants to study anthropology, and he definitely won't be joining Forrester International after college."

"Right. That's the problem. Trevor thinks his dad is punishing him because of that. I told him not to worry."

PART FIVE

TAINTED LOVE

CHAPTER 25

I LUMBER DOWN the hall on my way to the chapel. In one week, it will be mid-December. The time when high school seniors like me all over the country will get that early action decision email that may or may not change the trajectory of our lives. How will I feel if I don't get into Princeton? What if The Avenger sent that letter? I can only pretend that possibility doesn't exist. I feel anxiety coming on, so I shake off the unwanted thoughts and quicken my pace. The chapel is exactly where I need to be right now.

My eyes are closed, and I let the stillness shower me with calm. It doesn't take long before I sense a presence, so I open my eyes gradually. Only a few inches separate Sidney from me. Her icy stare throws me off balance for a brief moment.

She looks tired and scared beneath the veneer of sleek sophistication—the hair, the clothes, the makeup, even her handbag choice is flawless: a black and tan Celine luggage tote, a complete turnaround from our last encounter. I ignore her and close my eyes again. I won't get upset. I won't let her disturb my peace.

"About the incident in the girls' bathroom," she begins. "I was having a bad day. You don't need to go running off at the mouth to your friends about it."

I keep my voice steady, "We all have bad days. It's not a crime, last I heard. Besides, it was none of my business. I shouldn't have said anything."

"You can't help it. Being the do-gooder, good girl all the time. Makes me want to barf every time I see you."

"How awful for you," I snap.

"It's all an act. You're the biggest hypocrite at this school."

That word again. *Hypocrite*. It's been a constant reference with my stalker.

I stretch out my legs. "Maybe you're right. But the day your opinion starts to matter to me is the day I ask my parents to send me to the loony bin."

"I didn't come here to start a fight."

"Yes, you did. The minute you walked in here and saw me, you wanted a fight. So, bring it on, Sidney."

"You think I've been a pain up until now? You have no idea what I could do to you."

"You have way bigger problems than little old me. You might want to focus on those."

"What do you mean?"

"Anyone with eyes can see you're in a lot of trouble."

"Oh, look, Abbie went and got a degree in psychobabble. Where do you get off trying to play shrink with me?"

215

"You're a train wreck in progress. We're all just waiting for the impact."

She did it again. Brought out the worst in me. I should be sympathetic. She's going through a lot, and, from what I read in her email exchange with her mother, it's heavy stuff. All my good intentions fly out the window without consulting me when I'm near Sidney.

"Who do you think you are? You have no right to talk to me like that."

"I'll speak to you any way I please. You started this. What did you think I would do? Who do you think *you* are?"

"I can't wait for you to fall flat on your stupid face at Bedford Hills. I warned you. It won't last with Christian."

"Why do you want Christian so badly? You act as if he's a toy I stole from you and you want it back. He's a person. Does he mean anything to you?"

She glares at me. When she opens her mouth to speak, nothing comes out.

"I thought so. You just don't want him with *me*. Get used to it, Sidney. I'm not going anywhere. Can't wait for the New Year's Eve party. If you're nice to me, I will tell you all about it when I return. In the meantime, try not to die of jealousy."

CHAPTER 26

December 15th—Decision Time

MY CELL PHONE is blowing up. It's 5:01 p.m. The moment I'm supposed to find out if Princeton accepted me. Christian, Callie, Frances, and Trevor have all texted me, wanting to know the answer. Every high school senior, their family members, and teachers know the email was scheduled to go out at 5:00 o'clock today. I begged my parents not to text or call. I told them I would let them know as soon as I did. I'm home alone, in my room, the way I planned it. It's time to find out if the number one ranked university the United States (depending on who's compiling the statistics) has accepted me.

I see the "decision made" subject line right away when I login to my email account from my laptop. I open the email and click on the link, not bothering to read the message in the body. It takes me to the admissions status portal. My mouth goes dry, yet I'm starting to sweat. Adrenaline is pumping through me, and I'm breathing too fast.

I head to the bathroom and splash cold water on my face. I dry off with a small towel then head back to my task. I type in my username and password and boom; there it is: *We regret to inform you…*

I don't know how long I've been sitting at my desk. My legs are numb. My back hurts. I missed three calls from my mom and numerous text messages from my friends. I'm a failure. I couldn't crack the Princeton code. I'm not used to rejection. How should I handle this?

"Calm down, Cooper. Breathe. I don't understand a word you're saying."

My response is to wail even harder. I managed to get Ty on the phone, and when he answered, I broke open like a piñata. I can't control the hiccups, the incoherent words, or the pressure mounting in my chest.

"Cooper, did something happen? Please, you're scaring me. What is it? Why are you so upset?"

The poor guy is about to have a heart attack because he thinks I'm in danger, or something horrible happened. Ty has seen me at my absolute worst. He knows how to pick me up when I fall apart.

"I didn't make the cut. I didn't…I couldn't. Princeton said no, Ty. The Avenger sent that letter. She wants me to pay for my mistake. She wants me to suffer."

"Cooper, listen to me. You can't lose sight of all your achievements just because one school didn't admit you. And we don't know for sure if The Avenger is behind this. She could have been just psyching you out to make sure you dropped off the money. Princeton's decision may not have anything to do with her at all."

I remain silent during his little pep talk, mostly to get my emotions under control.

"Cooper, are you listening to me?"

"Yes, I'm listening. I know you're right. It's just hard to accept that they didn't want me."

"Admissions decisions aren't always black and white, Cooper. Many factors come into play, and Princeton knows you're going to be okay whether they accept you or not. You will get into a top college. When you do, you'll be glad that Princeton didn't pick you."

"You really think so? Because I thought Princeton was a shoe-in."

"You can go to *any* college you want. That's a privilege. No use crying over one school when you have so many options ahead of you."

I move away from the desk and stretch my cramped legs. Ty put the whole thing into perspective, just as I knew he would. In moments like these, I'm the luckiest girl alive because he's in my corner. We talk for a while longer, and he makes me promise I won't get depressed about one setback.

I deliver the news to my parents over dinner, and they take it almost as badly as I did when I first read the rejection letter. But their disappointment quickly turns to enthusiasm and optimism. All they can talk about is which offer of admittance I will accept of the multiple offers they're sure will come my way. Soon, the discussion shifts to how much Christmas shopping we all have left to do.

"THAT SUCKS, ABBIE," Frances says. "They're idiots in that admissions office. You're like the poster child for the Ivy League."

Frances, Callie, and I are chatting via FaceTime. My face is still swollen from all that crying I did earlier, and the girls wanted to come over right away when they first saw me onscreen. I convinced them I was done being a wreck over Princeton.

"It's their prerogative," I say. "At least it's over with, and I can focus on what's ahead."

"I wonder if The Avenger had anything to do with this," Callie says.

"The thought crossed my mind. But if this is all her doing, she would have called to brag about it," I reason.

"You could be right," Frances says. "But there's still the possibility that she could have sent that photo to Princeton."

"If that's true, then my life is about to explode."

CHAPTER 27

TWO DAYS AFTER Christmas, Christian loads my luggage into the back of his silver Maserati. I told him he didn't need to come back for me, that I would take a flight out to Dulles Airport where he could pick me up. Did he listen? No. I can't get mad at him, though. He likes spoiling me. The gorgeous Hermès Kelly handbag he got me for Christmas is the latest example.

"How's your dad?" he asks. We're zooming down the Mass Turnpike. Our flight is scheduled to take off at 12:30 p.m., so we should have plenty of time.

"Fighting the inevitable. Me growing up."

"What does he think I'm going to do to you?"

"It's not about you. He has a hard time letting go. I've never been away without my family before, except for the church youth group visit to Haiti, and travel for our school's Global Citizenship Program. I can say with confidence that my brother won't have to deal with my dad's overprotective behavior."

"Girls are different."

"Different how?"

"Delicate. I understand why your dad is freaking out."

"What?" I turn to him like he's suddenly sprouted horns.

"You've lived a sheltered life, babe. I'm not saying it's a bad thing. The stuff your parents taught you, that's your parachute. Now, it's about to be tested, and that scares your dad. He's worried it might malfunction, and you could get hurt."

"Wow. I had no idea you were this deep. You should consider majoring in philosophy instead of business."

He chuckles and squeezes my hand. "You're rubbing off on me. I think my IQ jumped twenty points since I started dating you."

"Imagine how much smarter you would be if we got together sooner."

"I tried. You avoided me like road kill. I had serious self-esteem issues because of you."

"You deserved it," I say, play punching him in the arm.

"What about now? Do I still deserve it?"

"When you first came to Saint Matthews, I thought you were just like all the others running around our school. Nothing I hadn't seen a million times before. Then I heard all the rumors, your reputation with girls, and that made me despise you even more."

His hands stiffen on the steering wheel.

"Then, everything changed. I didn't understand what was happening to me. My head gave me all the reasons I should stay away from you. Yet, it made me happy when you would show up at my locker. I couldn't let you know that, so it was easier to pretend I still hated you. I was so mad at myself."

"Why?"

"Because I wasn't supposed to like you or think about what you were doing before I fell asleep at night. Agonize over whether you were with someone. I wasn't supposed to be jealous and want to carve her eyeballs out with a knife, whoever she was."

There. I said it. The last of my barriers just came tumbling down. I want to stop the car, get out and run until I'm too tired to think straight. But I can't take back what I said nor do I want to.

He strokes my arm with his free hand, the other firmly on the steering wheel.

"My heart beats faster every time I see you. I miss you when you're not around, the way you smell, how you bite your fingernails without knowing you're doing it, your laugh when I fall for one of your tricks. I want to share things with you that I've never wanted to share with anyone else. Best of all, I like that you're simple and complicated at the same time, and you don't apologize for who you are."

Just when I think I have him figured out, he surprises me. I bask in his admiration, even though I know our entire relationship could blow up at any minute. I decide to tell him everything once we return from Bedford Hills.

"I don't know if I can live up to that portrait you have of me."

"You don't have to. You just do."

I look straight ahead and notice we're exiting the Mass Turnpike and heading toward Route 128.

"Why are we turning off? We're going to miss our flight to Dulles."

"We're not."

"Where are we going?"

"Relax, babe. It's going to be fine. I promise."

"Okay."

Route 128 is known for its gridlock traffic. Around this time of the day, traffic is much more agreeable, although that could change at any moment. I have no idea where we're going or if we'll make our flight. I'll just have to trust him like he asked.

We take exit 30B, which leads to Hanscom Field, a public use airport in the suburban town of Bedford. We pull up to a tan building. I see airplanes on the ground, close to the building.

"No freaking way," I say, barely believing my eyes.

He grins from ear to ear. "Anything for my girl."

Christian explains that Hanscom is much less of a hassle than Logan Airport for private jet travelers. Then it dawns on me. He told Callie and France about this plan. That's what they meant when they said I wouldn't need an airline ticket.

"A Gulfstream?" I ask. A tall, barrel-chested man in a gray suit takes the luggage out of the trunk and into the airplane.

"The 650. It's faster and can fly higher than commercial jets."

"Your dad must really be in the holiday spirit to let you do this."

"He surprised me. I was going to ask, but he suggested it on his own before I had the chance."

"You're kidding, right?"

Mary-Ann, the flight attendant, welcomes us aboard and fawns all over us. Christian chit chats with the pilot, Ron. The interior of the jet is luxurious, elegant gold and white sofas and chairs in a living room-style configuration. A table is already set up with fresh fruit and other yummy snacks.

We land at Dulles, where a limousine is already waiting. Forty-five minutes later, we're in Langley Forest, a posh neighborhood in McLean, Virginia. Each house we pass is bigger and more luxurious than the one before it. Fifteen minutes afterward, we pull up to the iron gates of an estate. A security guard in the booth opens the gate, and we drive down a long pathway toward the house.

When the driver opens the doors for us, and we exit the car, I take in the splendor of the place—a massive, three-story, Georgian-style mansion built of intricate stonework. Large white columns run from the top of the balcony down to the front entrance. A uniformed butler appears and takes my luggage from the trunk of the car into the house.

We enter the foyer, and a massive yet elegant double staircase pops into view to our left. Christian's mom is there to greet us. "Pleased to meet you, Mrs. Wheeler," I say, extending my hand.

"Call me Katherine. I want you to be comfortable during your stay with us. We're delighted to have you."

There's a glamorous yet understated air about her. With long, flowing locks the color of midnight, she's a dead ringer for actress Catherine Zeta-Jones.

"You both must be starving," she adds. "I'll let you get settled in, then you can join me for a late lunch."

When I arrive in the suite I'll be occupying for the next four days, my luggage has already been unpacked and put away. The room is opulent, warm, and welcoming, in pastel blue-and-white accents, plush carpeting, matching armchairs with a table at the center, and a fireplace. I look toward the double doors leading to a balcony. I make a quick call to my mother to let her know we arrived safely, and she shouldn't worry. There's a knock at the door, and I answer it. Christian strolls in.

"Do you like the room? We can change it if you don't."

"It's a great room and fine the way it is."

"My mom is right. You should feel at home here."

"I do. Your mom is much different than I expected. She's normal. I mean that in a respectful way."

"You were expecting a blonde, Barbie doll, social-climbing trophy wife, weren't you? And then when you arrived, you thought she would fly in on a broomstick, act snobbish, and bark orders at the staff."

"No, I wasn't. That's so cliché. Okay, maybe I was. A little."

Katherine McClellan graduated top of her class from the University of Virginia Law School and clerked for Supreme Court Justice Ruth Bader Ginsburg. According to Christian, one night at a cocktail party in Georgetown, Alan Wheeler saw her across the room, and that was that.

"It's okay. My dad likes smart, normal women. I inherited that trait from him," he says, winking at me.

He comes closer and presses his forehead against mine. "Will you let me kiss you now? You wouldn't on the plane. I was sad all the way down here."

I step away from him. "Hmm. I don't know. You don't seem that sad to me. You're going to have to convince me. Show me your sad face."

He puckers his lips and gives me a droopy-eyed look. "That's the worst sad face ever."

"Okay, how about this," he says, letting his chin drop into hands, his eyes blinking rapidly.

"I don't think you're taking this seriously. I'm heading downstairs and taking my lips with me. Can't say for sure when we'll be back."

I pretend I'm about to head out the door.

He pulls me back. "What if—?"

"Just shut up and kiss me."

I wrap my arms around his neck and press into his body. He pushes me backward until I collapse on the bed with him on top of me. He moves my sweater up past my bra, and when I feel his lips on the naked skin of my stomach, I gasp with pleasure. I feel his fingers fumbling with the button on my jeans. I hear the ripping sound of a zipper being opened, and I shudder.

His hands grab the waistband of my jeans, and he tugs. My brain switches gears, and the word stop is loud in my consciousness. I grab his hand and hold it still.

We sit at the edge of the bed, our breathing now under control.

"Sorry, I wasn't trying to be a tease. I got swept up in the moment, and it felt—"

"I know. Me too."

"Your mother is downstairs, and it wouldn't be right." I walk away from him, and lean against the dresser while I straighten my sweater. "I mean, I really want to, boy do I want to. It's just that it's a big deal to me, and I can't take it back if—"

"Abbie, it's okay if you're not sure. Don't stress about it. Come here," he commands.

I walk over to the bed and sit beside him. "You don't have to defend your decision to me," he says, stroking my arm. "I'm fine with whatever you want. I hope I didn't make you feel any pressure. I'm just happy to spend time with you."

I look at him, through narrowed eyes. "How come?"

"How come what?"

"How come you're so calm and understanding about this?"

"I know my so-called reputation freaked you out at firs. But I don't want to ruin what we have. You actually see me, Abbie. Do you know how special that is?"

I rest my head on his shoulder and loop my arm around his. "Yes, I know how special that is."

CHAPTER 28

A LAN WHEELER IS anything but the stern, stuffy CEO I expected when we sit down to a steak dinner. The swanky dining room has dark wood paneling, a fireplace with expensive paintings above it, and lush Persian rugs. He's a man with a towering presence, a wicked sense of humor, and eyes that miss nothing. His son takes after him in looks and temperament.

"Christian tells me you want to save the world," he says to me.

"He exaggerates."

Katherine pipes up. "Don't understate your ambition. Dedicating your life to the service of others is something to be admired and celebrated. What made you want to become a surgeon?"

"I found an old copy of *Time Magazine* in my Dad's study when I was twelve. The cover story was titled *Heroes of Medicine*. There was an African-American doctor on the cover. I'd never seen anything like that before. I was in awe. When I read about the incredible work some of the doctors featured in the article were doing around the world, I knew I wanted to be part of that one day.

"Then I got to the story on Dr. Keith Black, the man on the cover. He's a neurosurgeon and the article talked about how he would often take on the most difficult cases, cases other doctors had given up on. I was intrigued. He explained how he would sneak in while the brain was asleep and get out before it woke up. That was it for me."

Silence. Christian leans over and whispers in my ear, "I'm so hot for you right now."

I try to keep a straight face. I won't look at him.

"That deserves a toast, young lady," Mr. Wheeler says. "If there's anything I can do to help you achieve your goals, just say the word. And tell your father he has nothing to worry about."

I thank him for his generous offer and apologize for my dad, who just about threatened him. He brushes it off and says, as a parent, he understands why my dad is neurotic.

After dinner, Christian and I watch a movie in the home theater. We spend more time trying to keep our hands off each other than watching the movie. By the time the final credits roll, we both need to be hosed down with ice water. He promises to give me a tour of the property tomorrow, which could take forever. There's a lot to get through: ten bedrooms, twelve bathrooms, tennis court, basketball court, an Olympic-sized, indoor swimming pool, a bowling alley, a wine cellar, a ten-car garage, and a helipad on the roof, plus all the outdoor attractions of the property. I'm most excited about him showing me his art, though.

I WAKE UP disoriented, my breathing loud and rapid. I sit up and rub my eyes, then fumble in the dark for my cell phone on the nightstand. I turn it on and see it's 1:43 a.m. A horrible dream woke me up. A giant clock was chasing me, just like that famous boulder scene in *Raiders of the Lost Ark*. The ticking got louder and louder, as it gained speed. I stumbled and fell, and when the clock was about to devour me, I woke up.

I'm determined to go back to sleep but end up entangled in the comforter from tossing around so much. Eventually, exhaustion takes over, and I fall into a deep sleep.

The crowd erupts with loud cheering when the ball enters the net with a big swoosh. The Washington Wizards take the lead. I snack on popcorn and enjoy the action on the hardwood floor from our courtside seats. Christian grins up at me and then pulls me into a kiss. The crowd let out a collective, aww. We separate to see what the commotion is all about. We look up and see our image on every Jumbotron in the arena. I cover my face in embarrassment. Christian just laughs.

Stillness falls over the arena. I remove my hands from my face. I gasp at the new image on the Jumbotron. Everyone stares at me and shakes their heads. They are angry, accusing. Christian gets up and walks away.

On a 160-foot wide TV screen in high definition for the entire country to see is the photo The Avenger sent in the mail. It shows on every screen. I can't escape it. I look for Christian, and he's nowhere to be found. Fans leave their seats in droves. Families with children give me the death stare. The players and the court disappear. I call out for Christian, but he doesn't answer, doesn't come back for me, even though I tell him how sorry I am. The arena is empty now, and I'm alone. I hear mocking laughter. When I follow the direction of the sound, I see Sidney. A tree grows out of her head. She is dressed in an all-black costume, a gown with sculpted shoulders and long bell sleeves.

"I told you hypocrites always get caught by their own lies. I tried to warn you, but you wouldn't listen. Now, everyone knows you're a phony, and you've lost Christian forever. He's not coming back, Abbie. He's done with you and wants you to disappear." She extends her hand. "Come with me. I can make you disappear."

Then she laughs and laughs, a self-satisfied triumphant laugh that goes on for eons.

"Stop it, stop it. Please, stop."

I hit the floor with a thud then feel my way through the darkness toward the lamp on the nightstand. Once the room is illuminated, I climb into bed but don't get under the covers. Instead, I turn into a blubbering mess. I reach for my cell phone to call Christian, and there's a nasty surprise waiting for me—a text message, a photo of mom during an appearance on *Wake Up America*.

BLOCKED NUMBER

What do u think the headline should be?

BLOCKED NUMBER

Daughter of Cooking Network Star Busted for Drugs

BLOCKER NUMBER

It's perfect, don't u agree?

How naïve of me to think I can control the outcome of this game before it affects my family. I can barely handle the personal attacks, but now, she wants to involve my mother, who could be forced to resign from her job on *The Cooking Network* if this photo gets out. Sales of Mom's cookbooks could tank. Her reputation could be ruined. She worked so hard to carve out this niche for herself after she gave up her career in the scientific field. This can't be taken from her too.

The hiccups won't stop. If I try to go back to sleep, I'll go out of my mind, so I text Christian. Minutes later, I answer the knock on the door and let him in. He's half-asleep, his hair sticking up all over his head.

"I keep having nightmares, and I'm afraid if I go back to sleep alone, they'll return. Sorry, I dragged you out of bed. Having a needy girlfriend moment, yet I don't feel bad about it."

"It's okay, babe. You shouldn't feel bad. I'll stay with you until you fall asleep."

When I open my eyes, the room is bathed in sunlight.

Christian lies next to me on the bed, making adorable snoring sounds. My first thought is getting him back to his room before someone sees him leaving mine.

I nudge him. "Christian, it's morning. Wake up."

He just grunts and then rolls over. Then I hear Katherine's voice from outside the door.

"Abbie, are you in there?"

I break out in a cold sweat. Mrs. Wheeler can't find her son in my bed. There's just no way to explain that and make it sound innocent, even if it is.

I open the door just enough and put on my brightest smile. I didn't even have a minute to brush my hair and look presentable.

"Good morning. Sorry, it took me so long to answer; I'm just waking up."

"That's alright, hon. Have you seen Christian?"

"Christian?" I repeat like a parrot. "Is he missing?"

"He's not in his room, and he hasn't made it downstairs yet. He has a trip planned with his father today. He needs to get ready."

"Have you checked his studio? Maybe he decided to paint early."

Her eyes light up. "Ah. You might be right. Thanks, Abbie."

I tickle him until he starts moving. "Christian, wake up. If you don't, I'll pour cold water on you."

"You're a mean girlfriend," he mumbles.

"You love that about me. It's the secret sauce of our relationship. You have to leave now. Your mother was here looking for you, something about a trip with your dad. If she asks, you were in your studio, painting."

He sits up and yawns. "The trip with my dad is off. You and I can spend all day together."

"Great. Now, leave before someone sees you."

"No good morning kiss?" he teases.

"No time. Come on," I say, tugging at his arm.

"Fine. I know when I'm not wanted." He pretends to pout.

"I don't want your mother to think badly of me."

"Impossible. She loves you."

"She just met me yesterday."

"No, she didn't. I've been telling her all about you and sent her pictures."

"You what? Okay, we can talk about it later, but right now, she's looking for you."

He drags himself off the bed and heads for the door. I'm right behind him like some overbearing, helicopter parent. When he opens the door, his mother is standing there, her hand in mid-air about to knock. Way awkward.

"Hi, Mom," Christian says. "Dad canceled the trip, so no worries."

Mrs. Wheeler has a look that confuses me. I can't tell if she's amused or upset, so I ramble. "Nothing happened. I was afraid of the nightmares, and Christian, he tried to help. What I mean is, he helped me fall asleep. No, that's not right. The nightmare didn't come back after he showed up."

She's definitely not amused. I have no choice but to tell the truth.

"I'm sorry I lied earlier. I knew it would look bad if you discovered he was in the room with me, and I didn't want you to think badly of me."

"If you say nothing happened, I'll take your word for it."

"She's telling the truth, Mom," Christian says in my defense. "She called me at three o'clock this morning because she was having nightmares and couldn't sleep."

"I'm sorry to hear that, Abbie," she says, her voice softening. "I hope you'll get a better night's sleep tonight."

"Thanks for having my back," I say to Christian after his mother leaves.

"I was just confirming the truth."

CHAPTER 29

H IS STUDIO IS neat and organized, with multiple windows to let in natural light. A vintage French chair sits against the wall. Paint brushes and paints in various types of containers rest in a large cubby. A table with a computer is at the center of the room. His work is displayed on several easels and on the walls. He stands behind me as I observe the work.

"You like movement and energy." I point to a painting depicting a polo match in progress, and another with men working at a construction site.

"Life is always moving and changing. It's one big energy flow, and I feed off that energy when I paint."

I'm drawn to a painting across the room on an easel in its own little space. I move closer to get a better look. A little boy, about four or five years old, chases after a dog in the park. His smiling mother takes chase, too, her black hair flapping in the wind.

"Is this your favorite?"

"How can you tell?" he asks, looking over my shoulders.

"It's you and your mother. You remember that day?"

"Yeah. It's one of my happiest childhood memories."

"Why is that?"

"It was just me and Mom that day. No pawning me off on the nanny."

I turn my attention away from the painting and touch his face. "She has regrets. She thinks she won't have a chance to rebuild her relationship with you once you leave for college. She told me so at lunch. It must be bugging her for her to say that to a stranger."

"She should have thought of that before."

"She's thinking about it now. You could share some of your work with her. Show her that painting."

"I don't know," he says, pinching his nose. He strolls toward the desk in the middle of the room.

I join him and take his hand in mine. "It could be a fresh start for the both of you."

"You're too optimistic. She's not interested in my art."

"Has your father seen any of it?"

"A couple."

"So, why not your mom?"

"If she was interested, she would have asked. Dad did. He's a jerk sometimes, but he took an interest."

His shoulders tense up. I don't want to push the issue any further. He'll come to his own conclusions and do what he thinks is best. "Thank you for sharing your art with me. I'll cherish the memory."

"Do you like it?"

"Of course."

"You can be honest."

"I like your use of color and how deliberate your brush strokes are, as if each one has a strategy behind it, so it won't be the same as the next. I like how you interpret what you see. There's optimism in your perspective."

He kisses me on the cheek, and then hugs me tight. After he releases me, I ask, "What was that for?"

"You continually amaze me. Words can't explain how you make me feel."

He walks away from the desk and moves toward the French chair set against the wall near the window. He sits, and rests his hands on either side of his head. He stares at the floor, not saying a word.

I walk over and kneel before him. I palm his face with my hands and force him to look at me. "I don't have the words to explain how you make me feel, either," I whisper."

He grins at me bashfully. "Talking is overrated, anyway."

I get on my feet, and squeeze in next to him on the chair. I bury my face in his neck and close my eyes, inhaling the scent of him. "I agree."

We don't need big emotional words. All we need is just the silence because sometimes, that's the best way to be heard.

CHAPTER 30

T HE GIRL IN the mirror looks like she belongs on the cover of *Vanity Fair's* Hollywood issue, with her sophisticated updo, flawless makeup, and glamorous evening gown—a white, one shoulder, Armani Privé number that gathers at the waist and cascades to the floor. The side slit is a little risqué for my tastes, but Callie has been pressing me to take chances with my wardrobe.

A gentle knock on the door signals that it's time to head downstairs to the ballroom and have an evening I will never forget. I open the door wide. Christian and I stand there, gawking at each other like two besotted fools. He's impeccably groomed in a tailored tuxedo that fits his form to perfection.

He speaks first. "I don't think we should go to the party. Someone will try to steal you from me, and I'll have to beat him up."

"No way. It took me half a day to get ready. You just had to shower and put on a tuxedo. I've been plucked, scrubbed, poked, pulled, and squeezed. Between the

240

facials, body wrap, manicure and pedicure, waxing, and the hair and makeup sessions, I deserve my reward."

"If I'm a good boy, will I get my reward too?" His eyes glitter like sapphires.

"Who says I want you to be a good boy?"

I shoo him away when he leans in for a kiss. I don't want to ruin my makeup. I tell him I'll meet him downstairs after I do a final once over in the mirror.

Waiters in white dinner jackets and black slacks serve appetizers, hors d'oeuvres and champagne in the ballroom foyer. A full bar is in operation, and a few leather armchairs are peppered throughout the space. This party is the perfect place for a heist. The amount of bling alone would make the thieves instant millionaires if they could penetrate the ironclad security put in place for the ball.

Christian heads to the bar and returns with two orange and cranberry juices. He hands me one. Before I can take a sip, someone taps me on the shoulder. I turn around slowly and come face-to-face with Kerri Wheeler. She's stunning in a black, strapless evening gown. Her smooth, golden bronze complexion and striking gray eyes add a glossy richness to her appearance. The long, tangled brown mess she sported in high school is now cut in a sleek, honey-colored bob.

"Hi, Kerri."

"Little Abbie Cooper," she says, her eyes wide. "That is some dress."

She knows I hate it when she calls me Little Abbie

Cooper. It was her way of putting me in my place when she was chasing after Ty, letting me know I was just a kid and Ty would never see me as anything more.

"We've all changed, Kerri."

"Hey, cuz," she says, addressing Christian. "Can you give us a couple of minutes?"

"Sure, I get it. Girl talk." He kisses me on the cheek. "Don't wander off too far."

"So, you and my cousin," she says, sitting in one of the leather armchairs we found unoccupied. I take a seat, too, and place my juice on the end table. A waiter comes by and lowers a tray piled with smoked salmon and cream cheese cucumber bites. Kerri waves him off.

"I was surprised when he told me the two of you were a couple."

"Why is that?"

"Come on. You're you, and Christian is a free spirit."

"What are you really after, Kerri? You didn't pull me aside to do a personality assessment."

"Still the straight shooter. When it's convenient."

"Meaning what?"

"Nothing. Just don't hurt him."

I can't contain my irritation. "I love him. Why would I hurt him?"

Kerri is eerily silent. She tinkers with the mixed cluster diamond bracelet on her wrist. Pandemonium breaks out in my head. Where did that come from? When did it happen, exactly? Is Kerri going to tell him I said that?

"So Christian doesn't know how you feel?" Her attention is focused on me once more.

"No. I haven't told him."

"Don't worry about it. He adores you. Still don't get it, but whatever."

"You don't have to get it, Kerri. We just click." We haven't seen each other in years but Kerri still knows how to push my buttons.

"So, you're over Ty?"

"What?"

"Let's keep it real between us, Abbie, she says, edging closer to me. The smell of her perfume tickles my nostrils. "You wanted to rip my head off for dating Ty. You had it bad for him. The fact that the two of you are still close friends tells me—"

"That we're close friends. Don't create drama where there isn't any, Kerri."

"He was your first love. A girl doesn't just get over that."

"I'm with Christian. Period."

"I'm serious about you not hurting Christian," she says. "You'll have to deal with me if you do."

"Deal with you about what?"

I'm relieved to hear his voice. Kerri and I look up at him.

"Kerri thinks she's a mother bear and it's her job to protect you from me."

"It wasn't easy convincing Abbie to take a chance on me," he says to his cousin. "Stop giving her grief."

"Still don't get it," Kerri mumbles as she leaves us to go mingle.

I'm refreshing my makeup in the ladies' room when two girls appear on either side of me. One of them spills out of a blue ball gown. The other, decked out in lavender, floor-length halter-top dress looks like she's in desperate need of food. Her collarbone alone could be classified as a lethal weapon.

"So, you're Christian's girlfriend," the skinny one says.

What am I supposed to do here? Give her confirmation? I have no idea who they are and why they would care.

"Maybe she doesn't speak, Leah," the one in the blue gown says to her friend.

"Why do you care who Christian is dating?" I ask.

"We just want to know how you pulled it off," Leah responds.

"Pulled what off?" I ask.

"Christian doesn't do girlfriends, right, Chelsea?" Leah asks her friend. "He's more of a hookup kind of guy. So, I'm wondering how long before he dumps you. You made it this far, so I guess that means you haven't hooked up yet. Once you do, you're history."

My stomach tightens. I can't let them see how much they've affected me. I roll my eyes at them. "How would you know?"

The sly, knowing glance exchanged between them is all the answer I need.

"Both of you?" I must be a masochist for asking this question.

They shake their heads with stupid grins on their faces, as if they just won the grand prize on some cheesy reality show.

"And you're friends?"

"BFFs," Chelsea says.

I press my hands to my stomach, and concentrate hard, not wanting to throw up. The last thing I need is to embarrass myself in front of these girls.

Leah points to me and laughs. "She's praying she doesn't get dumped."

They giggle. I don't open my eyes until they leave. I knew who Christian was before we started dating. I just didn't think I would run into his past in his home. Does this change anything? I'm more confused than ever.

CHRISTIAN AND I head into the ballroom for the sit-down dinner. Katherine told me she was going for a modern elegance theme, and she made it happen. Swarovski Strass Crystal Chandeliers dangle from the high ceiling with painted murals. Tables are covered in gold silk tablecloths, with gold and ivory silk overlay. The crystal stemware with gold accents and white dinner plates with gold trimming, together with massive bouquets of white flowers, including calla lilies, orchids, and English garden roses, give the event the unmistakable mark of opulence and grandeur.

"What happened in the bathroom?" Christian asks the moment we sit down. We've barely acknowledged the other guests seated with us.

"I think you're old enough to know what happens when boys and girls go to the bathroom."

He frowns. "Are you okay?"

"I'm great," I say, tapping my feet to the beat of the live band's rendition of Frank Sinatra's "The Best is yet to Come".

"No, you're not. Did Kerri say something that upset you?"

"What makes you say that?"

"You went cold on me."

It hurt, what those girls said. I don't want it to be true, but what if it is? What if it was his plan all along? I can't breathe. Tears pool in my eyes. I bury my hands in my face and turn away from him.

"Babe, please tell me what's going on. Who hurt you?"

"You did," I say between ragged breaths.

He removes my hands from my face and wipes my tear-stained cheeks with his fingers.

"What did I do?"

"Leah and Chelsea."

Expletives tumble from his lips. I've never heard him swear since we've been together.

"That's in the past, and I didn't know they were friends. What did they say?"

"That you'd dump me the minute...the minute." I can't even say it. I swallow hard.

"Look into my eyes," he commands. "I've never lied about my feelings for you. I would never hurt you like that, Abbie. If you don't believe me, I'll walk away and never bother you again."

My bottom lip quivers. I know he's telling the truth. Why do I allow myself to doubt him? Why can't I just accept and trust his actions? Is it because of the guilt that's been festering in my bones, the knowledge that my lies will demolish what we've built once school resumes?

I take a deep breath and exhale slowly. "You're right. You've been wonderful. I'm sorry I flipped out. It wasn't fun hearing them talk about hooking up with you and how I would end up like them."

"They're jealous and want you to feel insecure. The only reason they're here is because Chelsea's aunt is on the Board of Directors for the foundation. She scored them invitations."

"No more meltdowns, no more doubt. I promise."

Dinner is scrumptious, and I plan to stay away from dessert. Before Christian and I hit the dance floor, we pose for pictures. Callie wasn't kidding. The place is crawling with press. I've been introduced to celebrities all evening (I haven't embarrassed myself so far), but one, in particular, has me curious. Nicholas Furi just walked into the ballroom with a glamorous Hollywood Starlet on his arm.

"Christian, look," I say, nodding in their direction. "I'm snapping a photo and sending it to Callie."

"Are you sure you want to do that?"

"You're right. It will only fuel her rage about the divorce."

"We should say hello. I'm sure he'll like that."

"If I exchange pleasantries, I'll feel bad about ratting him out to Callie, which is exactly what I intend to do."

While Christian and I are busy debating, Nicholas Furi sneaks up on us, without his companion.

"Christian, I think you have the prettiest girl at the ball as your date."

I turn around and come face-to-face again with the male version of Callie. Same raven black hair and cobalt blue eyes that look like they're always cooking up mischief. He's smaller in stature than he appears on television. He could be mistaken for a prom date instead of a world-famous movie director.

"Mr. Furi, it's good to see you again," I say.

"Please, Abbie, call me Nicholas. We're past the formality."

He asks us how we spent the holidays and if we're excited about graduation and our plans afterward. Christian and I both know what he really wants is to talk about Callie. Soon, Nicholas whisks me off to the dance floor. Christian is annoyed because it was our chance to begin dancing the night away. I shoot him a sympathetic glance.

In my heels, I'm at least two inches taller than Nicholas, but it doesn't bother him as he twirls me around the dance floor. "How is Callie?"

"She's disappointed in you."

"I know. She blames me for the divorce. There's so much she doesn't know."

"So, why don't you tell her?"

"I have to protect her."

"From what?"

"It's complicated, Abbie. She's all I have left that matters to me. I can't lose her."

"Are you asking me to talk to her?"

"She doesn't take my calls or answer my texts. On the rare occasion that she does, she's openly hostile. She's siding with her mother in the divorce."

"I don't know what I can do to help. If you have something to say to her, if her understanding of what happened is wrong, you have to let her know. I can't do that for you."

"I just need some time alone with her to explain things, certain situations she's not aware of."

I'm dying to know what things and situations Callie may not be aware of, but that's between Callie and her Dad, so I clamp down on my nosiness.

By the time our dance is over, Nicholas has convinced me to talk to Callie on his behalf. He said he would fly up to school to visit her so they could talk.

After my chat with Nicholas, Christian refuses to let me dance with anyone else. We spend the rest of the evening in our own little world.

CHAPTER 31

A BRAND NEW year has begun. It's 2:00 in the morning and I lie flat on my back, staring up at the ceiling. I can't seem to fall asleep. Christian and I toasted the New Year with sparkling apple cider. He said I was a good influence on him because if I weren't present, he would have had the hard stuff. I want to remember every detail of my visit: every smile, conversation, the sights, sounds, and smells, but especially every moment I spent with Christian here.

The screen of my cell phone lights up, casting a glow around the room. I answer, and soon thereafter, I open the door and let him in. He sits next to me on the bed.

"Couldn't sleep either?"

"No. I want to show you something important," he says, holding up his phone.

"What is it?"

"My heart."

"I don't understand."

"It upset me that you were so hurt by what Leah and Chelsea said to you. I don't want you to ever doubt me again."

"I won't. I don't know why I freaked out like that."

He wraps one arm around my shoulders and scrolls on his phone with his free hand. "These are the text messages my mom and I exchanged about you. We have our issues, but when you agreed to go out with me, I couldn't believe it. I had to share that with her."

I'm so touched by the gesture that I feel my tear ducts are about to burst wide open. "That's between you and your mother."

"I have to show you. Maybe it will explain how I feel better than I could ever say with words. Please, let me do this."

"Okay."

CHRISTIAN:

She said yes. Can u believe it?

KATHERINE:

Who said yes?

CHRISTIAN:

Abbie Cooper.

KATHERINE:

Yes to what? You're not making sense.

CHRISTIAN:

She agreed to go out with me.

KATHERINE:

I thought you went out with lots of girls. Is this important?

CHRISTIAN:

YES!!!

KATHERINE:

Oh. Is she a nice girl?

CHRISTIAN:

The best girl.

KATHERINE:

I'm happy for you then.

He scrolls to the next message.

KATHERINE:

I've never seen you this excited about a girl before.

CHRISTIAN:

I've never met anyone like her before.

KATHERINE:

Tell me about her.

CHRISTIAN:

I'll tell you more when we talk, but she's smart and funny and doesn't take crap from me.

KATHERINE:

She sounds perfect for you. You get out of control sometimes.

I read several more text messages, each one more

252

intense than the previous one. It's as if he was writing diary entries about his feelings for me by texting his mother. I rest my head on his shoulder. I want to capture this moment and keep it locked away so no one, and nothing can taint it. The last text floors me.

KATHERINE:

How's it going?

CHRISTIAN:

I don't know how to describe it.

KATHERINE:

Use words.

CHRISTIAN:

How do know? How did you know that you loved Dad?

KATHERINE:

Heading to a meeting. Let's talk about this when I get home.

CHRISTIAN:

Should I call Dad? I need to know now.

KATHERINE:

No. I'm glad u came to me.

CHRISTIAN:

Okay.

"I don't wonder anymore," he says to me. "I know."

I stay quiet for a beat.

His voice cracks. "You don't feel the same way."

"I'm just thinking."

His shoulders sag. I turn his face toward me. His wet, dull eyes make my heart ache. "I want you to remember us like this. The ball, your studio, when you slept next to me so I wouldn't be afraid of the nightmares, Thanksgiving, coming to my locker every morning. All of it."

He looks down at the floor and murmurs, "Are you breaking up with me?"

"No, but you might end things between us. If that happens, I won't regret letting you in and trusting you with my heart. Weird, since I'm a control freak."

He stops staring at the floor and focuses his attention on me. He cracks a smile. "I don't know why you think I will break up with you, but now that you've told me how you feel, that's not happening."

"What about graduation? We leave Saint Matthews in four months."

"We'll take it minute by minute, day by day."

How can I make plans for a future that may never come? How can I think about spending every day with Christian when at any moment, my deception will attack like a tsunami, and wipe out everything we've created?

"What's wrong, babe? Why are you sad?" He strokes my cheek. I can't look him in the eye because I'm about to start sobbing, and I may not be able to stop.

"Look at me?" he pleads.

I reluctantly meet his eyes. "What's going on? You can tell me anything, and I'll do my best to make it better for you. I swear."

I whimper like a wounded animal. I'm incapable of speech so instead, I kiss him. He's caught off guard at first, but then he reciprocates. He rains kisses all over my neck, my face and chest. When he nibbles on my earlobe, I can barely breathe. I fall backward into the mattress. He leans over me, his sensuous gaze lighting me on fire. The unspoken question is asked and answered. He bolts from the room and returns what seems like seconds later. We resume what we started, and I welcome the fever—content to let it take me to that place it's been dying to show me.

"Did I hurt you?" he asks, half asleep.

"No."

"Liar."

"Yes, but I don't care."

"How come?"

"I love you."

PART SIX

THE CRASH

CHAPTER 32

I TEXT CHRISTIAN, asking him to meet at Joe's Pizzeria after school and then slip my phone into the side pocket of my bag. Everyone looks like they're suffering from holiday hangover. I know I am. I arrive at my locker and ignore everyone around me. I have English Lit first period. Ugghh. I have to see Sidney's face. At least Trevor will be there to play peacemaker.

"What is this?"

When I turn around, I see Christian holding up his phone. His eyes are cold and vacant as if I'm some object of his loathing. I feel a chill that my turtleneck sweater can't combat. I want to be anywhere but here, standing at my locker, facing his disappointment and anger.

I take the phone from his stiff fingers and glance at the image. I don't even have the energy to be angry. The dreaded photo sent by The Avenger stares back at me from the screen of his smartphone. With trembling hands, I give it back.

"Well?" He's fuming, irate that he has to ask for an explanation a second time. What can I say when bigger problems are looming? The photo could go viral at any moment. I had tough words for The Avenger after the Black Friday money drop. Then I didn't get into Princeton. Now this. My attempt at retaliation is going to cost. A lot.

"That's why I wanted to meet after school."

"You knew about this?" he yells. A few people on their way to class level curious stares in our direction.

"I only knew it existed when it was sent to me," I say in my defense.

"When was that?"

"Before Thanksgiving."

"And you didn't tell me?" He almost chokes on the words.

"I was too ashamed," I confess. "I thought I could make it go away before it got to this point."

"How did you plan to make it go away?"

"I can't talk about it right now." My vague response is like throwing gasoline on the fire.

"We talk about it right now. If you have a problem, we can get you help."

"Who sent you the photo?" I ask him.

"I don't know, some anonymous person. When was it taken?"

"I don't know."

He inches closer to me. "What's going on, Abbie? Why did someone send me this?"

"I'll answer your questions this afternoon, and tell you everything. I promise."

"We said things to each other. Looking at this image, you didn't mean a single word of it. If you did, you would have trusted me with whatever *this* is. I was wrong about you. You're not different. You're just a liar who put on a good con job."

With those soul-crushing words, he walks away from me.

I can barely put one foot in front of the other as I attempt to walk all the way to class. My heart's been carved up into little pieces. I could just die now. When I arrive in class, I crawl to my seat and put my head down on the desk, ignoring the chatter of classmates around me. If anyone says anything to me, I'll shatter like a cheap toy.

"Abbie, are you okay?"

It's Trevor. I lift my head from the desk and look up at him. He adjusts his glasses. He peeks closer at me. Are you crying?" he asks, his voice soft.

"It's over," I whisper. "Christian and I are done. Happy freaking New Year to me."

He blinks in confusion. "Frances said the trip went great, and Christian's parents loved you. What happened? You guys just got back."

"Lies, Trevor. Lies. They always come back to bite you where it hurts most."

"But you don't lie."

"Don't I? Anyway, it was fun while it lasted, and now, I'm the newest addition to the Christian Wheeler Fan Club. Hooray for me. I'm so freaking special."

He opens and closes his mouth, unable to find the right words. That's because there aren't any words that can make up for the fact that I sabotaged my relationship with Christian by keeping the truth from him.

The conversation with Trevor ends when Ms. Morris, my guidance counselor, pops into the classroom. "Abbie, can you follow me? Bring your things with you."

Trevor and I look at each other. My classmates gaze in my direction and let out a collective "ooh." People are usually hauled out of class for one of the two Ts: trouble or tragedy.

SEATED IN THE office are the headmaster, Dr. Kellogg, and the Dean of Academic Affairs, Ms. Lana Weeks. Ms. Morris takes a seat, and so do I. Dr. Kellogg sits behind his desk, looking the scariest I've ever seen him look.

"Do you know why Ms. Morris brought you in here?"

"No, sir, I don't."

"Some serious allegations have been made against you, Abbie," Ms. Weeks says. She's a slim brunette with her hair pulled back in a bun, and large glasses. We've always held each other in high esteem. By the look on her face, that's over now.

"What allegations? We just got back from the holidays."

"Dr. Kellogg received a disturbing message early this morning," she says. "We have to address it right away."

"I wasn't around after Christmas, so I have no idea what this is about."

Dr. Kellogg straightens his tie. "Abbie, someone sent an anonymous message accusing you of using drugs to enhance your academic performance here at Saint Matthews."

It's time for my command performance. Fake it til I make it confidence. "Well, that's just ludicrous, Dr. Kellogg. You know my record from the day I arrived here as a fourteen-year-old freshman."

"We know. Which is why this is so upsetting," Ms. Morris says.

"There's more," Dr. Kellogg says. "These are not simple allegations. There's a photograph of a young lady engaged in drug use. Her face is barely visible, but—"

"But what?"

"She resembles you."

I scratch my head. "Some random person sends you a note accusing me of something I would never do, accompanied by a photo of someone who supposedly looks like me, but you can't tell for sure. Yet you still haul me into your office and treat me like a criminal?"

He doesn't care for my defiance. "There's a zero tolerance policy regarding drug use of any kind at this institution. It's our obligation to investigate all claims involving drugs. The consequences are severe if anyone is found guilty."

"If it's proven that any student uses drugs on the premises, it calls for immediate expulsion," Ms. Weeks says.

I cringe inwardly. Ms. Weeks is talking about expelling half the student body if they were to ever launch an investigation.

"I didn't do anything wrong. I don't know what you're accusing me of and why you're trying to scare me."

My strategy to get out of this is simple. Deny, deny, deny.

"We have compelling evidence. We have to take this seriously," Dr. Kellogg insists.

"What evidence? I would like to confront my accuser. I would like to see this so-called evidence. I've worked hard every day since I've been at this school, and I'm not about to let someone snatch that from me. Especially someone who doesn't have the guts to make him or herself known."

"We've called your parents. A meeting is set for this afternoon."

He just pushed a dagger through my heart. Crap! I can't talk my way out of this. "Why?"

"For one, they need to be made aware of the situation, and two, we need to discuss how to resolve this and figure out what options we want to exercise. You can return to class for now. We'll let you know when your parents arrive."

Just like that, I'm dismissed. I don't return to class, however. I head to the chapel instead. The chill returns, and I can't stop shaking. I can't be expelled; I just can't. What am I going to tell my parents? What if The Avenger sends the version of the photo with my face in full view? Dr. Kellogg says the face was blurred. It was meant as a warning to me that she's not messing around. My hands are shaking so badly, I can barely pick up my ringing cell phone from the side pocket of my bag. Blocked number.

"Happy New Year, Abbie. Did you miss me? I sure hope so because I missed you like crazy."

"Why don't you just drop dead, Sidney? Stop pretending that you're someone else. I know it's you. I know you're behind this."

"I'm going to call you in exactly three days with your next assignment. Let's give the bureaucrats in the main office a chance to cool down. In the meantime, don't mess this up. Rumor has it that Princeton didn't want you. How unfortunate it would be if you met the same fate with Brown or Cornell or Yale. Tick, tock, Abbie."

She just stuck a blade in me, and she's turning it slowly. I don't doubt for a second she could do what she just threatened. She's right about one thing. I am running out of time.

"Oh, by the way, I'd like to offer my condolences," she says chuckling. "I heard your relationship with Christian died a pretty painful death."

"You're going to die a pretty painful death when I'm done with you."

"You'll have to catch me first, and we both know you won't."

"I will."

"I bet you won't."

"Watch me."

CHAPTER 33

W HAT THE HECK is going on, Abbie? Your father is livid, and so am I."

Mom is on the line, and she's not happy.

"I don't know, Mom. Dr. Kellogg is acting like I committed the crime of the century, all based on some murky picture from an anonymous source. The whole thing is just stupid."

I'm still holed up in the chapel. I need divine intervention if I'm going to survive this hurricane.

"We should meet beforehand. I don't understand who would accuse you of using drugs. The idea is ludicrous."

"That's what I told him. I don't think he believes me. He's anxious to pin something on me, which is strange. We've always gotten along. I thought he liked me."

"We'll get this sorted out, sweetie. I'll see you soon."

After I hang up with Mom, I send out a new text message.

ME:

Need your help one last time. Sidney has completely lost it.

DAHLIA

???

ME:

Will tell u face-to-face.

I arrive in the cafeteria for lunch with my girls. I'm not hungry. In fact, the thought of food makes me want to gag. I plop down on the chair; my shoulders hunched over.

"We're so sorry, Abbie," Callie says. "What's the latest?"

"My parents are on their way here. You know my dad. He'll go nuclear on Dr. Kellogg. I can't afford to make The Avenger angry right now. She's threatening to send letters with the photo to the other schools I'm applying to."

"She's playing you," Frances says. "She already got fifty grand from you, and she won't stop."

Neither Frances nor Callie has any lunch in front of them. This is not the way I thought we'd spend our last few months of high school together. Frances is right, which is why I need Dahlia's help more than ever. This time, she really is the only person who can help me beat The Avenger.

"I'm going after Sidney hardcore," I say. "I want her diary. No more hesitation."

"You're such a bad-ass," Frances says. "I want to be you when I grow up." She gives me a high-five. So does Callie.

"How are you going to get the diary?" Frances asks.

"I can't give you the details of the plan. That way, if I get caught, you can say you don't know anything, and it will be the truth."

"What an awful beginning to the year, huh?" Callie says.

"Well, last year ended with a bang, so I have to hold on to that," I muse.

"Are you and Christian really over or is this just a fight?"

"I think we're done for good, Callie. You should have seen the way he looked at me. He called me a con artist. I wanted to die right there on the spot."

"Where does Christian get off, acting like the moral police?" Frances asks.

"He's mad that I didn't tell him," I explain. "He was blindsided by that picture. He has always been straight with me, about everything. To find out that I kept something this big from him hurt him a lot. But right now, I have to suck it up and deal with my pain another time."

"He'll be fine," Frances says. "You're right, though. You have to put that aside because there are bigger problems like you not getting kicked out of school."

"I know," I say and drop my head down on the table. "I need you guys to help me stay sane, remind me what our lives were like before all this trouble started.

Otherwise, I might end up in a psych ward, with only the voices in my head for company."

"Okay," Callie says. "My dad went out and bought me a Rolls-Royce Phantom. He said it was an early graduation gift. He probably figured you would tell me he showed up at the Wheeler's party with his latest skank and wanted to placate me. How stupid does he think I am?"

I sit up straight in my chair. "So you won't meet with him? Callie, I think you should. When I spoke with him, I got the feeling that the situation goes much deeper than we imagine. Don't you think you owe it to yourself to hear his version of what happened?"

She sighs. "I don't know, Abbie. I'm a coward, I guess. I don't want to be lied to or handled."

Frances chimes in, "It's like Abbie says. Give him some face time, and after that, you can do whatever you want. You don't want to damage your relationship long-term, wondering what he had to tell you and if it would have made a difference in the way you see things."

Callie lets out a puff of air. "I'll consider it."

"What about you, Frances?" I ask.

"I start my internship at the newspaper tomorrow after school. It won't do any good for my applications to Columbia and Northwestern, but it will be a boost to my resume. And next month, I'm heading to San Francisco with my parents for the Chinese New Year celebration."

"That's cool," I say. "Is your sister going?"

"Penny will be touring, again. My parents will be forced to adopt me as their favorite child."

"I'm sure you'll have a blast," Callie says.

Our conversation is interrupted when Sidney makes a sudden appearance at our table, startling us.

"What do want, Sidney?" I can't control the hostility pouring out of me.

"I just had to come over. I heard the most devastating news that you and Christian broke up after such a long time together. What was it, five minutes? You should have listened to me."

Frances glares at her. "Don't be a hater, Sidney. Christian still adores Abbie, and so do his parents. Can't say the same for you. Wait, hold on a minute," she says, holding up her hand dramatically. "You've never met his parents, have you? You've never seen the inside of Bedford Hills, and you never will. Now, run along."

Sidney bites her bottom lip, then backs away from the table. "I hate all you bitches. Drop dead," she says, her voice thick with emotion. Then she turns on her heels and walks away.

DR. KELLOGG DOES the introductions in his now crowded office, which includes my parents, my guidance counselor, and the Dean of Academic Affairs. "Sorry to call you in on such short notice under these circumstances," he says to my parents. "We didn't want to waste any time tackling the issue."

"Let's hear it then," my dad says to him.

He launches into the same speech he gave me about how serious the accusations are, the repercussions if they're true, and the school's zero tolerance policy. The rest of the administrators in the room just nod in agreement.

"Dr. Kellogg, can you explain to my wife and I how you plan to go about validating these claims?" Dad asks. "Seems to me you're putting too much stock in baseless allegations from an unidentified source instead of looking at Abbie's record here at Saint Matthews. She has been a model student in every way."

The headmaster removes his glasses and places them on his desk. "You're right, Mr. Cooper. Abbie has been an exemplary student, which is why this is so shocking. The girl in the photo bears an uncanny resemblance to her and the kind of behavior the young lady is engaged in...."

"We'd like to see the picture," Mom says.

Dr. Kellogg puts on his glasses, shuffles some papers, picks out the photo, and then hands it to Mom. She's stone-faced as she passes it to dad. His expression mirrors hers. They're thinking the same thing. *It looks like me.*

Dad swallows several times. Mom maintains her granite-hard stare.

"You can see why we're concerned, Mr. and Mrs. Cooper," Ms. Weeks says.

"What I see is an image representative of the digital age in which we live," Mom says. "Anyone with a rudimentary understanding of Photoshop or similar programs can create an illusion that can fool even the experts."

"Is it possible that this complaint against Abbie is just a smokescreen?" my dad asks.

"What are saying, Mr. Cooper?" Ms. Morris asks, leaning forward in her chair.

"Allegations of drug use were made against my daughter. Each of us sitting here knows it's a ridiculous notion. If they're accusing her, I wonder what's going on at this school that they don't want you to know."

Ms. Morris fiddles with the pen in her hand, and I can hear Ms. Weeks grinding her teeth. Dr. Kellogg makes a show of clearing his throat and shuffling papers on his desk.

"Because of your record here and the circumstances surrounding these allegations, we'll let you off with a warning this time," he says looking at me. "But this has to be included as part of your permanent record."

"That's not happening," my father says. "It's unwarranted and unfair. I don't see any reason for it."

"Mr. Cooper," Dr. Kellogg says, as if my dad is a toddler trying his patience, "we have rules here. Abbie is not above the rules."

"No argument from me on that point. However, adding this to her record implies wrongdoing on her part. There's no concrete proof of that. If we were in the court of law, this case would be tossed out in minutes."

I was right. Dad went nuclear on him. No one in the room misses the subtle threat behind his words.

"We all want what's best for Abbie," Dr. Kellogg says.

"Great." Dad stands up, shakes Dr. Kellogg's hand, thanks him for his time and cooperation, and then leaves the office with Mom on his heels.

DAHLIA MEETS UP with me at the end of my Spanish class. I stay seated. She enters as everyone leaves, and then takes the seat next to me.

"So, can you help me?"

"Hold up. Before I say anything, we need to come to an agreement."

"About what?" My patience is hanging on by a thread. It has to be tonight. The Avenger said I had three days before she calls with her next blackmail scheme, and I need to get ahead of her.

"So, what's in it for me?"

"I don't know, taking down Sidney. Being my hero."

"Yeah, yeah. That's all good, but I'm sticking my neck out for you, again. I need something valuable in exchange."

"Dahlia, you haven't said anything to me, and as far as I can tell, your neck is still firmly on your body. I don't see any stretching here."

"Alright, Abbie. Listen up. I need a favor too. You help me, I help you."

I should know that's the way the world works, quid pro quo. "Okay, Dahlia, what do you want in exchange for helping me?"

"You and Callie are tight, right?"

"Yes. So?"

"So, Nicholas Furi is the biggest movie director in the world with his own production company. If he wants a movie made, it gets made."

"You've lost me."

"You don't think I would walk away from SMA without getting the hookup, did you?"

"So, you want Callie's phone and email?"

"You know for a smart girl, you're really dumb."

"I didn't come here to get insulted, Dahlia. Are you going to help me or not?"

"Look, I'm going pre-law once I get accepted into Georgetown. And at some point during college, I'm going to need a good internship that can help me get into a top law school—like an internship in the legal department at Pacific Pictures. If that doesn't work, I'm flexible. Callie's father can use his contacts at the movie studios to get me in. I'm not picky: Paramount, Warner Bros., Twentieth Century Fox, DreamWorks, whichever. Any one of them would be just fine with me. As long as I can add that to my resume and impress law school admissions at Harvard and Columbia."

I can't blame her for her ambition. I just wish I knew in advance that there would be a hurdle to getting her help.

"All I can do is talk to Callie. I can't guarantee her dad is going to remember their conversation two or three years from now."

"That's where having Callie's contact info comes in handy. See, you're not stupid after all."

I glare at her, and she has the nerve to smile back at me. "Can you get me access to Sidney's diary?"

"Ask me a hard question."

"I'm going to hurt you if you don't stop it."

"Sorry. I'll give you a break. I know you're nursing a broken heart since you and Christian ended your relationship. Yes, I know where she keeps it."

"Where?"

"In her sock drawer."

"Really? That's so cliché."

"It's Sidney. She's vindictive, not imaginative."

"So, what's the plan?" I ask.

"Why are you asking me? This is your show."

"I don't know the rules of residence life that well. You're the Resident Assistant. I thought you would have this part of the plan figured out."

"Okay, you got me."

"Invite me over. I'll hang out in your room, and while everyone is at dinner, open her room and let me in. You'll have to be the lookout, though."

She rakes her hand through her hair. "It's not that complicated, Dahlia. You let me in, I grab the diary, and I'm out."

"How are you going to put it back?"

"Haven't thought that far yet."

"You should."

"Don't you think I know that?" I scratch my head. "I have a better idea. I can take snapshots of the diary entries that interest me."

"That could work," she concurs. "Taking the whole diary will create too much drama, mostly with getting caught trying to return it."

"Exactly. Are there cameras in the hallway?"

"No, just the main lobby area."

"Good. So, we have a plan?"

"Do I have a choice?" she asks, shrugging.

"Nope. It has to be tonight, though."

"What? You never said that before, Abbie. Tonight is too soon."

"Why not tonight?" I ask.

"Why tonight?" she counters.

"I want to bring this nightmare to an end. I'm exhausted."

"Did something else happen?"

"It's Sidney. There's always something. I promise this is the last time I'll ask you to get involved in my problems."

"You promise? This is it?"

"Promise."

PART SEVEN

DIARY OF A MEAN GIRL

CHAPTER 34

THERE WAS NO high-octane drama like in the heist movies when I took photos of Sidney's diary entries. I visited Dahlia just like we planned, and while everyone was at dinner, she unlocked Sidney's dorm room, and I walked in. The diary was exactly where Dahlia said it would be.

It's after eleven o'clock at night. In two days, I'll get the call. I sit on my bed, my stomach in knots. What if I don't like what I read? What if I don't find anything I could actually use to shut down Sidney and catch The Avenger? These are the questions I didn't ask myself when I decided this was a good idea. It's too late now.

I click the camera icon on the phone and tap the image that begins the series of photos. I scroll through to the beginning, give myself an anti-wimp pep talk, and dive in. Within seconds, my pep talk starts to unravel.

September 13th

Jessica told me he was hanging around her locker, staring at her like a lost puppy. So disgusting. No way I'm letting that overachieving ice queen get close to Christian. He's just crazy enough to invite her to Bedford Hills to piss me off. If anyone is getting an invitation, it's going to be me. Besides, what would people in our social circle think if she showed up? Anyway, she would never go out with him. I see the evil glares she gives him at general assembly and during lunch in the dining hall. Definitely not interested. But just in case she thinks that she actually has a chance with him, I'll have to shut her down and put her in her place. Looking forward to it!

No surprises there. This happened at the beginning of the school year. Sidney is never shy about expressing her feelings. Round two.

October 24th
She showed up with her crew at Evan Mueller's Party, and that wasn't the worst. She and Christian were all over each other. Barf. But the best part was when she went postal and shoved a text message in my face, which I barely read. I didn't need to. I was laughing my butt off, though. The ice queen was thawing right before my eyes. Good times.

More ranting about Christian chasing me, her attempts to insult me into submission, and what a miserable failure that strategy was. Based on the number of skipped dates, she's doesn't journal regularly.

November 13th
I hate her. I wish she would stop calling and emailing me. My shrink says my anger is justified. Duh. Do I need

her to tell me stuff I already know? Patty just sucks! She's not my mother, and doesn't deserve to be called a mother. She's faking like she doesn't know why I don't want to talk to her. She knows what he did to me, and she's told me to keep quiet because it would cause a massive scandal and destroy "a lot of lives." "Think of the greater good, Sidney," she tells me. Whatever. What about my greater good? She doesn't care about me. All she cares about is my dad becoming president and the idea that the creep who raped me can make it happen. She wants to be First Lady so bad that she's willing to throw me under the bus. Barf.

Every time I see him on TV or at some event with his ugly wife and dumb ass kids, pretending to be the All American Family, I want to scream. I want to tell the world he's a rapist, a lying pig, a hypocrite, and the worst kind of human being ever. He said if I told, no one would believe me because I was a little slut. I had a plan for how I was going to take him down. Alan Wheeler. He's the only one I know powerful enough to give that psycho what's coming to him. Christian was my ticket until Abbie Cooper came on the scene and ruined everything. She'll pay for her meddling. I'll make her regret the day she crossed me.

I can't breathe. A five thousand pound elephant just sat on my chest. I put the phone down and place my hands on top of my head. Poor Sidney. Tormented by the assault and then betrayed by her own mother. She sees me as an enemy, an enemy to the justice she deserves. I can't count the many ways this is messed up.

I still don't understand how blackmailing me for money is supposed to help her, unless she's refusing all financial assistance from her parents or family members.

I should stop reading, but I can't. I continue.

November 27th

I decided not to go home for Thanksgiving. I won't be able to stand either one of them acting like they're so happy I'm home, and we're the perfect, happy family. Taylor is so lucky she doesn't have to deal with this crap. Moving to Japan to teach English was the best move. As soon as I graduate, I'm moving overseas for a gap year. I don't know where yet. I might even decide to attend college abroad. I'm applying to a couple just to keep my options open. It's quiet here today. Almost everybody is gone. Only the international students and messed up people like me stayed behind. They'll have a big dinner in the dining hall for us.

Sometimes I wonder if my parents would miss me if I go overseas or just called it quits altogether. They'll probably sigh with relief, especially Patty. What would be the best way to do it, though? Jumping from the bell tower at Saint Matthews might work, but I want to look fabulous on the way out, and turning into cottage cheese from the impact is not a hot look. Driving my car into traffic? I think pills would be the best way. I could tell my shrink I can't sleep and get her to prescribe sleeping pills. That way I can control everything, what I wear, how my hair looks, the position in which I'm found. It would be epic.

She wouldn't do it, would she? Her psychiatrist is supposed to be helping her. This doesn't sound like someone who's getting the help she needs. Now I'm involved. What did I get myself into? I don't think she would do it. Life is one big, endless drama to Sidney, so it's hard to know if she's serious about this. I'm not sure what I should do. She's in a lot of pain as far as I can tell. But it's getting late, and I can't figure this out just yet. I want to finish reading, though.

December 11th

My dad called today. He's pushing me to the breaking point. Seriously, I wish he would just go away and never come back. He's all freaked out about me applying to Harvard, which would be a total waste of my time. He keeps talking about his friend who's on the Board of Trustees putting in a good word on my behalf. Whatever. I'm not applying. First off, the regular deadline is less than a month away. Secondly, I had to take drastic measures to get the grades I have now. He would go batshit crazy if he ever found out. You know, he has to protect his reputation and all that. Parents are so dumb, and so is the administration here. They never see what's going on right under their noses. You can get anything you want at this school. Name it, and for a price, it's yours. That always cracks me up whenever I pass the headmaster's office. Clueless. We all made a pact never to reveal the identity of our supplier. Kellogg would crap his pants if he knew who it was.

CHAPTER 35

THE SOUND OF tires screeching startles me. I look up and see a gray sedan has stopped mere inches from me. I stare into the face of the horrified driver. It takes me another split second to realize that I was so caught up in my disturbing thoughts, that I was almost killed by oncoming traffic. The adrenaline kicks in. I run all the way from the street to the main building. I collapse at my locker, struggling to catch my breath, trying not to think about the fact that I could have been gone in an instant.

I didn't sleep a wink last night. After I read Sidney's diary entries, I discontinued spying on her computer. She's talking about ending it all, and I'm at a loss. I don't know what to do about it. I'm now seriously beginning to question my original assumption that she's The Avenger or, at the very least, an accomplice. Sidney only offers a vague hint that she may be the one behind the blackmail (*I'll make her pay for her meddling*), but she stops just shy of a full confession. Why the hesitation? It's not as if she's expecting anyone to read her private thoughts. She confessed that she was raped, which is as gut-wrenching as it gets. So why not admit that she's been stalking me and making threats too?

I pick myself off the floor and start exchanging textbooks. Unfortunately, I have to face Sidney this morning but I can't allow my feelings to get in the way. I must do two things today: First, leave a note about Sidney in the Safe Box at the front of the classroom without being seen; second, I'll make one last attempt to determine for good if she knows anything. When Trevor pops up next to me, looking like his pet just died, I figure my day is going to suck.

"What's wrong?"

"I'm so sorry, Abbie. He didn't mean it. He's been depressed since you guys broke up, and I think Sidney took advantage."

I steel myself against what's coming next. I exchange the books in my locker. "Took advantage how?"

"She threw herself at him. He was too drunk to care."

"Just say it."

"Christian slept with Sidney. I'm informing you because you're my friend, and Sidney is going to make sure she tells you in a way that will hurt you. I figured if you knew ahead of time, it might soften the blow."

"Christian is an adult. He can do whatever he wants. How do you know this anyway?"

"Saw her coming out of his room late last night. Sneaking out, actually. I confronted him, and he admitted it."

"Oh. I see."

"That's it? You know it didn't mean anything with Sidney. He's miserable, Abbie. I'm not just saying that because he's my friend. He doesn't care about anything. I'm afraid of what he might do to stop hurting about the breakup."

"I'm sorry your friend is hurting. Not my problem."

"Abbie, it's not like you to be so cold-hearted."

"Trevor, I got my own problems. I can't take on anyone else's. I'll see you in class. I just need another minute."

"Okay," he murmurs and leaves.

I slam the locker door with such force that I almost dislocate my arm. I want to curl up in a corner somewhere and die. I mean it this time. Just die, so I won't feel anything.

He did it on purpose, payback for keeping the truth from him. He knows how I feel about Sidney, and he did it anyway. That's just hateful.

"Is Abbie having a bad day? Well, I have some news that might cheer you up."

I turn around and glare at her. "Yeah, yeah, you slept with Christian. Don't care. Now, go away."

I can see the let down on her face. My preemptive strike worked. Thank you, Trevor. The longer she lingers, the closer I come to falling apart. Sidney was practically frothing at the mouth in her eagerness to tell me what happened between her and Christian moments ago, her only goal my complete humiliation. But because of what I know, I struggle to see her simply as the vindictive girl she's proven to be time and time again. I see someone who suffers in silence because the people who are supposed to help her betrayed her. Tragic. Yet, I also have to remember that I'm fighting for my future.

"What else do you want, Sidney? Do you want to make another threat? Go ahead. I'm standing right here. You don't have to hide behind anonymous calls anymore."

She folds her arms and backs up a couple of steps. "Are you serious? Someone is stalking you? I thought you made up that story."

"You know full well it started back in the fall. Cut it out. Just tell whoever you're working with to stop it."

"What are you talking about?"

I get more desperate by the second. I see my future turning to dust right before me. I try again, in the hopes that a miracle will occur and free me.

"Look, we have dirt on each other. We're even. Let's just call off this nonsense."

"Dirt?"

"Don't play innocent."

"You're flipping out again, Abbie."

"I am flipping out. I'm asking you, no, begging you—please, if you know anything about who's been stalking me, tell me. You're hurting. I get it. But you can get better, Sidney. A gap year is a good idea. It will give you a chance to put some distance between you and what he did. You have to take back your life. You can't let him win. Trying to punish me won't help you heal. Can't you see that?"

She backs up even further, desperate to get away from me. "How do you know all that stuff about me?"

I wasn't prepared for that question because I've been preoccupied with her heartbreaking story and getting her to admit she's been harassing me. Oh, boy. How do I remove my foot from my mouth?

"Never mind about that. Our information isn't as safe as we think. The important thing is we end this now."

"We'll end it for sure. I'm going to destroy you. I'm going to call my dad and have him and his friends at the NSA, CIA, and FBI cause major problems for you and your family. You'll be living under a bridge, eating out of a can for the rest of your miserable lives."

"The same dad who allowed a grown man to violate you in the most heinous way possible, and he was too weak and selfish to do anything about it? That dad? He should be prosecuted right along with the creep who raped you. So should your narcissistic mother."

The minute the words leave my mouth, I know it was a mistake. I not only confirmed that I had violated her privacy, but I also took a deeply personal tragedy and stuck a knife in the wound. When Sidney starts tearing up, I follow suit. "I'm sorry, Sidney, I didn't mean it. The past few months have been draining."

I reach out to comfort her, and she slaps my hand away. "You're going down, Abbie Cooper. You messed with the wrong girl."

CHAPTER 36

I SKIP DINNER, so I can stay in my bedroom and boohoo in private. If Sidney isn't behind the plot to ruin me, who is? And why? When I looked into her eyes earlier today, something inside me stirred. She was telling the truth. I left a note in the Safe Box in English Lit class. All I said was that Sidney needed help because something terrible had happened to her. That only makes me feel a little better. If Dr. Campbell approaches Sidney, she'll know I was the one who informed on her. Oh, well, that's the least of my troubles. I have to find out who wants to take me down before it's too late.

A knock on my bedroom door spurs me into action. I jump up from the floor and wipe my eyes with the sleeves of my T-shirt.

"Abbie, it's Mom. Open up."

I let her in. Something heavy is on her mind. She parks herself on the bed and signals for me to join her.

"What's going on? You've been distant, and I walk in here to find you in tears. I suspect your odd behavior has to do with the meeting in Dr. Kellogg's office. Who is the girl in the picture, Abbie?"

I stare at the wall. It's time to stop running and stop lying. "Me."

I turn to look at her. That's the thing about my mom. She never yells, not even when my brother and I deserve it. It's because of her rough childhood and a mother who beat on her every day.

"Care to explain yourself?" she asks, calmly.

"It happened while you were in jail two years ago. They were going to expel me because I wasn't keeping up with my schoolwork. I flunked a couple of major exams and was in danger of the same thing happening in other classes. Plus, I was missing a bunch of homework assignments."

Mom gets up from the bed. Her hands are clasped loosely behind her back as she paces. "Go on."

"I heard about Adderall from some kids at school, and they told me the person who could get it for me. So I bought some to help me study longer, so I could get my grades back to where they used to be."

"How long did this go on for?"

"A couple of weeks. Then I stopped because I didn't feel right. I knew it was wrong, and you and Dad would be ashamed of me."

"So somebody found out, and that's what the picture is about?"

"Yes, ma'am. I know it looks like I was about to use cocaine, but it wasn't. I swear it was Adderall."

"You crushed the pills."

"Yes."

Mom shuts her eyes tight. When she opens them, they convey her true feelings: *how could you?*

"This is bad, Abbie. Do you realize this person could send the picture with your face clearly in view for everyone to see? There could be hundreds of pictures like this floating around out there. You're four months away from graduation, and you could get kicked out of school before you get your diploma. There are legal ramifications if this happens. Your father will fight the school, trying to prove it's not you in the photo, regardless of whether or not they can confirm its origin."

"I'm sorry, Mom. I don't know what else to say. I made a mistake, and I tried to cover it up."

"I'm disappointed in you, Abbie. I raised you better than that."

I can't stop the tears. Next thing I know, I'm in a full-on ugly cry. It gets louder and louder, like a hungry baby demanding to be fed. Then Mom starts bawling too. She stops her pacing and comes to sit next to me on the bed. She hugs me tight.

"I'm sorry I wasn't there for you, sweetie. What you did was wrong and dangerous. But I think you were punished enough when I was in jail, so it doesn't make sense to visit that idea."

We break apart and wipe our tears. "Your father will be devastated. The most important thing right now is for us to come up with a strategy before this turns into a disaster that will take years to salvage."

THE NEXT MORNING, at precisely 7:36 a.m., I receive a text message that will profoundly change my life.

FRANCES:

Sidney is dead.

Shock, grief, confusion, and despair conspire to suffocate us as we shuffle into the auditorium. Dr. Kellogg called an emergency meeting of the entire school. Somehow, my friends have found me among the four hundred plus students. We hold hands and say nothing. Some around us weep quiet tears while others are more vocal in their grief. No questions are asked about what happened, when or how. It's up to the school leadership to deliver the grim details.

Our headmaster looks like he has aged since I saw him yesterday. He takes the stage and signals for us to take our seats. The school chaplain stands to his left, and Mr. Collins, the Assistant Head of School to his right. He adjusts the microphone.

"Today will go down as one of the most difficult days in the history of Saint Matthews Academy, certainly the most difficult day in my tenure as Head of School," Dr. Kellogg begins. "I've been tasked with delivering heartbreaking news to you all. Early this morning, we lost a beloved member of our community.

Sidney Bailey Shepard, a friend, mentor, and classmate was found dead at the bottom of the bell tower."

A collective gasp erupts from the auditorium. Loud wailing starts up again. Dr. Kellogg is prevented from stumbling and falling by Mr. Collins, who grabs his arm in time.

She went the cottage cheese route. Sidney said she wanted to look good on her way out. I don't know why this diary entry pops into my head. Perhaps it's a numbing mechanism because the alternative is too painful to consider, that I may have pushed her from the bell tower because of our discussion yesterday. The note I left didn't make a difference. That was only twenty-four hours ago. Maybe Dr. Campbell didn't have time to act. I can't believe Sidney did it. The girl I spoke to yesterday was the same as always. There were no signs to indicate she would jump only hours later. I start to hiccup. Callie squeezes my arm.

"Sidney was full of life and had a promising future ahead of her," Dr. Kellogg says. "She had much to offer the world, and her light was extinguished too soon. Her family has been informed of this tragic event and will be here shortly. Details of a memorial service will be forthcoming."

He moves away from the microphone, and the school chaplain, Pastor Reynolds, takes over. "I'm available for grief and spiritual counseling. My door is wide open. Please walk through it."

The girls and I leave the chapel with our arms around each other's waists. On the way out, I spot Christian leaning up against the wall beside the main door. I tell the girls I'll catch up with them later. His face is red and swollen, his hair a wild mess and his clothes disheveled.

"Hi."

"Hey, Abbie."

We stand there like that for a few beats, awkward, raw, unguarded, not knowing what to say. I do the only thing I can do, the only thing that makes sense. I pull him into my arms and hug him tight.

"I can't believe she's gone, Abbie," he says.

"Me, neither. I just saw her yesterday."

"Why? I don't understand why she would do this," he says.

"I'm sure she had her reasons, Christian. Reasons none of us understands."

At least she went out on her own terms, right or wrong, I want to add. Instead, I hold him tighter. When we separate, I take another look at him.

"You're too skinny." It comes out more like an accusation instead of an observation.

He serves up a weak smile. "Maybe I should eat more."

"Maybe you should."

More awkwardness. "Well, I should be going," I say. "It's a tough day for everybody."

He grabs my arm. "Abbie, about the way things—"

"It's in the past," I say, hastily.

"I acted like a jerk. I should have supported you and tried to understand what was going on with you. I regret that. I'm sorry. Can you forgive me?"

"Your reaction came from an honest place. There's nothing to forgive."

"Some kids were talking about holding a candlelight vigil at the bell tower. Will you come? It's tonight."

"I don't know if Sidney would approve. You know how she liked to call me a hypocrite."

A genuine smile appears on his lips. "She really hated you, didn't she?"

"As only Sidney could. There was a certain flair in her contempt for me. I admired that in a warped kind of way. Even when she gave me the finger, it was dramatic."

"Can I call you or text you?" he asks.

"That's a bad idea, Christian. We should just leave it alone."

"I don't want to," he insists, determination springing from him. "I miss you. I don't ever miss anybody, Abbie. The minute I walked away from your locker that day, I knew it was a mistake. When I tried to fix it, to fix us, you wanted nothing to do with me. You avoided me at school and wouldn't return my calls or texts. Your friends stopped talking to me. Callie gives me the silent treatment, and Frances just looks at me like I'm dead to her."

A soft giggle escapes me. My girls always have my back. But I can't forget what he did, although to bring it up now would make me seem petty. Still, I have to call a thing, a thing.

"You missed me so much, wanted to fix us so badly, that your answer was to sleep with Sidney?"

He winces and then glances at the big exit sign over the double doors. "I was trying to forget us," he says, his voice weak. "Being reckless was the only way I could make it from one day to the next. That way I didn't have to feel anything. It didn't work, obviously. I want things to go back to the way they were. I don't care about that photo."

I edge closer to him and turn his face toward me, forcing him to look at me. "You can't keep punishing yourself. We both handled it poorly. You don't have a monopoly on guilt and stupidity."

"Did you ever find out who took that picture of you?"

"Let's not talk about that today of all days," I say.

He looks at me confused, but I offer no further explanation.

Callie, Frances, and I decide to spend lunch period in the student lounge. The cafeteria is a ghost town anyway. A few other souls are seated around the TV set, watching a movie.

"It doesn't seem like Sidney to commit suicide," Callie says. "She liked living too much. Mostly to torment other people."

"Maybe it was the drugs," Frances says. "She took too much, and it rewired her brain."

"I know why she did it," I say.

Two pairs of inquisitive eyes focus on me. I tell them the sordid story of what Sidney was going through, the real reason she wanted Christian so badly, and how indifferent her parents were to her pain and struggle.

I ended with our final confrontation yesterday at my locker. I wish I could take it back.

"You couldn't have known she would do it," Frances says. "Her problems were bigger than you. Than any of us."

"She wanted to escape. To go someplace where it didn't hurt so much," I say. "Guilt is eating me up. She didn't share this with anyone except her psychiatrist. I violated her privacy, thinking it would free me from the threat hanging over my head. Now that she's gone, I don't know."

"This is not your fault, Abbie," Callie says.

"What did Christian say?" Frances asks.

"He's in shock as we all are. He apologized for the way things ended between us, said he was wrong."

"It's about time he acknowledged he acted like a douchebag," Frances says.

"So it's really over? We can go back to our normal lives?" Callie asks.

"What do you mean?"

"You don't have to worry about having your life trashed because of that picture. Sidney is gone. If she had an accomplice as we suspected, she might back off too. Game over."

"Game not over. I don't think Sidney was The Avenger."

Frances and Callie stare at me, speechless.

"What are you saying, Abbie?" Frances asks.

"We don't have any proof pointing directly to her. Everything we've done so far has been for nothing." I start to hiccup again.

"It's the guilt talking, that's all," Callie says, rubbing my shoulder. "You feel sorry about what happened to Sidney, and now she's dead. You don't have to feel guilty, Abbie. You couldn't have known."

"If Sidney wasn't The Avenger, then who is?" Frances asks.

"That's the scariest question of all," I say.

PART EIGHT

IVY LEAGUE SWAGGER

CHAPTER 37

I HAVEN'T HEARD from The Avenger since Sidney died. No threats, no demands for money, and no feeling like my world will blow up at any moment. I decided not to attend the Platinum Ball this year. I can't think about partying when there's a chance I may not even graduate from Saint Matthews. The girls stand in solidarity with me, even though I insisted they should attend the ball. Christian and I have eased back into our relationship. He even started coming to the house again. I think Sidney will always be a part of us, no matter how we try to deny it.

I sit at my homework desk and boot up my laptop. The remaining schools I applied to for regular decision sent out their emails this afternoon. The pressure is off now. Even if I receive only one acceptance letter, it will still be a great school. Ty was right. Princeton wasn't the end of the line for me.

At the very top of my email inbox is a message from Brown University Admissions. My hands freeze, afraid to click on the email. I'm seconds away from learning my fate. My nerves hurt if that's even possible.

I double click on the mouse.

There's a brief note that a decision has been made and a link to login to my application status portal. I can barely type in my username and password.

I read the first sentence of the letter, then the second. I read it again. Excitement starts to build in every cell in my body. I want to scream with abandon, but instead, I start weeping. I'm overwhelmed with relief. I got in. They accepted me.

I leave my room and walk down the hallway that leads to the stairs. I slide down the banister, yelling for my mother. She appears at the bottom of the stairs, looking tense.

"What is it? Why are you yelling?"

I don't answer. I grab her arm and pull her up the stairs and into my room.

"Look," I tell her, gesturing to the laptop.

She leans in closer and reads the message. She pulls me into a crushing embrace, but I don't mind. We don't say anything, content to absorb the moment.

"I'm so proud of you," she says.

"I know."

We release each other, and Mom's already thinking ahead of me. "We should celebrate, you know."

"This is just the first one, Mom."

"You're right. Were there any others in your inbox?"

"Oh. I haven't checked yet. Brown was at the top."

"Why don't you check the others too?"

I wipe my sweaty palms on my jeans and get to work.

Decisions from Duke and Johns-Hopkins came in earlier, mixed in between all my other, mostly junk emails. I can't handle the stress, so I give Mom the username and password to the application status portals for all the schools.

"You check them out," I say to her.

"Are you sure?"

"Yes. I'll just sit on my bed."

The clock on the wall is ticking loudly. I've never noticed that before or perhaps my anxiety has amplified the volume. Mom has been clicking away at the computer for what feels like forever. After a minute or two, she stands up and announces, "I need a drink."

The earlier thrill of getting into Brown disappears like someone who fell into quicksand. It doesn't make sense. I was sure I would get into Duke and Johns-Hopkins. Mom attended both schools, and she's an active alumni. The rejection hurts.

"Sorry," I whisper.

"Why should you be sorry? I need a drink. The oldest and most expensive wine we have in the cellar. No. This calls for champagne."

She's pacing, mumbling to herself.

"I got in?"

My heart begins to soar. Mom ignores me and continues her rant.

"First, I have to call your father. No, wait, he's about to head into a lecture. I'll text him instead. Oh, there's so much to do. I have to call both your grandmothers and your Uncle Michael. Oh, I can hardly stand it. My baby...."

I don't hear the rest of her sentence. I get my butt off the bed and look at the open acceptance letter from Duke. I can't stop beaming. I close out the Duke letter and pull up the second screen to read the Johns-Hopkins acceptance. Soon, I'll hear from Cornell and Yale. I sit still, just taking it all in.

CHAPTER 38

THREE DAYS LATER, I turn eighteen, but I want no big fuss or special treatment—only to spend time with the people I love. The good news bus rolled into town, and it isn't going anywhere. I was accepted into Cornell, too. My guidance counselor, Ms. Morris, said she was proud of me. Frances got into her first choice college, Northwestern University. And Callie? She'll be heading off to the Fashion Institute of Technology in New York this fall. As for Christian and Trevor, they did just fine too. Later in the evening, we'll celebrate my birthday and getting into college.

A FedEx package arrived for me while I was at school. Mom stashed it on the sofa in my bedroom. I dump the box on the bed, and then rip it open. Inside is another box with a giant, pink ribbon. I untie the ribbon and peek inside. I pull back the delicate pink tissue and remove the item from the box.

It's a stunning pink Indian sari made of silk with a floral design. The edge of the wrap and bottom of the skirt are finished off with tightly woven gold embroidery stitching. Wow! Ty must have enlisted the help of his dad's younger sister to get this made. She still wears the traditional Indian garb, even though she tends to favor Western-style dress. I remove the card from its envelope.

Saw a sketch for this and thought you should have it.

Happy Birthday, my princess.

Ty

How strange. Ty always calls me Cooper. What is this new thing? He said he couldn't make the celebration but wouldn't miss my graduation. I take a photo of the note and text it to my girls to see what they think.

"MOM, NO ONE can eat this much food. There are only nine of us here. Where do you think we're going to put all this?"

"Your friends can take doggie bags back to campus, and we'll store the rest. I won't have to cook for a month."

We're gathered in the kitchen, enjoying the spread that mom put together for my birthday celebration. Mini turkey meatballs, crab cakes, pulled pork and burger sliders, coconut shrimp, fruit and cheese platters, mini cheesecakes, white chocolate tarts, and of course, the three-tiered birthday cake (chocolate, vanilla, and red velvet) designed to look like pink and white polka dot gift boxes with a single stiletto as a topper.

My brother, Miles, sits at the kitchen table, stuffing his face with dessert because Mom never allows him to have this much sugar. He's taking advantage of the special occasion. Christian is stuck to my side. He says he's afraid I might tumble down into a hole somewhere, never to be heard from again. He's back to his usual gorgeous self. He was wasting away for a little while. Trevor couldn't join us. He was summoned home the minute he received his acceptance letters. His dad wants to discuss his future at Forrester International. Poor Trevor. He's not going to win this battle.

"I'm just here for the presents," Frances says. "When do we get to open them?"

"It's Abbie's birthday," Callie reminds her as if Frances forgot.

"I know that. But we're her best friends. We get to be nosy. No waiting until we leave to open them, Abbie."

"Okay, Frances," Mom says. "You girls can be nosy all you want after we make a toast. Miles, find your father. It's time for the toast."

"I'm right here," Dad says, entering the kitchen. "My little girl isn't a little girl anymore. I'll make the toast and then retreat to my man cave to drink myself into oblivion."

"Dad, come on."

"Just kidding."

We gather around the island in the middle of the kitchen. Mom hands us each a champagne flute, but only she and dad are drinking the real thing. The rest of us have to settle for sparkling white grape juice. Mom nods at Frances. I guess they worked something out beforehand.

"To the most awesome, fabulous, smart, and fearless chic I know," Frances says. "Happy Birthday, Abbie."

I start to tear up as we clink our glasses together, and everyone says, "Here, here." We all take a swig and place the glasses on the island counter. Christian kisses me on the cheek and pinches my butt where no one can see his hand. I play it cool but can't stop grinning.

"Now, for the presents," Frances says.

"Not so fast," I say. "I have an announcement to make."

Everyone pipes down. "I got my last email late this afternoon. Yale accepted me. They're offering a full academic scholarship."

My eardrums are about to shatter from the fanatic screaming of my friends. My mother hugs my father. Christian hugs me so tight I might pass out from lack of oxygen. Miles squeezes Callie and Frances. He lingers a little too long. I can see the mischief in his eyes. He can't wait to brag to his friends that he hugged his sister's two hot friends. I'm sure he'll add some spice to make the story more interesting.

"We need more champagne," Mom says to Dad. "Why don't you kids go on to the family room? The presents are all piled up in there. Then you can come back for birthday cake."

Mom doesn't have to tell us twice. We trip over each other to get to the gifts. Christian follows us while Miles remains in the kitchen with my parents.

"Open this one first," Frances says, shaking a box with gold wrapping and white ribbon.

"I agree," Christian says, sitting on the arm of the couch, right next to me.

Frances hands me the gift. I rip the wrapping off to find a paper bag colored box underneath with the logo of a famous shoe designer in white.

"Where's the card?" I ask excitedly.

"Who cares?' Frances says. "You can read it afterward."

Callie finds the card on the floor, and hands it to me, and I rip the envelope and reach inside for the card. I read a very private message from Christian. I look up at him and smile. I'll keep the message just between us.

"The present is from Christian," I tell the girls.

I open the box and gasp when I discover what's inside: a gorgeous python, peep-toe pump in a combination of smooth butter-yellow, pale-green and dark-brown—my first pair of stilettos. I've never worn heels this high before, five inches, but as Frances says, who cares. I lift one shoe out of the box and hold it up so the girls can see.

"Now, that's a Louboutin. Jennifer Lawrence wore one similar on the red carpet recently. Christian, you have excellent taste," Callie says, nodding in his direction.

He smiles proudly.

"Where would I wear this to?" I ask.

"Um, hot college parties. Hellooo," Frances says.

I turn to Christian and whisper, "Thank you for my birthday present. It's my first."

"Seems to be a habit with you and me," he whispers back.

We're all back in the kitchen for birthday cake. I lean up against the island in the center. Miles tells me my phone is ringing. I left it on the kitchen table. I walk over to it and see a strange number. I answer the call anyway.

"Hello."

"Hi, Abbie. Did you miss me? I sure hope so because I missed you like crazy."

For a moment, it feels like my heart has stopped beating, and bone-chilling fear takes over. I now have irrefutable proof that neither Sidney nor her supposed accomplice is behind the threat. "Who...who are you?" I squeak.

"Abbie, what's going on?" Dad asks. All eyes are focused on me.

His question jolts me out of my haze. I end the call. "It's a wrong number, Dad. They just sounded a little creepy. Perhaps some kid prank calling."

He accepts my explanation and returns to eating his cake. My friends know something is up. I tell Christian and my parents I want to show my friends something in my room, and we'll be right back.

I toss the phone on the bed and lie on my back. Callie leans up against the dresser. Frances pulls out my homework chair and sits.

"Who was that?" Frances asks, her tone anxious.

"The Avenger," I say.

"What?" they ask at the same time.

"It's the same voice. She asked the same lame question, whether I missed her or not."

My phone rings again. I know it's her. I pop up into a sitting position and answer the call.

"Why did you hang up on me?" she asks. "Don't do that again."

"Who are you? When does this end?"

"It ends when I say so, Abbie. Now listen up. I was blindsided by the whole Sidney dying thing. I figured I should lay low, you know, give you time to fake grieve. Now, I'm back with your next assignment, as promised. A hundred thousand dollars cash in the next forty-eight hours.

"The drop-off will be the dumpster behind the fast food joint on Route 30 in Framingham. Be there at 11:00 p.m. with the cash. If you decide to get cute, you know the penalty. Don't be fooled, Abbie. You're a long way from safe. Acceptance letters can be rescinded. I'll disappear after I send my little gift, of course. Kellogg won't even give you time to clean out your locker; he'll want you gone so badly. Ciao!"

"What did she say?" Callie asks. Both girls join me on the bed.

"She wants double the amount of the first drop in two days. And she doesn't go to St. Matthews."

"What makes you say that?" Frances asks.

"Someone who goes to our school wouldn't threaten to disappear weeks before graduation."

CHAPTER 39

I DON'T KNOW how I managed to convince Lance to help me one last time, but I did. He's waiting for me in the chapel's first row. I sit next to him.

"So, you got a complicated challenge for me, Mama?"

"It's the only kind you like."

"True. Lay it on me."

"I thought it was Sidney, but I was wrong. The only way to catch this girl is to infiltrate her phone."

"Whoa. That will take some major firepower. You're not playing around."

"She's not playing around, Lance." I tell him about the phone calls and the extortion, leaving out other crucial details. I get creative with the truth when I explain why this is happening.

"I need a week to come up with something."

"I don't have a week. She said I had two days. I don't want to sit home this fall, Lance. My acceptance letters could be rescinded based on her lies."

He lets out a puff of air. "I really want to help you, but I don't know if I can do this."

"Yes, you can. Please, Lance. I'm not going out like this. I tried everything I could think of and got nowhere. I have no more moves left to play in this game. Look, I'll pay you. I know what I'm asking is huge, and it's only fair I pay you for your time. How much?"

"I can't take your money."

"You took a huge risk for me by getting the surveillance footage of the locker. Now I'm asking this. Don't you need to buy hardware or software? I don't know how this would work exactly."

"Software. I would build the program you can install on your phone."

"Doesn't this software exist already?"

"I can check, see if something is already prepackaged, and I can modify it, but I don't think so. I'm going to have to go without sleep for the next two days."

I touch his arm. "I'm sorry, Lance. I'll make this up to you somehow."

"Like you said, we can't let you go out like this."

"I have the voice sample. I'll email it to you. Maybe there's a clue in there that can help."

"Sure, whatever you got."

PART NINE

TICK, TOCK

CHAPTER 40

15hrs, 30 minutes to deadline

IF ANYTHING GOES wrong with the plan, my life will come crashing down for sure. So far, I've been able to avert disaster but my luck is running out.

I'm at my locker. Sidney's death is still a presence with us. The ritual of back and forth between classes and hanging out in the hallways has been subdued since she left us. I suspect her ghost will always inhabit these halls. I pull my phone from the pocket of my sweater when it rings. I can't afford to miss any calls today. It's Lance.

"Hey, Mama. I compared the samples you emailed me. They don't match. It's not the same girl."

Given the events of the past several weeks, this is not surprising news. I move my neck from side to side. I know my stress levels will rise as the day wears on. Who is she? Why did she target me? What does she want? It can't be all about the money.

"You there, Mama?"

"Yes, Lance, I'm here. I heard you."

"I'll run the samples again. I think it's possible that sample B is not a girl."

"Pardon me? How is that possible?"

"Whoever was stalking you with those calls could have used voice-altering software to hide their true identity. It's easy to get. You can change your voice from male to female and vice versa, use accents, whatever. The possibilities are endless."

A lump forms in my throat. My brain scrambles to find a logical explanation, one that would fit perfectly, like the pieces of a jigsaw puzzle. One that wouldn't make me feel like a four-alarm blaze is about to consume me.

"Thanks for the update, Lance. Let me know what you find out."

I hang up, and my anxiety climbs higher than a jetliner gaining altitude. When I hear Christian's voice right behind me, my breath hitches.

"What are you trying to find out, babe?"

He deserves the truth. At this point, I'm doing it for selfish reasons—to free myself from the feeling that I betrayed what we shared and never set things right.

"Follow me to the student lounge. I have a story to tell you."

So, I do. I leave nothing out, including the fact that Ty gifted me the fifty thousand dollars I needed to pay off The Avenger.

"I didn't do it to hurt you, Christian. I just wanted to be that girl you put on a pedestal. I wanted to tell you so many times, and I kept putting it off. I wanted to tell you at Bedford Hills, but I didn't want to ruin the trip. I figured you would break up with me for lying to you, and I wanted to have good memories of that time. I was going to confess everything when we got back. It was too late. When you walked away from me, in my mind, you had written The End on our story. That meant I didn't have to tell you. Then Sidney died."

He closes and opens his mouth a few times before finally forming coherent words, "That's why you're working with Lance?"

"He's helping me figure out who it is before the deadline tonight."

"What if he can't?"

I sigh. "He will. My future is literally in Lance Carter's hands. It's obvious that this person wants to use me as his or her personal ATM. It won't end with tonight. He or she will find a way to keep asking for more."

"I'm disappointed that you didn't come to me for help. That cuts deep, Abbie."

"There's no excuse for what I did. And I'm sorry I lied to you."

"Did you think I would judge you? You know I would never do that."

"I was desperate to be the girl you thought I was. The girl I thought you needed."

"You are. That doesn't change because you made a mistake. That night when I met your family for the first time, you defended me to your dad. You wouldn't let him run me over with criticism and disapproval. So why do you keep punishing yourself because of one mistake? You'll make plenty in your lifetime. Are you're going to freak out every time you do?"

"I need intense therapy to work that out."

He chuckles. "Maybe you do."

"I wish Sidney had that and more," I say. "Maybe she would still be with us today."

"You don't know that for sure. Sidney was Sidney. If this is how she wanted to end things, no amount of therapy was going to stop her. But her parents are losers."

"The worst kind."

"What are we going to do about tonight?"

"Pray really hard that Lance's program works?"

"I hate to even suggest it, but we may have to go to Kellogg with this."

"No way. I'm not giving up."

"Hear me out. The element of surprise may work in our favor. Whoever is doing this would never expect you to go to the Head of School. I can give you the money, but you're right, it won't end. You have to think about your safety too. We don't know what The Avenger is capable of besides blackmail."

"My father went postal on Kellogg during that meeting. To go back and admit it was me, I don't know."

"He has more serious problems. That's your ace. If what Sidney says is true, that there's a drug ring operating in the school, he has to investigate."

I know he's right. When Sidney died, I told my parents they didn't have to worry about this coming out. Now, I may have to inform them they have only a few hours to come up with an alternate strategy. Knowing Dr. Kellogg, he would turn every dorm room upside down until he found something. The implications are much bigger than someone extorting money from me.

"I'll check in with Lance in an hour, then call my parents."

"Cool. I'm here to support you. Whatever you need. For the record, I'm not mad that you turned to Ty. He's a good guy."

"You had to get that in there, huh?"

"As long as he doesn't cross the friendship line, we're good."

"That's so sweet. You're jealous."

"Yeah, I'm jealous."

"Don't be," I say stroking his face. "I'm all yours."

Someone interrupts our kissing. It's Dan Cosgrove, Head Prefect, and Captain of the boy's Lacrosse team.

"Dr. Kellogg asked me to see if I could grab you before class starts," he says, addressing me. "You weren't at your locker. I figured I would try my luck here. He wants to see you in his office, ASAP."

"Do you know what it's about?"

"Dr. Kellogg never explains himself. You know that."

"Thanks, Dan."

I gather my bag and stand up.

"You were so smooth just now, all casual," Christian says. "You're freaking out inside, aren't you?"

"Yeah. What could he possibly want with me now? Unless that psycho sent another picture."

"Stay calm no matter what he says. Don't answer any questions that might get you in trouble. Tell him you have nothing to say until your parents get here. With their lawyers."

"Right."

"Text me the minute you get out, and we can meet up here again. I might get yelled at for showing up late to my next class, but this is more important."

CHAPTER 41

"AM I IN trouble?"

"Have you done something you should be in trouble for?"

I can't tell if he's being serious or just teasing me. I sit across from Dr. Kellogg in his office yet again. I seriously need to break that habit. He takes off his glasses and places them on the desk.

"Full academic scholarship to Yale. That's impressive, young lady. Your entire resume here at Saint Matthews has been impressive. You make us proud."

I almost fall out of my seat. I can't believe it. Is this the same man, who not too long ago threatened me with expulsion?

"Thanks, Dr. Kellogg. It means a lot coming from you."

"I wanted to apologize to you for the way I behaved the last time we met. I should have trusted what I know to be true about you."

"You had a job to do."

"That's right. However, I want to be clear. I'm not apologizing for bringing you and your parents in here. I would be remiss in my duties if I didn't. I only wanted to say that I rushed to judgment based on questionable information."

His praise makes me feel all kinds of guilty about making a stink when he initially hauled me into his office. What was I supposed to do? Confess and watch my life crumble because of one bad judgment call?

"I'm sure my parents understand your actions, Dr. Kellogg."

His gaze is relaxed, and all his pearly whites are visible. Shocking. He must be having a great day.

"I brought you in here for another reason." He picks up a cream-colored monarch envelope from his desk and hands it to me. I reach over and take it from him.

"Mr. and Mrs. Shepard found this amongst Sidney's things. They're hoping she explains why in this letter to you. It may help them heal from their terrible loss."

I look down at the envelope. My name is written in bold, sweeping strokes in heavy, black ink. Sidney never did anything halfway, even in death. "Thank you, Dr. Kellogg."

He nods, and I get up to leave. As I turn the doorknob to exit his office, he says, "Good luck at Yale, Abbie. Don't forget to come visit us."

I promise him I will and shut the door behind me.

FOURTEEN AND A half hours until deadline. I send Christian a quick text letting him know that things went okay with Kellogg. I head to the chapel right out of my psychology class. Two students are already present, but they occupy the back rows. I plop my bag next to me, rip open the envelope, and begin to read from the matching paper inside.

Dear Abbie,

If you're reading this, it means I'm gone. I bet you're wondering why I did it, why I went the cottage cheese route. You want to know why I'm writing to you when even God knows I hate your stupid guts. This may sound strange to you, but you're the only person who gave a damn. When you said my parents let me down, and they should pay for letting him ruin my life, I wanted to punch you in the mouth. When you told me I could get better, and I shouldn't let him win, I wanted to believe you because you've never lied to me. But I'm not strong like you, Abbie. I was just good at faking it. I didn't have the strength to fight both him and my parents. They would never let me go after him. Even if I did, I would end up right where I am now, totally wrecked. Don't feel bad for me, though. This way is the best way. I'm doing it my way.

For what it's worth, I believe you, about the stalking. Sometimes the people closest to you don't always have your back. And one more thing, Ms. Goody. You fell hard for Christian, didn't you? The bad boy you swore wasn't good enough. I still hate you for stealing him from me, but the truth is he wanted you so bad. Barf. Anyway, I'm out. Don't cry too hard, hypocrite.

Hating your guts for eternity.
Sidney Bailey Shepard

I close the note and place it back in the envelope. Time slips away from me as I sit, unable to move. Was I surprised she wrote me what amounts to her suicide note? Yes. But that was Sidney, always keeping me off balance. I'm intrigued by the comment about people not always having my back. What did she know? What was she trying to tell me?

My phone pings, a new text message.

CHRISTIAN:

Are you okay?

ME:

I'm fine.

CHRISTIAN:

What did Kellogg want?

ME:

Felt bad about accusing me of cheating. We're good.

CHRISTIAN:

Are you sure?

ME:

Yes.

CHRISTIAN:

I'm worried about you.

ME:

I'll be okay. You'll see.

I glance at the digital clock on my phone. Time to resume my school day as if it's normal when it's anything but. Fourteen hours until deadline. I'm tempted to call Lance again, but I squash the urge.

CHAPTER 42

Six hours until deadline

LANCE'S PROGRAM ISN'T ready yet, and I'm officially freaking out in my room. To add to my stress, there's no guarantee The Avenger will call me before 11:00 p.m. in order for the plan to work. I don't have a way to provoke her into calling me. Once she realizes I won't pay up, will she send the incriminating photos right away or wait until the morning? Will I have to implement Plan B and ask my parents to wake up Dr. Kellogg in the middle of the night for an emergency meeting?

My phone rings, and I grab it off the bed. It's Lance.

"Please tell me it's ready."

"Sorry, Mama. It's a complicated process, and I'm encountering some issues that could take a while to resolve. We're six hours out, and I don't know if I will have it ready in time."

I whimper into the phone.

"Look, I'll do what I can. I haven't showered or eaten since I took on this project. My teachers will believe me when I tell them I've been sick because I'll show up to class with bloodshot eyes."

"Please know that I appreciate everything you're doing, Lance. I'll find a way to pay you back."

Two hours later, I look over the speech I've written. I can't walk into Kellogg's office and throw myself on his mercy without a plan. My debate team skills will come in handy. I'll keep my points short but compelling. I have to grovel with dignity.

I find Mom in the family room, curled up on the sofa listening to some program on her tablet. She removes the earbuds as I approach.

"What's wrong?" she asks. "Please have a seat."

I prefer to stand. It's best to get it all out. "There's something about the photo I didn't tell you, something that's been going on for months, and I'm sorry I didn't say anything earlier, but I thought I could handle it on my own, and now I may not be able to, and it involves you and Dad, too, and I know I've let you down, but the person who sent the—"

"Abbie, slow down, catch your breath," she says.

I almost had everything out before she interrupted me. Now I have to go back to the beginning.

"Now, pace yourself and breathe. What is it? What's been going on for months?"

I open my mouth, and nothing comes out.

"Sweetie, you're scaring me." She swings her legs off the couch and sits ramrod straight.

"Um... I...."

My phone rings. I reach into the pocket of my sweatshirt. Lance. It's time. Four hours until deadline.

"Mom, I forgot I was supposed to meet my lab partner at the school library. I have to go."

"Fine. What were you about to tell me?"

I stick the phone back in my pocket. "Just thanks for being cool about the whole ugly Adderall episode. Dad, too. I've been stressing out about it for months, how much I disappointed you guys."

"Everybody makes mistakes. Next time, come to us first instead of trying to cover it up. That only leads to deeper trouble."

I MEET UP with Lance in the student lounge. Three and a half hours until deadline. Dinner is over, and the lounge is busy. No one will pay attention to us. I approach him where he's seated at the far corner. He has a good view of the entire space. I take the seat across from him.

"Is it a go?"

"Only one way to find out. Give me your phone so I can install it."

I hand him the phone, and he explains what he's doing.

"The program is on this Micro SD card," he says, holding up a device that looks like a flash drive. "The program will download to your phone from it. Once the download is complete, I'll remove the card, and then comes the big test."

After he removes the card, he explains further, "I'll call your phone and then hang up. A code should appear in your incoming call log. Send a text using the code. I'll call you again, and it will activate the program. I'll step out of the room, and you should be able to hear me and any surrounding noise because the external microphone will be turned on."

He calls and hangs up. Just like he said, the code appears in the incoming call log. I'm excited, and agitated— like someone on caffeine overload. He steps out of the room after I send a test text message to the number in the log. I listen. I hear nothing at first, just dead air. Then I hear him whistling. Success!

It's 8:00 p.m., three hours until deadline. The lounge will close in an hour. The earlier crowd has thinned out, down to a couple of die-hards with their noses in textbooks. Lance offers to stay with me, but I convince him to leave. Christian sends me a text to check on me. I assure him I'm fine, and it will be over soon. I tell him the program works and convince him it's not a good idea to come hang out with me. I have to do this alone.

At 8:30 p.m., The Avenger still hasn't called. I remove my sweatshirt and place my phone in the front pocket of my jeans. I put my hair up in a hurried ponytail to get it out of my face and off my back. My eyelids are sweating too. I cross my arms and start to pace.

At 8:50 p.m., my phone rings. I carefully extract it from my pocket and answer.

"Do you have my money?"

"It's not yet 11:00 p.m. Calm down. Why so anxious? You didn't call me before the Black Friday drop."

"I wanted to tell you don't even think about shorting me. Every single dollar of the full hundred grand better be in that bag. No excuses."

There's desperation in her voice as if her life depends on everything going smoothly tonight. What's different about this drop? Not that I'm complaining. I needed her to call to set this trap in motion. The cocky girl I've come to know has disappeared, replaced by someone who is genuinely frightened. "You'll have your money. You're too clever for me, anyway."

"Are you giving up?"

"No. I'll play your game until I catch you."

"Dream on, Abbie. Just make sure you're not followed. I'll be watching from a safe distance."

She hangs up.

I crash into the chair I occupied earlier. My limbs are weak. I pull up the call log. I take a minute to calm my frayed nerves. I send a text message to the code that appears in the log. This allows the program to download to The Avenger's phone, giving me access to his or her external microphone, just like it did when Lance and I conducted the test. The lounge closes in less than ten minutes. My head feels like it's about to explode. I sit still and press the phone close to my ears.

"Don't touch it. How many times have I told you not to touch my stuff?"

"Chill, dude. Stop leaving your crap all over the place; then I won't have to move it."

That's all it took for my world to shatter.

PART TEN

---◄━◆━►---

A FAREWELL TO FRIENDS

CHAPTER 43

I RUN AS fast as my legs can carry me, out of the main building and toward Westman Towers. It's dark. I'm not familiar with the terrain at night, but my rage spurs me on. I continue my breakneck speed, ignoring the burning in my chest and my tiring legs. I thunder into the lobby and don't even slow down to acknowledge the stunned prefect manning the desk. I take the stairs two at a time.

When I arrive at my destination, I pound on the door, my breathing loud and angry. He opens the door, and I barge in. I barely notice the look of surprise on his face. He closes the door behind him. I'm hyped up on pure adrenaline, but I need my breathing to return to normal, so I can speak. We just stare at each other. All the stress and rage and fear of the past several months crash into me all at once. I pounce on him and start hitting him, punching him, biting him.

"Stop hitting me!" he yells.

I won't be deterred. The betrayal is excruciating and raw, a raging fire out of control.

He dodges a few blows, but I'm too blinded by rage to anticipate his next move. His hand lands in the middle of my chest, and with one powerful shove, I stumble backward and run into the desk near the window. For the first time since I barged in, I realize his roommate Daryl is absent. One brief exchange between the two of them gave me my life back.

"Why, Trevor? Why did you do this to me?"

He stands in the middle of the room, his hands shoved into his pockets, showing no remorse or guilt.

"I like you, Abbie. A lot. But there was something I needed badly, and you were the only person who could get it for me. Your secret gave me the leverage I needed to accomplish my goal."

"So, this *is* about money?"

"Well, yeah. I needed money, and you could get it for me because you wanted to protect your secret. It's not complicated."

My head spins. So many things don't make sense. "Your parents are wealthy."

"That's the thing," he says, pacing the small space. "The parents cut me off. People were breathing down my neck, people who could do bad things to me if I didn't pay."

"You're a gambler?" I ask, the question barely registering in my brain. "You extorted money from me to pay off gambling debt?"

"Don't be such a hypocrite, Abbie. You were inhaling Adderall like it was candy. Kyle Davidson's drunken rant was what set all of this in motion."

I frown. "Kyle Davidson graduated last year. What does he have to do with any of this?"

"How do you think I got the photo? Kyle and I were hanging out in his room one evening, enjoying an alcoholic beverage or two. Then he started bragging about how he had a picture of this popular girl getting wild, and I wouldn't believe who it was. I thought he was talking about naked pictures or something, so I convinced him to send it to me so I could see."

"Kyle would never do that."

"The fifty thousand dollars I got from you says he did."

Trevor explains that the photo surprised him, but he never gave it another thought until his gambling debt started mounting and his father diminished his financial support.

I sit on his roommate's bed, my legs unable to support me. "Frances is one of my best friends. You've been to my house. I thought you were my friend too. I blamed Sidney the whole time."

"That was the plan."

"What?"

"It was no secret that you and Sidney hated each other. All I had to do was throw in a couple phrases she would use. Implicating her was easy. As long as you believed it was her, you wouldn't suspect anyone else."

"That's why you changed your voice to female, using voice-altering software. To guarantee I would believe it was a girl and most likely Sidney."

"Now you're getting it."

I think back to Sidney's diary entry about the person who is supplying drugs to students. She said Kellogg would crap his pants if he found out who it was. With Trevor's gambling debts, it made sense.

"Are you dealing drugs too?"

"I had to keep my girlfriend in the lifestyle to which she's accustomed."

"You're blaming your despicable behavior on Frances?" I want to hit him again, but I know it won't do any good.

"I'll be back in my dad's good graces soon, and this whole ugly episode will be behind me."

"You won't get away with this, Trevor."

"I already did," he says, removing his glasses. "I didn't think you would catch me, though. I was prepared to walk out of here with your hundred grand, in addition to the killing I made dealing. My debt would have been wiped out. How did you track me anyway?"

"I'm smarter than you."

"Don't be mad, Abbie. I wasn't really going to rat you out."

"You almost ruined my life, and you think it's a joke? Frances is going to kick you out of her life for good."

"We're all but over, anyway."

My eyes wander around the room.

"You can look all you want, but you won't find anything linking me to those phone calls or the money drop. No one will believe you."

I pull out my phone from my coat pocket and hold it up so he can see. "I disagree, Trevor. Everybody will believe you did it because you told them in your own words."

"What are you talking about?"

I replay the confession he just made. The cockiness vanishes. I stand up and get in his face. He backs up, but there's nowhere to run. He bumps into the door.

"I beat you, Trevor. You're a hundred thousand dollars short of what you need to pay off your debt, and I figured out it was you. What do you think the people you owe are going to do to you when you can't pay them back?"

I ask him to get out of my way so I can leave. I turn the doorknob and realize there's one perplexing question he hasn't answered.

"How did you get the note and the list in my locker without being captured by surveillance cameras?"

He looks at me with something resembling hatred in his eyes. Then he breaks into a big, cocky smile. "That was the easy part. Whenever I met you in the lounge to go over homework or study for a test, you usually had the books for other classes spread out as well. I slipped the note and the list in the same way, when you were distracted and conversing with other people."

CHAPTER 44

T HE NEXT DAY, a distraught Frances calls me on
my way to school. Trevor has disappeared. No one
knows when he left his dorm room or the campus, not
even his roommate. His belongings vanished along with
him. I tell Frances to meet me in the chapel and bring
Callie too.

"What's going on, Abbie?" Frances asks, her arms
crossed. "Do you know where Trevor is?"

"No. I don't think he wants to be found, either."

"What do you mean?" Callie asks.

"Frances, please sit down," I say.

"That's okay," she says and continues to pace the
aisle.

"What I have to say will help you understand what
happened with Trevor. I spoke with him last night."

That statement stops her in her tracks. "Last night?
Where was this?"

"In his dorm room. Please sit. I have a spot saved
for you," I say, pointing to the seat in the middle of
Callie and me.

Frances finally obeys. I have to face them both when I deliver the blow. It just makes sense to stand when I do.

"This bit of news will scare you and hurt you and make you angry. But you'll be fine. We all will."

"Just say it, Abbie," Frances says, staring at the glossy polish on her fingernails.

"I found out who has been stalking and blackmailing me all these months. That's why I went to see Trevor last night."

"He knew who was behind it?" Frances asks.

"Yes."

"I don't understand," Callie says. "If Trevor knew who it was, why didn't he say something?"

"Because it was him all along. Trevor was the one behind the threats and extortion."

"Are you sure you're okay?" Frances asks. "The stalker is a girl. Why would you make up a story about Trevor being the stalker?" Her forehead wrinkles and she squints at me.

I pull out my phone from the side pocket of my bag and play the recording for them.

At the end of the recording, no one says a word. I've had a few hours head start to grapple with the shock factor. Frances starts tearing up and crosses her arms over her chest. I understand how she feels. Hiccups give way to a river of dark tears. I sit with them. In that moment of profound betrayal and sadness, we don't need words to express how we feel.

"He's not coming back, is he?" Frances asks through her sniffles.

"I doubt it," I respond.

"He's on the run?" Callie asks.

"I think so."

"What will you do with the recording?" Frances asks.

"Delete it. I only recorded it so you guys could hear him confess in his own words. He's gone. We don't need it anymore."

CHAPTER 45

I T'S A GORGEOUS Saturday morning in the middle of May. The sun seeps through the window, telling me I must hurry. I pull back the curtains and smile at the extra cars parked on our street, then return to the mirror for a final once over. Callie's creation, a beautiful white dress made of lace and cotton, flounces out just above my knees. It's cinched at the waist with a silver belt. I pick up the single white calla lily from the bed and place it above my right ear.

I scan the room to make sure I don't forget anything. My eyes are drawn to the large frame resting against the closet door. It's the painting of Christian and his mom in the park when he was five years old, chasing after that dog. He said he couldn't think of a better graduation present because it was my favorite painting from his collection. It's a gift I will cherish always. My present to him was a DVD collection of the best western movies ever made. He told me that he loved old westerns on our first date, and according to my dad, and *All the Buzz*, a well-known pop culture website, my choices were spot on.

"Abbie, you're going to miss your own graduation if you don't come out of this room right now."

It's my dad. I open the bedroom door, and he walks in, looking handsome as always in a dark gray suit, white dress shirt, and navy blue silk tie with polka dots. His eyes well up when he gets a good look at me. Dad doesn't usually get emotional, but this is a special day for him, too. He opens his arms wide, and I walk into his embrace.

"Your old man is profoundly proud of you. You make being your dad the best job in the world. I love you more than I can ever express."

"You're not bad yourself," I reply and extract myself from the bear hug. "Ready to be the dad of a soon-to-be Yale freshman?"

He flashes that megawatt smile at me.

"Then you need to be the dad of a Saint Matthews graduate first. Let's go."

AFTER THE CEREMONY, graduates and their families exit the large tent set up for the event and embrace the vast, open space, and cloudless sky. All the senior girls sport white dresses, and the guys wear navy blue jackets, a tie, and khaki slacks. My parents are beaming, and Miles is fussing with his tie. Grandma Naomi drove up from Ridgefield, Connecticut, and my Uncle Michael and his wife, Analise, flew in from Mom's home state of Louisiana. I know Ty made it to the ceremony, but I haven't seen him yet.

"Hey, Abbie, let's grab a spot at the gazebo for pictures before all the other families get the same idea," Dad says.

"I'll meet you guys there."

I raise my hand to shield my eyes from the sun. I scan the crowds to see if I spot my girls, Christian or Ty. I decide I'll have to text them to find out where they are. I feel a hand on my shoulder. I turn around to find Lance grinning at me, Dahlia at his side. I can't help it. I rush into his arms and give him a great, big hug.

"You, too, Dahlia," I say, and I hug her after I release Lance.

"Congratulations on getting into Carnegie Mellon," I say to Lance.

"Thanks. I got a full ride too. Funny how the school just happened to have that money available the minute they accepted me. You wouldn't know anything about that, would you, Mama?"

"Me? I have no idea. But you deserve it, Lance."

"Girl, you are something else," Dahlia says shaking her head. "Yale's going to have their hands full with you."

We have a good laugh and take a few selfies. We promise to keep in touch, and they go off to be with their family and friends. Lance saved me, and this was the only way I could repay him. I asked my parents to use the money they would have spent on my tuition on Lance's instead.

I join my family at the gazebo, and we take a million pictures, laughing and goofing off all through it. Then

I notice someone approaching us. Christian. When he gets closer, my parents leave us alone, dragging the other family members with them.

"I've been looking everywhere for you. My phone died, so I couldn't text you."

"Here I am." I wrap my arms around his neck, and when he leans in, we exchange a passionate kiss.

"I'm going to miss that."

"That's right. Think about that when you leave for Greece in a few hours, and when you leave for college. You can't get kisses like that in Texas."

"I know. Levitron-Blair has a major presence in Austin. It just made sense for me to attend college there."

"I agree. UT Austin is the best place for you."

"Well that may be true but what about us?"

"We don't tell each other stories about how college won't change anything. It will."

He jams his hands into the pockets of his khakis. "So, what do we do?"

I think about it for a moment. There's no script that explains how to handle a transition like this. "We never forget."

"I know I won't," he says. "I made a painting of you."

"You did? You never mentioned it before."

"Because it's just for me."

"What does it look like?"

"The way you looked, gliding down the grand staircase at Bedford Hills the night of the ball. You were enchanting. That's how I will never forget."

"The morning after the ball, when you showed me the text messages from your mom. That's how I will never forget."

I brush a loose lock of hair away from his eyes. "You made me do things I didn't think I could. You helped me exhale when I didn't know I was holding my breath. Thank you."

"You're welcome, Abigail Lillian Cooper. I'll do anything for you."

"You may regret that offer one day."

"Never."

"You're the most persistent person I know."

"How else would I have found out how incredible you are?"

My text message ring tone interrupts us. I glance at my phone.

MOM:

Where are you?

"It's Mom. They're looking for me."

Christian pulls me into his arms. I savor the moment and don't want it to end. When we break apart, he strokes my arms. "See you later this summer? I want to come visit you before I leave for Austin."

"I would like that," I say.

After Christian leaves, I can barely form an intelligent thought. I fan my face with my hands to stop the tears in their tracks. They ignore me. I receive a new text message. Callie says she's rounding up Frances and wants to know where I am. I tell her I'm still at the gazebo. I text Mom back to let her know I'll be on my way to the car in a few minutes.

Callie and Frances come into view and join me inside the gazebo. It's quite cozy.

"You guys are still coming to the house afterward, right? We can all celebrate together before you go home. Christian just took off, the jet's already on the tarmac."

"I don't think that's going happen, Abbie," Callie says.

"I don't understand," I say. "That was the plan."

"The plan changed," Frances quips.

"Why?"

Callie explains that she spoke to her father and learned that her mother is a functioning alcoholic who was unfaithful to her father throughout the marriage. "All three of us are leaving for Cannes tonight for the Film Festival. When it's over, we're taking Mom to a private clinic in Switzerland so she can get treatment without it being all over the tabloids."

"Callie, I'm sorry to hear your mom's sick. But I'm glad for you that your family is working through those problems. Are you still getting your own apartment when you move to New York or will you live in the dorms?"

"I still don't know yet. At least we'll be close to each other, only a two-hour drive away."

"That's a good thing. Why do you have to attend college in Chicago?" I ask Frances.

"Because it's Northwestern," she answers with her trademark attitude.

I want to remember us like this: young, carefree, and full of promise. We take a bunch of pictures with each other's phones. That way, we'll each have a piece of our final moments together, as eighteen-year-old high school graduates.

"This is it," Callie says.

"There is this invention called a smartphone," I tease. All three of us lean against the railing of the Gazebo, holding each other's hands as if we could force time to stand still.

"Do you think Trevor will ever stop running?" Callie asks, staring off into the distance.

"I don't know," I say.

"Do you think we'll be best friends forever?" she asks.

"I hope so, Callie. I hope so."

We hug each other, and then I watch my best friends walk off into their futures. I hope we can keep the promise that our lives will always be connected.

EPILOGUE

—◦—

THE GIFT

Three months later

"Y OU GOT A package in the mail," Mom says as she rushes out the front door. "It's on the kitchen table."

I do an about face and return to the kitchen. On the table lies a package wrapped in thick, plain brown paper. My name is written neatly in block letters. There's no return address. I shiver, and it has nothing to do with the central air conditioning or the fact that I'm wearing a tank top and shorts.

I have a seat and open the box. I pull out a slab of something wrapped in aluminum foil. I peel away the foil to reveal stacks of cash tightly bound by duct tape. When I get over the initial shock, I can say with certainty the money amounts to fifty thousand dollars. I put it aside and notice a plain white envelope at the bottom of the box.

I open the envelope. Inside is a postcard. On the

front is a generic image, a country road surrounded by lush, green vegetation. The back reads:

"Forgiveness is a virtue of the brave."
—*Indira Gandhi*

You're fearless.

Goosebumps appear all over my arms. I hope Trevor's okay, wherever he is. As for forgiveness, only time will tell how fearless I am.

My cell phone rings, and I answer it. It's Ty calling.

"Cooper, are you all packed? I have a feeling we'll need multiple cars to transport all your stuff to campus."

"Yeah. I'm mostly done with packing."

"Are you okay? Don't tell me you're fine. I can feel that you're not."

"I'm okay, Ty. Just thinking about someone I once knew."

"The past can be a dangerous place to visit, Cooper."

"Speaking from experience?"

"Yes."

"Can I ask you something?"

"Sure."

"What was the note that came with my birthday gift all about? You said Happy Birthday, my princess."

"You know what it means, Cooper. I don't need to explain it to you."

After I hang up, I want to mull over his words, but that will have to wait. Ty insisted that I shouldn't pay him back the money, that it was a gift. Well, turns out he was right. I grab my purse and head out the front door. The scorching summer heat beats down on me, but I don't mind. I hop in my car and head toward the Healing Hearts Foundation, a rape crisis center on Worcester Road in Framingham. I want to put a smile on their faces today with a fifty thousand dollar donation in memory of Sidney Bailey Shepard. I know exactly what she would say. She would tell me I'm a Ms. Goody, Goody who can't help herself. And for the first time, she wouldn't call me a hypocrite.

###

A SPECIAL PREVIEW OF AUTUMN OF FEAR

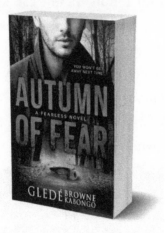

An ambitious girl with a promising future, a charming manipulator with a diabolical secret—the truth will destroy them both.

When Ivy League co-ed Abbie Cooper wakes up in a hospital bed barely alive after a violent assault, her world comes crashing down. She has no memory of the attack or her assailant, and no idea how she ended up in the Emergency Room.

As she grapples with the horrific aftermath, Abbie is determined to uncover the truth about what happened that night. But to catch a monster, she must piece together the events in the weeks leading up to the assault. Why did charming senior Spencer Rossdale take a sudden interest in her, and why did her quiet study group partner Justin Tate want to meet with her alone?

The deeper Abbie digs into the events leading up to that fateful night, the more she unravels a stunning web of lies that stretch back decades. Revealing them will change everything but the truth is the least of Abbie's problems. A vicious predator is watching her, and he's willing to kill to protect his secret.

CHAPTER 1

AFTER

P AIN EXPLODES THROUGHOUT my body like Fourth of July fireworks. I groan, but no one comes to help me. I move my arms. Blinding, savage agony. When I try opening my eyes, my lids won't budge, as if they've been sealed shut by an industrial sized staple gun. Where am I? Why am I in such hideous pain?

I hear a woman's voice, soft and sympathetic, almost a whisper. "Poor thing. She'll never be the same. What that monster did to her is unspeakable. How does anyone come back from that?"

Wait. What happened? Why won't I be the same?

I move my legs slowly. They work fine. I should try speaking. Maybe they didn't hear my groans before.

"Hello?" My voice cracks. I'm tired. So tired.

Footsteps approach. "Abbie, can you hear me? Are you awake?"

It's the woman's voice again. The one who predicted I would never be the same.

Then a guy says, "Cooper, can you open your eyes?"

1

Hot tears drizzle down my cheeks. It's Ty. He's here. Everything will be fine.

"Ty, what's going on? Where am I?" With each word, I expend massive amounts of energy. I stop to catch my breath.

"You're in the hospital." His warm, comforting hands clasp mine.

"Why?" I croak.

A brief silence passes.

"Abbie, I'm Nurse Russo. We're going to take good care of you. Don't try to get up, hon. Can you open your eyes for me?"

My eyelids are heavy, and all I want to do is to go back to sleep. But I won't give in to the temptation. I blink a couple of times, and when I'm able to focus, I see Ty sitting next to the bed in a chair. His shirt is a rumpled mess. The sparkle in his usually mischievous hazel eyes has vanished, replaced with barely disguised anguish. He tries to muster a smile but it falls flat. *Am I dying?*

"How do you feel?" he asks.

"Like I just got run over by an oil tanker a hundred times."

I take in my surroundings. A typical hospital room with machines beeping, an IV bag, and heart rate monitor. A flat screen TV is perched on the wall. A finger pulse oximeter is clipped to my index finger, but even scarier, an IV needle is shoved into the flesh at the back of my hand and held down by white tape.

Ty squeezes my hand. "Nurse Russo is right, Cooper. We're going to take good care of you. I don't want you to worry about anything."

"Listen to your friend," the nurse chimes in. To my left, she fumbles with a blood pressure cuff. She looks to be in her thirties. A full, pretty face, auburn hair pulled back in a high ponytail, and blue scrubs.

She tells me she's about to take my blood pressure on the other arm and moves to the right side of the bed. My left arm throbs—a mounting pressure that demands my attention. I glance down. Most of the arm is wrapped in bandages.

"Was I in an accident? Ty, did you bring me to the hospital?"

He looks away from me.

"We'll get everything sorted out, sweetie," Nurse Russo says as she wraps the blood pressure cuff around my arm and squeezes the bulb. After she notes the results, she takes my temperature and then announces she's going to get the doctor.

After she leaves, I touch my face. It's swollen, and like the rest of me, aches terribly. My head is pounding, but I need Ty to explain why I'm here. Sleep tugs at me, inviting me to give in to blissful rest where I won't feel the pain, where there aren't important questions no one wants to answer.

"Why won't you tell me what happened, Ty? I was in some kind of accident, wasn't I? Was it a car crash? I don't remember it at all."

Ty's hands grip the sides of his chair, as if he's afraid he'll fall off. Before he can respond, the door opens and in walks a tall, slim man with thinning hair, and a short beard. Nurse Russo follows closely behind.

Abbie, I'm Dr. Gray. You gave us quite a scare, young lady."

Ty stands up. "Do you want me to leave, Cooper? This is the first time the doctor's had a chance to talk to you."

"No, please don't go. I need you to stay with me."

Ty has a special gift for consoling me whenever things go wrong in my life. I have a feeling I'm going to need his calming presence in the next few moments. However this turns out, I need my best friend by my side to help me cope.

Dr. Gray pulls up a chair next to the bed, across from Ty.

"How bad was the accident?" I ask. "Did anyone die? Was it my fault? Please tell me no one was hurt."

I blink back tears and then focus on Dr. Gray, who has on a poker face. Dr. Linwood had the same look when he told us Dad had stage two colon cancer.

"Abbie," Dr. Gray begins, "Nurse Russo tells me you don't remember how you got here or where you were before you arrived in the Emergency Room. Your injuries are extensive, and we're trying to piece things together."

"So it was an accident then."

Dr. Gray noisily clears his throat. "Not quite."

"I don't understand."

Ty takes my hand in his and squeezes again. When I look at his face, I see devastation and heartbreak, as if whatever they're about to tell me is so horrible, that they can't even comprehend it themselves.

"Tell me," I insist. "What kind of injuries?"

Dr. Gray takes a deep breath, removes his glasses, blows on them and returns them to his face. "From what we've been able to gather, you were badly beaten and thrown out of a moving vehicle."

A vicious chill hits me at the core of my being, a paralyzing shock that knocks the wind out of me. *I can't breathe.* Why is the room spinning? The iciness settles into my stomach, heavy and merciless, as if it wants to crush the very life out of me. *I can't breathe. They made a mistake. It was a car accident.*

I suck in air in shorts bursts. My emotions run wild, screaming a million questions. I'm a good person. I'm nice to everyone. Who would do something so horrible to me and why?

CHAPTER 2

AFTER

I LOOK AT their faces, from one to the other. There's something they haven't told me yet, something even worse than my wounds. Dr. Gray begins to describe my injuries in detail.

"From what we can determine, you sustained severe blows to the head and face, and a sprained arm. The arm injury could be from the impact of being thrown out of the vehicle, when you hit the asphalt. You were unconscious when you were found a few hundred yards from the ER entrance."

I screw my eyes shut. For a moment, everyone in the room disappears behind a dreamlike fog, leaving me to wrestle with this seemingly impossible puzzle. Was I in the wrong place at the wrong time, a random crime victim? Why can't I recall what happened?

I will my mind to conjure up a memory, a name or place, a face, smell or sound. Nothing. Not even a shadow, real or imagined. There's an empty space in my brain where those details should have been stored for retrieval when I needed them.

"Abbie, there's more," Dr. Gray says. Something in his voice tells me that I had better brace myself. Ty won't meet my eyes.

"What do you mean there's more? How much more?"

"As I said earlier, you were unconscious when you were admitted. Naturally, we had to run blood tests and conduct a thorough examination to determine the cause. You sustained multiple bruises and scrapes from the impact, in addition to the severe sprain in your arm."

Dr. Gray looks down at his notes, but not because he needs to be reminded what to say next. He's gearing up to tell me that other horrible thing.

"Your attacker also drugged and sexually assaulted you. The toxicology results will reveal exactly what drug was in your system. It's the reason you may not remember the assault."

Everyone in the room is silent with solemn expressions. My brain seizes. I can't comprehend what I just heard. I lie here, not moving, not thinking, and not feeling. After a minute or two, I hear a pathetic whimper, a gut-wrenching snivel from some poor, unfortunate creature that needs to be put out of its misery. That creature is me. Ty wraps his arms around me, wipes my tears and whispers comforting words. I bury my head in his chest, and hot, bitter tears soak through his shirt.

I don't know how long we stay like this, but when I pull my head up, the room is empty. My guess is Nurse

Russo and Dr. Gray wanted to give us some privacy. They should be back soon. As Ty fluffs my pillow and helps me get comfortable, a hundred unpleasant questions bounce around in my head: How do I break the news to my parents—and do I even want to? Will the police catch the monster who did this? Will I ever feel safe again, or am I condemned to, for the rest of my life, look over my shoulder?

"How did you find out I was here?" I ask Ty.

"The last call on your phone log was from me. Your phone was powered off and the screen cracked in multiple places. Maybe the attacker shut it off so you couldn't be tracked, but the phone still worked. Thank God the hospital called, Cooper. I've never been so scared in my life. When I couldn't find you at the party, I thought I would lose my mind.

"By the time it was over, it was coming up on one in the morning and I still hadn't heard from you. I went into full-fledged panic. I knew I couldn't report you missing because the police would wait until twenty-four hours had passed to file a missing person's report. I only had to wait for a couple of hours, though. That's when the hospital called."

I turn over what he said in my mind. I remember a party at a house in Bethany, but the details are vague. I squeeze my eyes, trying to get my memory to cooperate, to understand the missing hours between when Ty last saw me and when he arrived at the hospital. Total blank.

"You don't remember, do you?"

"No. I only recall being at a house. It was a party to celebrate our win in the big game." I squeeze my eyes again, hoping my memory will throw me a crumb or two. "I talked to a bunch of people. You were there with Kristina. I hung out with Spencer. I don't remember anything after that."

"That's good. At least you remember being there. That can be useful. Spencer helped me look for you, but we couldn't find you anywhere. I should let him know I found you."

"Please don't give him any details. Make up a story or something. He's a nice guy, and I had fun with him, but you're the only person I trust to see me like this. I don't want to see or talk to anyone else."

"You don't have to explain it to me. I get it." He looks away and pinches the bridge of his nose, then scoots off the bed, heading toward the sink. After he splashes water on his face and dries off with paper towel, he returns to the chair next to the bed.

"I'm going to take good care of you, Cooper, and we'll find the monster who did this."

I don't answer right away. Instead, I take short, deep breaths to pull myself back from the brink—the brink of an abyss that wants to suck me into its black hole of perpetual hurt and torment.

"It's hard to explain where the physical wounds end and the emotional ones begin. It's as if they form this massive ocean of confusion and chaos that wants to drown me."

9

"Let me get the doctor and nurse back in here," he says and takes off.

A few minutes later, my head is throbbing and the ache in my arm has increased ten-fold.

"How bad is it?" Nurse Russo asks, as she enters the room. "On a scale of one to ten."

"A hundred," I say between pants.

Ty pulls up in the chair again and holds my hand. He says nothing.

Nurse Russo appears at my left side. "We'll adjust the medication in the IV so you can be comfortable. And Dr. Gray will be back to see you shortly."

After a ton of questions about my medical history and a battery of additional tests, Ty and I are once again alone.

"You're going to be okay, Cooper. I promise. You already have your own room at my place. We're going to get through this together. You're not alone."

Moisture gathers in his eyes as he delivers the little peptalk. He has always known the right things to say and do, ever since we met as young teenagers. But nothing in our relationship prepared us for this.

"What about you, Ty? You have your own stuff to worry about. You're in the middle of your remaining medical school applications. I know you still have a couple of interviews left, plus your regular class and lab schedule."

"Don't worry about me. I'll make it work somehow. I just want you to be all right."

The medication is kicking in. My eyes open and shut as exhaustion sweeps over me, and the promise of rest beckons. I would give anything to go back to being a carefree college student, to before I ended up in a hospital with gaps in my memory. I want to go back to the time my body was whole instead of violated, a time where brokenness didn't circle my consciousness like a vulture. Does my attacker recall the moment I fell unconscious or the moment he threw me out of a moving car? I'd give anything to find out the truth, to learn who did this and why.

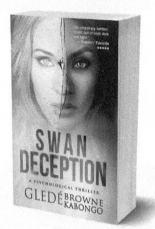
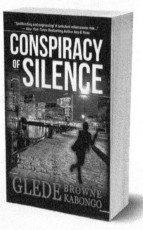

ABOUT THE AUTHOR

Gledé Browne Kabongo writes intense psychological thrillers—unflinching tales of deception, secrecy, danger and family. She is the author of the *Fearless* Series, *Swan Deception*, *Conspiracy of Silence*, and *Mark of Deceit*. Her love affair with books began as a young girl growing up in the Caribbean, where her town library overlooked the Atlantic Ocean. She was trading books and discussing them with neighbors before Book Clubs became popular.

Gledé holds both an M.S. and B.A. in communications. She was a featured speaker at the Boston Book Festival and has led workshops on publishing and the craft of writing. She hopes to win an Oscar for screenwriting one day. Gledé lives outside Boston with her husband and two sons.

Visit Gledé at **www.gledekabongo.com** to learn more.

CPSIA information can be obtained
at www.ICGtesting.com
Printed in the USA
LVHW091252180919
631465LV00001B/58/P